Pamela Rowlands Smith moved to Dorset from Kent upon marriage in 1963. Writing and selling short stories soon became a way of life . . . and then she and her two daughters found Tyneham. Subsequently, a strange chain of events led her to write OUT OF TIME to mark the fiftieth anniversary of the evacuation. While currently dividing her time between Dorset and Gower, she is still often to be found in Tyneham, which is where her spirit lives.

# OUT OF TIME
## Tyneham Revisited

## Pamela Rowlands Smith

**Dorset Publishing Company**
WINCANTON PRESS, NATIONAL SCHOOL, NORTH STREET
WINCANTON, SOMERSET BA9 9AT

**Publishing details.** First published 1994.
Copyright Pamela Rowlands Smith ©1994. Published by Dorset Publishing Company at the Wincanton Press, National School, North Street, Wincanton, Somerset BA9 9AT (telephone 01963 32583) with distribution in Dorset being undertaken by Maurice Hann from 36 Langdon Road, Parkstone, Poole, Dorset BH14 9EH (telephone 01202 738248).
**Printing credits.** Typesetting by Reg V. Ward, Holwell, Dorset, output by Daisywheel, Wallasey, Merseyside. Printed by Wincanton Print Company, at Wessex Way, Wincanton, Somerset.

**International standard book number** ISBN 0 948699 38 8

FOR

JOANNA, CAROLINE, APRIL AND YVONNE

AND FOR

LILIAN, MARGARET AND MARK BOND

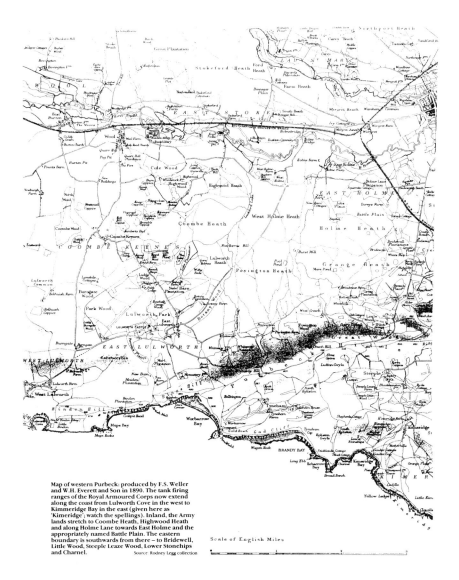

Map of western Purbeck: produced by F.S. Weller and W.H. Everett and Son in 1890. The tank firing ranges of the Royal Armoured Corps now extend along the coast from Lulworth Cove in the west to Kimmeridge Bay in the east (given here as 'Kimeridge'; watch the spellings). Inland, the Army lands stretch to Coombe Heath, Highwood Heath and along Holme Lane towards East Holme and the appropriately named Battle Plain. The eastern boundary is southwards from there – to Bridewell, Little Wood, Steeple Leaze Wood, Lower Stonehips and Charnel.

Source: Rodney Legg collection

Scale of English Miles

# TYNEHAM
## by Lilian Bond

I shall not cross the sleeping hill
Nor take the homeward road again,
The whispering woods, the hidden vale,
The soft winds call to me in vain.

I shall not see your blinded face,
Dear house now crumbling slow to dust,
I will not gaze upon your death
Who gave me life to hold in trust.

Your kindly hearthstone has grown cold,
Yet silently your faith you keep
(Mute victim of the strife of men)
With generations long asleep.

They say your beauty haunts you still,
Wrought out through all the patient years,
And breathes an immemorial peace
Transcending mortal hopes and fears.

The peace of God, dispensed to men
With hearts to service consecrate
In loyal thraldom to the land
And courtesy to small and great.

So, dying, in your old grey stones
Unmeasured memories remain,
The long-lost silence of the world,
The grace that will not come again.

Although reference is made to persons who exist,
or who have existed, the characters in this work
are without exception fictitious.

# The Story Behind OUT OF TIME

From the very beginning it was clear that this book just HAD to be written. After visiting Tyneham for the first time, in 1976, I went to my library and asked whether they had any information on the village. Expecting no more than some magazine articles or newspaper cuttings, I was handed – much to my surprise – the book TYNEHAM – A LOST HERITAGE by Mrs L.M.G. Bond. Reading her graphic account of an idyllic childhood spent in Tyneham's manor house and of her family's subsequent exile (along with that of all former village occupants) owing to the War Department's broken promise, I was soon firing on all cylinders.

My telephone directory revealed that a Lieutenant-Colonel A.R. Bond lived at Creech Grange and I immediately wrote to him. His widow very kindly telephoned me the following morning, to put me in touch with Major-General Mark Bond – heir to Tyneham House – who now lived in Owermoigne. I heard from him by return of post, with an invitation to telephone for an appointment. I did this at once and later that week (on 27 May) he welcomed me in to his home. As he was serving overseas at the time of the evacuation in 1943, he said that the best person to help me would be Philip Draper, who lived on the Arne peninsula. The Major-General readily gave his blessing to the writing of my novel and, at a later date, to the use of his Aunt Lilian's beautiful poem TYNEHAM as my frontispiece.

The day that I posted the letter to Philip Draper I also went to Worbarrow to start absorbing atmosphere. Up there on the cliffs, I did a spot of pilfering – removing a small piece of Purbeck stone from one of the ruins. This I placed under my pillow ... and soon started dreaming many remarkable dreams about Tyneham.

Philip Draper telephoned straight away on receipt of my letter and we arranged an appointment for the following week. Visiting him and his wife at their cottage on the shore of Poole Harbour, right at the tip of the peninsula, I discovered in time that the stone I had taken was from the ruin of their old home! Like the Bonds, the Drapers couldn't have been more helpful and I left two hours later clutching a fat file containing documentation, letters, photographs etc. covering Tyneham's history from the 1943 evacuation to the present day. The file was on loan to me for as long as I needed it.

A friend who knew what I was up to and who made many visits to Tyneham with me during my research, rang one day to tell me excitedly that her church (St Mark.'s, West Parley) had just acquired the bell from St Mary's, Tyneham. Coincidence? There were to be many, many 'coincidences'.

An early visit to Tyneham coincided with the arrival of workmen to open up St Mary's for the first time since the evacuation. Although it was in a dangerous condition and members of the public were not permitted within, I was permitted. April Butler (of the church-bell!) was with me and it was a weird feeling to walk where for so long no-one had walked. Later, we walked over Gold Down and Gad Cliff to Kimmeridge with the five children (one borrowed) we had brought with us. That evening April rang to say that when she returned her 'borrowed' child to the girl's grandparents, she mentioned my book – only to be told by Mr Tice that he served in the same Masonic Lodge as the late Lieutenant-Colonel Bond. Startled, I asked who Mr Tice was. For, unbeknown to April, I had named the fictitious family who lived in Tyneham House Tice. He was a friend of hers, living in Wimborne.

During research through old newpapers at the 'Echo' offices in Bournemouth, I discovered that dates in 1976 (and again in 1993) fell on the same days as during 1943. Harvest Thanksgiving in all three cases was held on 3 October.

The fact is, there have been two versions of my book – the first, entitled THE TYNEHAM GAP, written back in 1976, with this version, OUT OF TIME, written in 1989 and updated in 1993. There was a very good reason why THE TYNEHAM GAP never saw daylight. More on that anon.

Conversing one day with my elderly neighbour's daily help, Lily, I learned that her mother was cook to Mrs Bond at Tyneham House!

On 8 September, having completed my research and having typed umpteen pages of notes, I began writing the final draft. There was, though, one major gap in my work, this being that despite all my efforts to do so, I had been unable as yet to get even a glimpse of Tyneham House, which was sealed off from the public both by the army and by Cowleaze Knap and the grouping of some tall trees. Without so much as a sighting of this, and with a huge lack of writing experience, I lacked the confidence to have my heroine actually living in the House. I did not know it then, but unless she lived there my story could not possibly become the story I wanted it to be. This will be self-evident to its readers.

April suggested that, in order to see Tyneham from a new angle, we walk from Lulworth to Arishmel. By then we had visited 'my village' in every kind of weather except a gale – and there seemed little hope of one on this lovely, calm day. But we wondered all the same whether our Guardian Angel might manage something. Between Lulworth and Little Bindon we experienced a bit of a breeze, which had worked itself up to quite a wind by the time we reached the cliffs above Mupe Bay. Arrival on the Swine's Back, overlooking Arishmel, saw us clinging to a fence to avoid being blown over the cliff by a considerable gale!

Finding I needed some facts about Corfe Castle, I mentioned this to April, who told me that only the previous day her mother-in-law had arrived with a book on the Castle's history. April loaned me the book, together with a leaflet belonging to her son. Mention was made in the leaflet that Corfe is the old Anglo-Saxon word for gap and that the Castle is so named because it is situated in a gap between hills. It also stated that 'Mr Bond of Tyneham' had written a longer work about the Castle, available on request.

That same afternoon, as I drove near St Mary's Convent, Branksome, I remembered reading in the 'Echo' that Lilian Bond now lived there. So I trespassed, just wanting to see the building that housed the author of the book that had started me on my journey. As I rounded the last bend, an elderly lady waved to me from a window on the top floor. She was not wearing a nun's habit. As I waved back, I wondered . . . could she be Mrs Bond? I'll never know, but I'll always believe that she was.

Next, I needed information about a Devonshire bull, and mentioning this to April, joked that ideally I'd like to set hands on a James Herriot novel giving such facts. His would be the kind of treatment I needed. Next morning, the post brought the October edition of 'Reader's Digest', including an excerpt from a James Herriot book entitled 'Danger – Beware of the Bull!'

April had rung me in fine fettle saying she had called in at her local baker's to find the woman serving her in raptures over an amazing sunset she had seen the previous evening. Several times, describing this spectacle, the woman mentioned the word 'gap'. Unable to contain herself, knowing that a sunset featured in my book, April asked: "Did you by any chance see the sun set over Tyneham?" The woman had of course – and for me to do it justice on paper, *I* needed to see it too. We made two abortive attempts before the seemingly ludicrous thought came to me that, in THE TYNEHAM GAP, Edward did not take Adelaide to see the sunset until *after* Harvest Thanksgiving. As it turned out, the very next occasion when weather conditions indicated a likely sunset came on 4 October – the day after harvest!

I arrived ahead of April in the car park above Tyneham. There was just one other car in the vicinity and it was empty. Then I saw a woman, walking with a stick. She approached me and in due course told me she had been an artist, but that since her husband's death six months before all her artistry had been blocked. She had come here to Tyneham seeking inspiration. This was like coming face-to-face with my fictitious heroine – also an artist unable to paint since losing her husband! April could hardly believe her ears when I introduced Mollie Brodie to her and told her her reason for being there.

The curator of the Wareham museum put me in touch with Percy Best, a local inhabitant with a long memory, who wrote me a letter setting out some valuable information about the Telecommunications Research Establishment at Worth and stating that the man to help me with my fishing questions was Anthony Marshall of Gaulter Cottages, Kimmeridge.

On Monday 25 October (my birthday) April and I visited the Marshall home, where Mrs Marshall kindly provided all the information I needed, plus a bit more for good measure.

Well, THE TYNEHAM GAP never found a publisher and languished on a shelf for a few years. While it was languishing, I was writing and trying to become as proficient as I knew I would need to be.

Then, early in 1986, I was with another friend, Yvonne Rice, in Corfe when – in the National Trust shop – she spotted a newly published book, LULWORTH AND TYNEHAM REVISITED by Rodney Legg. I had been in touch with Rodney (via Philip Draper) ten years earlier in the course of my research for THE TYNEHAM GAP and he had been most helpful. Now, through his book, he became instrumental in the birth of OUT OF TIME – for he showed me photographs of Tyneham House which set me on the path of finally seeing the site for myself.

The bluebells were in bloom when I drove one Saturday with Yvonne to Tyneham. Driving down to the village, I experienced a profound sense of coming home, and there was something magical about that morning. I started talking of trespassing, if necessary, and risking being blown up by a bomb, so great was my need to come home fully. Yvonne pointed out that if I was blown up the new book would never be written – which soon sobered me! In the car park was an army Land Rover. I drove over to this like someone demented, leapt from my Mini and asked the startled driver – a range warden named Brian Morgan – how I could arrange to see Tyneham House. When, he queried, did I wish to see it? To my reply "as soon as possible", he questioned mildly "would now be soon enough?" No, my hearing hadn't gone wrong. He meant it . . . but did I mind if he finished his sandwich?

Soon we were driving back up the hill we had just descended, in convoy with the Land Rover. Parking by a big gate that was securely padlocked, the warden unlocked it and told us that we were free to cross the field unaccompanied (he seemed to see that for me this was some deep experience) and to take our time. He would wait, if necessary, indefinitely. Sheep watched us as we crossed Cowleaze Knap. I could scarcely believe we were crossing it and that we would soon be seeing the sight I'd dreamed for so long of seeing. Then I was standing on Shoemaker's Lane, at the gate to the House of my dreams.

A sea of blue greeted me, amidst all the tangles of green – and, over there, by the old stone wall was one scarlet bloom on the Smithii rhododendron. There used to be so many . . .

Ah . . . used to be!

Was I now seeing, or was I still dreaming? Rounding the last bend and not knowing quite what to expect, I had certainly not expected such a ruin. Lilian Bond's old home had crumbled almost to dust . . . and yet . . . and yet there was still something left of the atmosphere that had for so long prevailed here. I soaked this up, wondering, marvelling, feeling at times like crying. I felt, for sure, a watchful presence there . . .

So Katharine was born and, with her birth and that visit came the confidence I needed to instal my fictitious family in the Bond family's cherished old home.

I wrote to Rodney Legg, thanking him for inspiring me to begin again – and he invited me along to see him in Wincanton. There, he had on his desk a letter from Miss Margaret Bond, Lilian's sister. He had answered this, he said, and subsequently gave it to me. Lilian had died by this time, but Margaret was living in a home for retired gentlefolk at Winfrith (close to the Rectory where, in 1943, the Bond family's books were stored in the new granary). I wrote to her and she telephoned by return asking me to pay her a visit. She was in her nineties by then, which I would never have known from the strength of her voice on the telephone.

I visited her twice altogether and she showed me old photographs and reminisced at length about the life that had been lived in Tyneham. During my second visit her nephew – Major-General Mark Bond – arrived and it was at this time that they both gave their blessing to my using Lilian's poem. I also received Lilian's publisher's permission to use it.

Margaret mentioned having lived, post-Tyneham, at The Hermitage, in Parkstone. On the morning after my first visit to her, I received from an estate agent (I had a vague notion of moving) details of a maisonette in a newly converted Parkstone property . . . The Hermitage! I went, post haste, to see it and there was immediately no doubt but that this was where Margaret had once lived. Hidden away in its own grounds from the main thoroughfare and hurly burly, it stood imperiously with turrets and with a character vaguely reminiscent of another house, in another time. I looked over the maisonette, which was lovely but which was impractical for me. Then I closed the door on another of the Bonds' old homes.

Needing some more information about the Telecommunications Research Establishment, I couldn't quite recall where I had acquired this before. Then, in a place where it had no business to be, I found a scrap of paper bearing the name and address of Percy Best. I wrote to him and was soon on my way for a visit. Yvonne was with me and we had no map of Wareham, but by this time felt that we had no need of such material things. Sure enough, using just instinct, I drove straight to Percy's home, with no false turnings.

And he was, of course, able to supply the facts I needed.

I had just introduced the character of Jeremiah to OUT OF TIME (my hero's name is Jeremy) when Yvonne and I visited Tyneham again. We made first for St Mary's church, which had by now long been open to the public and which contained all kinds of data about Tyneham past and present. Yvonne's feet took her for some reason to the pulpit, where she glanced down at the big, open Bible. Upon glancing, she gasped, for – quite differently from our previous visits – the Bible lay open at the Book of Jeremiah!

Having by now ceased to be overly surprised by the various things that kept happening, we headed for Ocean Seat to have our picnic. Seated up there, looking across to Long Ebb, we became aware of a lone figure striding purposefully in our direction. Upon reaching us, he introduced himself and enquired whether we knew it was Ocean Seat that we were sitting on. Before long, he and I were engaged in earnest conversation and had virtually forgotten Yvonne. When, some while later, he had gone, Yvonne and I stared at each other, disbelieving and yet believing . . .

You see, Chapter Two had started with Jeremy striding up from Long Ebb to Ocean Seat and engaging in earnest conversation with his future (but hitherto unknown) wife, Catherine.

After a chance meeting at the end of August 1993 with an old schoolmistress of my daughters, whom we hadn't seen for donkey's years, things suddenly started happening. For Miss Nightingale asked the question: "What's the news of the book, fifty years on?"

Yes – of course – we were fast approaching the fiftieth anniversary of the Tyneham evacuation. Now, without doubt, was the moment to publish OUT OF TIME.

Instinctively, I rang Rodney Legg at Wincanton Press to ask him if he would be interested in publishing it to mark this historic anniversary. He had, after all, already written my book's last few words (which I had taken, as part of my factual afterword, from his book TYNEHAM: DORSET'S GHOST VILLAGE). Rodney's reply? Yes, he would certainly be interested! The rest, as they say, is history.                                                      P.R.S.

# One

Somewhere I'll find her – somewhere, somewhen. I know that she is here, in this vicinity, because back in my youth she said she would be and from the start I could trust Katharine.

It is springtime. I have always returned in the spring, in my mind. Now, though, I am back in reality.

Blueness surrounds me – a whole sea of bluebells. We knew them as granfer greygles and they coloured our springs just as they are colouring this one. Amidst the blue, and the rampaging greens of weeds and ivy, what is this I see? A clump of poetaz narcissi, half hidden yet smelling sweetly. So shall I also see Banksia roses, Riccartonii fuschias and the old walnut tree that the rooks fed from so greedily? Maybe.

There is one scarlet bloom on the Smithii rhododendron, over by the stone wall. There used to be so many. But that was before Nature took over from the gardeners. Before suckers and creepers choked the shrubs and the trees that were once tended so lovingly.

I stand by the wide wooden gate that marks the entrance to our grounds and cannot see the House. Undergrowth gone wild conceals it from prying eyes. I am not at all sure that I want to see it. Better to remember it as it was than to confront its crumbling walls. Or is that cowardly of me?

I must find Katharine. Brambles and convolvulus cannot bar me from her. Nothing can, for I am finally back. How long it has been, since I lived here with Jeremy and William and, of course, Katharine! Why, it will soon have been half a century . . .

In some senses, it seems longer in retrospect. When we lost our home, we also lost our moorings. But I am not here to dwell on what was and nor am I bitter, though I am heavy-hearted. I am

15

here, purely and simply, in search of Katharine.

She told me, all those years ago, that I would return. Little did I dream, then, that I would be returning in these circumstances. It was fortunate for me that I could not see as she saw. It doesn't do, to see too far into the future. The seeing might make us fearful when, in fact, there is nothing to fear and much to be thankful for.

I must bear this in mind as I round the last bend of our drive. Rounding it, I stand stock-still and sigh.

Those well-loved walls which housed us have crumbled virtually to dust. There is left but a shell and the sadness in me is overwhelming. There is room, though, for relief that William and Jeremy are not with me. I would not want them to see the desolate scene I am seeing.

What is this? I come face to face with a warning notice:

ORDERS ARE MEANT TO BE OBEYED.

DISREGARD OF THEM HAS CAUSED <u>DEATH</u>

I cannot obey orders to keep out of my house. It might even be that my death is necessary for the finding of Katharine.

Memory directs my feet towards the medieval wing. And I hear my voice calling: "Katharine . . . Katharine."

Then there is silence.

The silence is broken by the sound of gunfire. Is the world again at war? I could believe that it is. I could believe anything.

A mist swirls in. Purbeck mists are invariably sudden, so I am not surprised by this one. It soon surrounds me, enfolding . . . obscuring.

"Katharine," I call again.

My voice echoes through the mist. Or is it echoing?

Now I know that it is not, for I can see Katharine. She is emerging from the oldest wing and she is saying my name. Then, she beckons.

# Two

Whenever Jeremy came home, we seemed to be back on our honeymoon. I imagine that the same applied to other servicemen and their wives during the war the world was still waging in 1943, but I tended to think that this just happened to Jeremy and me.

So it had been between us since our marriage in 1939. I wondered sometimes whether our bond went back before that – before, even, our first meeting. Did some bonds date from former lives? I would not find that surprising. And I seemed to see recognition in Jeremy's eyes as we met that first time. We met here, in Tyneham.

I had come with a friend, Yvonne, for a picnic and a walk. We both loved Dorset and in particular her Purbeck hills, which enclosed a special world. This was a world at peace with itself: a world of simple pleasures and of spectacular vistas. To stroll on Tyneham Cap, above Brandy Bay, was to be awed by the jagged splendour of Gad Cliff and by the beauty of Gold Down as it dipped to Worbarrow, while a climb to Flower's Barrow was rewarded with access to Ring's Hill and means of descent to glorious Arish Mell. Flower's Barrow was so high that at times that climb seemed almost vertical. From that lofty vantage point, it was simple to bring to mind images of prehistoric man defending his fortress with slings and stones. But then, I was ever fanciful.

So it could have been my fancy, when Jeremy first strode up from Long Ebb towards Ocean Seat, where we were picnicking, and seemed to recognise me. He has said since, though, that I was not imagining things. And we have both come to think that our mutual recognition belonged beyond this lifetime.

We talked then, like old friends, and I bless Yvonne for her understanding. There we were, two apparent strangers who had soon forgotten her.

I was nineteen and of the belief, until that meeting, that I had been in love before . . . that I knew how love felt. Well, I didn't. I knew nothing of love, before Jeremy's advent.

He was the other half of me, as I was of him. Without him I had existence, but I was not alive as I have been since. I was in limbo – waiting, I now see, for Jeremy and for the life he brought me.

That life was concentrated in Tyneham, where the Tice family had lived for four centuries. The House that we lived in was of Tudor origin, except for one wing dating back to the fourteenth century, and it stood apart from the rest of the village, sheltered from the sea winds by its plantings. So apart did it stand, there on the valley floor, that one needed to be half-way at least down the Cowleaze Knap before even a chimney could be seen between the trees.

I remember teasing Jeremy, the first time he took me to it, that his House could not possibly exist. No sooner had I begun to tease him than there opened a gap through which he pointed out to me the mullioned windows of the tall north gable.

This was my very first glimpse of Tyneham House, which began as a hall two storeys high, with an open timber roof of fine design, and which was extended in Tudor and Elizabethan times to its present imposing size. I doubt there was ever a more gracious manor, with a more tranquil atmosphere. Shabby, some furnishings may have been, but the House was not for show – it was home, and had been since 1543.

Jeremy was acutely conscious of its long history and of the forebears who had passed on to him this precious legacy. He had a deep sense of duty to them and to future generations, speaking often of the need to preserve his heritage. He spoke, too, of those who depended on him for their livelihood and of how he must never fail them. I loved him for his attitude, and for so many things. How I loved him!

"What are you thinking?"

Jeremy had asked the question. We were seated in the drawing-room as the sun was sinking and were alone for the moment. William, his grandfather, who lived with us – or, rather, whom we lived with – was out on duty as platoon commander of the Tyneham Home Guard and was due back shortly. Smiling at my husband in the glow from the log fire I told him: "I wasn't so much thinking as wondering."

He grinned, his grey eyes crinkling, and rose from his chair on the far side of the William and Mary fireplace. With unhurried stride, he came across to me and squatted at my feet, his arm on my knees. "I see," he said, as I smoothed an unruly lock of dark hair back from his forehead. "So you were wondering, just as I was, when this war will end."

"Yes." I had long since stopped being surprised by Jeremy's ability to read my mind. "I'd been re-living the picnic and the sight of a lone figure striding up from Long Ebb . . . "

"So had I, except that I was greeted by the sight of a girl taking a bite from an egg sandwich!"

I grimaced at him. "You're making it sound so unromantic, whereas I . . . I was trying to visualise future picnics, when the war is finally won and there's no need, ever, for you to leave me again."

Drawing my face down to meet his, Jeremy gently kissed my lips. Then he said: "When I have to leave, I always take you with me. You're never alone, Catherine, and never have been since that fateful picnic. We might be separated physically but you and I can't be, essentially. That said, this old war must eventually end and, when it ends, my love, how we'll celebrate!"

We spoke then at some length, in the gathering gloom, of the form our celebrations would take. We would permit ourselves a short break and would walk where walking was forbidden at present because of the sea-defences. Jeremy longed to take me across the cliffs to Kimmeridge, and to visit old friends of his at Chapman's Pool, and to show me where the best fossils were to be found, near Little Bindon. To walk in freedom with him would be to come close to heaven, and there was much to see locally that I had not yet seen on account of the mined beaches and other restrictions. While walking, in peace-time, we would find somewhere beneath God's sky that was wholly private and we would make love there, in summer's sweet air.

Though the war was still on and it was growing dark in the drawing-room, with Jeremy's arms around me and his lips brushing mine, I could believe as we spoke that peace had come and that we were out there, loving each other at the heavenly height of summer.

Then William walked past the east windows, along the terrace, and we knew that in a matter of moments he would be joining us. So Jeremy struck a match and lit lamps to either side of the fireplace while I pulled down the blinds and drew the curtains.

The world was at war again, bringing nightly raids by the Germans, and necessitating blackout regulations, and we were back in the drawing-room with its wainscoted walls of warm biscuit, its paintings and its Regency furnishings. On a small work table positioned in one east window stood a tall china jar filled years ago with pot-pourri. This had never been replenished, according to Jeremy, yet it still perfumed the whole room faintly.

As the door opened to admit William and one of the labradors that seldom strayed far from him, the grandfather clock struck six from the first-floor landing.

"Ah, so the lamps are alight!" William said with satisfaction, approaching the fire eagerly and seating himself in his favourite chintz-covered chair to warm his hands – Horus at his feet – and face the two of us.

"I thought, from outside, that you must be elsewhere, as the room was so gloomy. It's going to be another cold night. Can't say that I care for February. All that can be said in its favour is that spring is on its way."

The two men started conversing and I thought, as I often had before, how alike they were, both in looks and in manner. William was tall and spare, like Jeremy, and used to have the same dark hair. Now his was white, above a face that was still handsome, if lined. The wonder was that he did not look older than his eighty years, after all that he had endured, but he in fact looked at least ten years younger. Jeremy attributed that to this environment, which sustained in times of trouble and pain, and which calmed the soul unfailingly. William had needed the sustenance and calm after his daughter-in-law, Geraldine, died while giving birth to Jeremy. That was in 1913. The following year, Jeremy's father, John – William's only son – went away to war, returning at its end a broken man. His heart broke on Geraldine's death and now his spirit too was broken by what he had seen and done during the Battle of the Somme. He survived until 1927, but was withdrawn and lost to Tyneham whose management was left to William. Maybe it was all the responsibility that had kept William young – for he was still largely responsible, with Jeremy now away at war. I helped him, of course, to the best of my ability, but I was a woman and Tyneham had traditionally been managed by a man.

My menfolk were by now deep in discussion and I half listened for a time to their assessment of the world situation. Last month, Churchill and Roosevelt had met in Casablanca to plan future strategy and it seemed to William that this would include allied invasion of Sicily. The allies would defeat the Italians just as on 31 January the Russians had forced the German Sixth Army's surrender at Stalingrad. The war was going our way at last.

"Could fighting end this year?" I asked.

"I'd estimate that there's a good chance," William answered. "In my opinion, Mussolini's days are numbered, and Hitler's position is much weaker. The tide is turning for us, and the Germans will not be able to withstand the Second Front, when it comes. Is that your view, too, Jeremy, or am I being over-optimistic?"

"That would be unlike you," Jeremy smiled. "Hard facts are more your forte than a surfeit of optimism. For me, the turning point came with Montgomery's victory at El Alamein and the allied entry of Tripoli. I agree that we're well on our way to ending this bloodbath." Then he turned to me, saying: "So yes, Catherine, my darling – there's a strong possibility that before this year's out we'll have brought Jerry to his knees and I'll be home with you in Tyneham."

I sighed at this and said: "That's when you'll need to convince me I'm not dreaming. I've dreamed so often of leading a normal life with you, whatever normality might mean, and of a Tyneham with fishermen hauling in their nets again and with a rector in the rectory and with the rightful occupants restored to 'Sheepleaze', and no Nissen huts in the valley. Oh, Jeremy, we have so much to look forward to, haven't we?"

He hugged me, while William looked on indulgently.

There were RAF officers stationed at the rectory, and soldiers at 'Sheepleaze' – Philip Draper's house on Worbarrow Cliffs – forming part of the defence group set up to protect the Telecommunications Research Establishment at Worth Matravers against a seaborne raid. Other than their presence and the gunfire to be heard from the army firing ranges at Lulworth, we were not unduly affected here by the war. So I suppose it was wrong of me to complain, when I had so much to be grateful for. But I missed my man unbelievably when he was away and, though I tried not to, I feared for his safety. War was such a waste and there had been so much carnage. All I wanted was for this to cease and for my husband to return safely to me.

When the grandfather clock struck seven we made our way to the dining-room, which was reached via a lamplit corridor from the entrance hall and a short flight of stairs. Norman Ayles, our houseman, tended the lamps daily, trimming their wicks, cleaning and refilling them so that they were ready for lighting each evening. He then lit those that were needed on staircases and corridors before eating with cook in the kitchen and retiring. He retired early and rose early, as is the tendency in the country. I liked the long shadows and dark corners created by oil lighting and did not even slightly miss the electricity that lit and heated my family home in Hampshire. Maybe I would have missed it, though, had I been burdened with Norman's duties.

The dining-room faced south and east, so that from its windows could be seen the terraced flower garden and the hanging West Plantation as well as the haha and lawn. But not after dark, of course, when the blinds were down and the curtains drawn. I thought of this as the portrait-room, for its pale green walls were populated with an amazing array of Tice ancestors. Over the chimney-piece hung, in an elaborate frame, an unfinished Gainsborough copy of Rubens's Antwerp altarpiece "The Descent From The Cross". This fine work rather eclipsed some lesser works on the walls, but it was the faces that interested me more than the artistry. For they were all essential to Jeremy. Without them, he would not be. Dating back several centuries, his antecedents peered out from their frames as we ate and as we took our ease. Like us, they had lived and breathed and procreated (that is to say, Jeremy and I hoped to procreate), and like them we would one day die and look down from our frames on future generations. Could they SEE us? Oh, not with their painted eyes, but from wherever they had gone when they died. I imagined that they could, and that we would see them if we only knew how to look with our full sight. This had long been my belief, unfounded as yet. But I was fascinated with where we went after death.

I realised suddenly that William was speaking to me.

"Sorry," I said, stupidly. "I was daydreaming again. What did you say?"

"Just that there are two portraits missing."

"Are there?" I glanced round the room but could see no spaces. "Whose portraits?"

"Ours, dimwit!" Jeremy told me with a grin. "William wants us on the wall – and was suggesting an artist. Her name is Catherine Tice."

"She isn't too well qualified," I smiled. "Give her a landscape to paint, in preference to a portrait, any day – especially a self-portrait. She might manage you, though, since she's so familiar with your face."

"Manage me?" echoed Jeremy, after swallowing some of the delicious brisket Lily had prepared. "Is that the best you can summon, in the way of enthusiasm? I'm not sure that I want to be managed. I was thinking more in terms of being immortalised! And as for an artist being familiar with her sitter – I have my doubts as to whether that's altogether ethical. It certainly doesn't sound proper, does it, William?"

I threw my napkin at him, saying: "We'll just have to be improper, then! That is, if I take you on. We should perhaps wait till your face looks more lived in . . . and until I'm more experienced in portraiture."

"Don't wait for anything," advised William. "That would be a mistake. Waiting never pays. If something needs doing, it shouldn't be saved until tomorrow, but should be done yesterday. This, life has taught me. And if you're afraid of failing, Catherine, don't be. You won't fail. You've too much on your side – too much talent and too much drive, though you're a funny child."

William tended usually to temper his compliments, and often referred to me as funny. I could see why I was in his eyes, and why he still thought of me as a child. To someone of eighty, twenty-three must seem almost unweaned – and William was bemused by my artistic streak, finding it intriguing that I

24

frequently drifted off in to long reveries as in my mind I considered a composition or a technique. Not that there had been too much time, since the war's outbreak, to sketch and paint. I was kept busy on the land and assisting William in the day-to-day running of the House and estate. But a wonderful aspect of being an artist was that I could work on pictures in my head while using my hands for other things. How they had tried, at school, to make me more academic and less intent on pursuing an artistic career! They had failed, however, for I was no great scholar. I had been born, it seemed, to paint. "You're right," I informed William. "Not necessarily about my funniness, nor my talent, but about not waiting for an older face. Why wait, when the face in front of me is the foundation for all its future faces, and when . . . " The rest of my sentence went unspoken. This was war-time and it was family policy never to refer specifically to dire possibilities. We thought and spoke, as far as was within our power, phlegmatically. "Painting your portrait, Jeremy, will keep you close to me, even when you're back at sea."

"There are, of course, photographs you can refer to in my absence, should your memory fail you."

"As it's bound to!"

His face was better known to me than my own, though I was not going to be drawn on the subject of familiarity again. I had not studied my face with the love and the curiosity with which I'd studied Jeremy's. There was no inch of his that I did not know intimately and that I had not touched with my lips and my fingertips. And wherever he was, no matter how far from me, I could see him at will quite clearly. So there should be no problem in painting his portrait while he was gone. It might even prove to be good therapy.

Talk turned then to William's plans for planting and to the health of the schoolmistress, who had been ailing but continuing to teach nevertheless, such was her conscientiousness and love of the children attending her tiny school. William told Jeremy, too, of the Spitfire pilot whose plane ditched last month in Poole Bay, and who was saved by the local Air-Sea Rescue launch COMMODORE. This had occurred, he said, not long after a four-engined Halifax bomber from RAF Holmsley South, on the fringe of the New Forest, crashed in the grounds of Kingston Lacy House, seat of Ralph Bankes, whose illustrious ancestress, Lady Bankes, was known for having defended Corfe Castle against Cromwell and his Roundheads for two and a half years from May, 1643. The crew of the bomber, belonging to 58 Squadron, were killed and a stag was so terrified by the impact that it leapt through the House's dining-room window.

"So life in Dorset isn't altogether uneventful," Jeremy observed drily at the end of William's account. "It's to be hoped that Ralph's family were not dining at the time. What happened to their intruder?"

"I understand," William answered, "that it had to be put down. There must be simpler methods of stocking up with venison!"

He went on to mention that there had been problems again with the hot water cylinder at the rectory, which kept perforating. "The Air Force aren't using it as a dartboard, are they?" Jeremy asked. His question would have sounded facetious but for the fact that the soldiers at 'Sheepleaze' used doors as dartboards and wrenched shelves from the walls for firewood. "No, they aren't" William responded with a half-hearted smile, "At least, I don't think they are. It seems that the water could be at fault, so we've sent samples off for analysis, It might be that a copper cylinder is needed. The RAF have kindly offered to pay for it."

The telephone rang and William, who was expecting a call, excused himself from the table.

"Shall we go for a stroll?" Jeremy asked me.

"It's rather dark and cold," I said doubtfully.

"It won't be, once we're outside. There's a full moon tonight, and there'll be stars, quite apart from the searchlights. Besides, even if it were as black as pitch out there, I could still steer you around Tyneham – without a Tilley lamp – as if it were light."

"You've convinced me," I grinned, "even if in doing so you've made me sound like a ship!"

"Have I?" He looked surprised. Then another look stole into his eyes as, from his seat opposite mine, he studied me for a while. "I don't see you as ship-like. Shall I tell you how I see you, at this moment, Catherine?"

When, in a rush of feeling for him, I failed to respond, he went on: "You are, for me, the Virgin Mary that we see with Jesus on her knee in the window of St Mary's. Your hair, by lamplight, is like a halo, and there's something about your expression – something maternal. I must make a mother of you, my beloved."

I still could not speak. The love in Jeremy's eyes, and his perception of me as Mary, made me want to cry. As for making a mother of me – I wished he would hurry . . . wished we could dispense with the walk and retreat upstairs instead for the purpose of procreation and of releasing the tenderness and exquisite pain that was overwhelming.

Before releasing anything, we walked as arranged, warmly wrapped in overcoats and hats and holding hands. With my hand in Jeremy's, I felt as tall as he – taller even – and I felt capable of greatness. There was nothing that I could not achieve and there was no ordinariness in me. I was destined for immortality.

"Look," he said.

I looked where he was looking, and there was the moon, seeming to look back at us. It was immediately above, shining from a sky sprinkled with stars. How vast the universe, how astounding its Creator! I had read in a book by Vera Stanley Alder that each cell in our bodies formed a microcosm of our solar system, as did our cells in totality, linking us thus intrinsically with the universe. We were an essential element of it, as it was of us. But oh, how much of creation and its purpose was beyond our limited comprehension!

"Why do men fight?" I asked Jeremy, "when one glance at the

skies should suffice to show that we shouldn't be fighting? We're surely meant to be in harmony with our world and with our fellow humans."

"I'm sure that we are – but try telling that to Hitler and Mussolini! They wouldn't listen, just as I suppose there will always be those with hatred in them, and spite and greed." He smiled wanly. "Wars won't end until men learn that love is the key to living harmoniously. And first, man must find in his heart a need for harmony. I fear, Catherine, that such a need won't be surfacing this week, nor even this century." Taking me in to his arms, he held me securely, now whispering: "Love, if others but knew it, is the answer to everything – to our every need. Soon, soon, I'll start answering your present needs, and have you answer mine for me. But not quite yet. Let's walk further first, shall we?"

We were postponing the moment knowing that it would be enhanced by its postponement and also knowing that there were all too few such precious moments left to us this leave. Two days from now, Jeremy would be back at sea and we would have just our memories until he next returned to me. We were in the process of making those memories – and the making of them was bitter-sweet.

Our steps then turned toward Great Wood. Ahead of us, from the cliffs, powerful beams searched the sky for enemy aircraft, and out of our sight gunners were standing by to bring down any plane coned by these searchlights. There was an unreal quality to war-strategies and to all the deaths inflicted in the cause of freedom. Sometimes, at night, I would wake and would believe that it had all been a bad dream and that we were free to live our lives as we pleased. But then I would see that Jeremy was not beside me and would know that it was no dream. We were living the nightmare. Our war was real.

The Wood was lit eerily by the moon and stars and man-made beams. We walked among tall chestnut trees, elms and ashes, whose branches swayed and sighed in the slight wind. When a strong wind blew through Tyneham, straight from the sea, with the valley effectively like a funnel, it tormented the trees and sounded, even to our accustomed ears, like water rushing in, bent on destroying everything. We would hear the gale hit West Plantation with an almighty roar and would know that at any second the House would be hit. It was nerve-racking, waiting for this, the sole comfort being that our home had withstood countless previous such winds, so should withstand this one.

A weasel darted out from under some leaves right in front of us and then was gone again on some quest in the woodland. No doubt he was after a juicy mouse, or maybe a frog, or rabbit. "I used to keep ferrets as pets," Jeremy said. "Not that that was a ferret. Did you know that they can be quite affectionate?"

"No, I can't say I did . . . and I'll take your word for it. I've never looked for affection from a ferret, and am never likely to, now that I've found you!"

"Who, I wonder, found who? Not that it matters," Jeremy cupped my head lovingly in his hands, "as long as, between us, we did the finding. I don't know how I lived, my darling, without you in my life. I think it's time."

It WAS time, for going home and for letting go. So homeward we went.

# Three

Our bedroom was in the west wing and was known as the North Room. The view from its ancient mullioned window was of Cowleaze Knap, which had special meaning for us, and during Jeremy's long absences I would often sit on the wide window-seat and gaze across the trees to where he had proposed to me. Or I would look instead at our big four-poster bed, re-living different memories.

The west wing dated back to Tudor times and had such low doorways that even I needed to stoop to enter our room, which had wood-panelled walls and built-in shelves overflowing with books. We were above the stableyard which, in Jeremy's childhood, had echoed early each morning with the sounds of grooming – the ring of iron shoes on the cobbles, the clang of bucket handles, the coachman's laborious breathing as out there in the open he did his curry-combing, and the horses' snufflings. There were no sounds from the stables now that the brougham had made way for the motor-car and now that the coachman was drawing his pension. But Jeremy's description of the sounds from his boyhood had been vivid and from time to time I fancied that I could hear hooves out there on the smooth stones.

I fancied, too, that the faint scent of lavender in the room, which merged with the scents (if so they can be termed) of scrubbed floorboards, old furniture and dampness, reached me from some earlier era as I lay in my bed enclosed by dimity curtains.

It was perhaps the artist in me making me fanciful. I was given to all manner of fancies, especially when I was alone. There was less time for these, and less need, when Jeremy was home.

I looked at him now, tingling through and through to the sight of his head on his pillow. So often, I would lie imagining how it would be if he were lying there beside me, and now here he was . . . but not for long. Tomorrow, he would again be gone. I must not, though, think of tomorrow. To do so would be to spoil the hours left to us, and these must not be spoiled. They must be savoured.

And they would be, because there was only today to count on. I dared not think beyond . . . dared not think of the danger aboard Jeremy's minesweeper . . . dared not think of anything save my love for him. I thought of him as handsome, and so he was, even unshaven, with fine features, among them a hooked nose. This reminded me of noses I had seen on busts of ancient Romans. Well, with his ancestry it might even be that we could trace his family tree back to that lineage.

As I watched him, he stirred, reaching out for me spontaneously at the very moment of stirring. I was drawn to him and to his warmth, and soon we were back where we had been after last evening's walk.

But our lovemaking was now less urgent than it had been. It was almost leisurely, as we delighted afresh in our loving and in the bodies that fitted together so perfectly. Jeremy opened the door for me to yet further sensations and ecstasies. Hard to believe that we had been married for four years, when there was this newness and when each entry seemed the first time he was entering me. Oh, the joy of such belonging . . . oh, the agony!

Our love and longing again spent for the moment, we lay, limbs entwined, and slept for a brief while.

Then, his lips against my cheek, Jeremy asked me: "Do you ever feel . . . restricted by your body? That might seem a strange question, coming so soon after our bodies have behaved with such delicious freedom." He smiled slightly sheepishly. "But I meant it in the sense that . . . "

" . . . because we're embodied, we aren't as free as we might be?"

"Yes!" Propping himself up on one elbow, he said: "That's it, exactly! The feeling sometimes steals over me that to know true fusion we have somehow to leave our bodies. Not that that is exactly an option. My feeling, though, is often . . . strong."

Souls left, upon death. I shivered. He wasn't about to die, was he? I said lightly: "I've often felt, too, that because of my body I can't come close enough to you – which is odd, because no two people could come closer than we do. Or could they?"

My question had the desired effect on Jeremy who, answering it with a lengthy kiss, said afterwards: "No, they couldn't! And we couldn't do this if we were bodiless, could we? I'll never complain about restrictions again. Not," he added with a boyish grin, "that I was complaining. I wonder whether we've made . . ."

" . . . a baby? I'll be amazed if we haven't."

"So shall I," he sighed happily. "After last night, so shall I!"

We spent the morning sick-visiting. Cook's mother, who was once cook to Jeremy's great-grandmother, had been ill with pneumonia and Lily had been most anxious about her. Old Mrs Hodden was now feeling much better, but Jeremy wanted to see her before going off again to war. She was ninety-one and there were no guarantees that she would still be here when next he came home. Nothing in life was guaranteed, so it was best to see someone while you could be sure of seeing them.

Bumble Bee Cottage, where the Hoddens lived, was down near the gwyle stream, between Tyneham village and Worbarrow. It was small, but comfortable, and was set in a hollow surrounded by thickets. There were three approaches to it – from the sea road, from across the stream and from a western wicket. We approached from our side of the stream, via a steep stairway of uneven stone, and were soon enclosed by tall, spiny tea-plants and by the foliage of huge fuchsias that thrived here like weeds, never losing their leaves.

Lily had seen us arriving and now let us in. "T'is right good of you to come," she said as we entered her spick-and-span home. "Mother's that pleased. I'll take you to her, so's you can chat while I'm makin' our nammut."

Mrs Hodden, a plaid blanket wrapped round her knees, was seated in an armchair in the little living room, in front of a log fire. She was an older version of her daughter, who was plump, with short, straight white hair and rosy cheeks. Not that Mrs Hodden's cheeks were as rosy today as Lily's, and she had also lost weight. But the likeness remained.

"Elevenses sound like a good idea," Jeremy said, in response to Lily. "It's cold out there. And while you're in your kitchen, could you please put these in water for your mother?"

He handed her hothouse flowers which I could take part-credit for. I felt proud of the fact that I, who before coming to Tyneham could not differentiate between a thistle and a cowslip, had now relieved our gardener of responsibility for the hothouse and also to some extent for the flower garden. Our flowers were necessary to village life, since we provided arum lilies for the altar, as well as varieties for funerals, weddings and baptisms. George Warner had patiently taught me much about nature and about growing things. I was grateful to him for giving me a love of gardening.

While so thinking, I had watched Jeremy stoop to kiss Mrs Hodden's aged cheek and had at the same time seen her eyes mist. Now she said to him: "Were I still a meäden, I'd blush at bein' kissed by such a oon. T'is pleasin' to see you again, Mr Jeremy . . . and Missus."

"It's a pleasure to see you, too," Jeremy said, sitting in a chair near hers while I seated myself on the small flower-patterned sofa, "and looking so hale, as well. Was it a false rumour I heard, that you had been poorly?"

She smiled at him and in her smile I could virtually see the maiden that she had been  So she was still young, within. Souls did not age. They stayed ever the same, removed from time and space. But bodies, which were made of matter and were of the earth plane, decayed. Where were we, before we were given a body, and where would we be after our need of it ceased?

Lily arrived just then with cups of steaming tea. Coffee was extremely scarce and, besides, she knew that neither Jeremy nor I greatly cared for coffee. I was in fact acquiring a taste for tea made from rose hips and also from nettles, of which there were plenty. Why waste coupons on conventional tea, when Nature could provide a whole host of healthy alternatives?

Jeremy and I talked for some time with Cook and her mother, who thanked us for sparing Lily from duty during the bout of pneumonia. Then it was time to leave. As we were leaving, Mrs Hodden clutched Jeremy's hand in hers and said: "I shan' be seein' you again. I'm a wold 'oman and with the war on you're off athirt the sea. But we'll meet one day in heaven. God speed."

Thinking that by virtue of her years she might know something I did not, I found myself questioning: "Do you know where heaven is?"

"Why," came her answer, "t'is right here. Oft times I see my mother and father. As for my man – he was with me while I was umpty. But he said he hadn' come for me. Wadn' my time, see."

On our walk back to the village I said to Jeremy: "She's very sure, isn't she, of heaven's locality? I rather suspected she would be."

"Because she's an old lady?"

"Partly. She also has a serenity suggestive of having seen beyond death and been freed from fear. Dying doesn't trouble her. She calmly accepts the prospect of her dead husband coming for her at the appointed time and of their reunion. Her acceptance, I'm sure, is born not of faith, but of knowledge. I believe that the very old and the very young know things that we somehow lose in the interim. We'll find them again, won't we, Jeremy?"

"We shall," he readily agreed, smiling at me. "Why wait for

advanced age, when we can hasten its advantages? Besides which, I can't imagine being as old as Mrs Hodden is."

"For it to happen, you *must* imagine it. And don't forget that she's only old on the surface. Within, beneath that wrinkled skin, she's young. That's the conclusion I came to, when she smiled at you. The years don't touch our souls. So, although we might turn ninety and might become slow, we'll always be essentially the same as we are now."

Tightening his hold on my hand, Jeremy responded: "Supposing we don't turn ninety . . . or supposing one of us doesn't ? I'm not being morbid, darling – just facing, or trying to face, a possibility. We should discuss how the one left behind would cope."

I thought about this. It was not as if I had never considered it. Where love lived, such things had to be considered. "Neither of us will be left behind," I said then. "Oh, I don't mean we'll die simultaneously. That would be too much to hope, kindly though Providence can be. And it might well be that whichever of us is bereaved will believe, for a time, through grief, that he or she has indeed been deserted. But they won't have been. That is solely how it will seem. Knowing that the soul lives on, can you imagine straying far from me, just because you've left your body, or being strayed far from?"

"No, that's beyond my imagining," said Jeremy, holding and kissing me. "We would know the true fusion that we can't know now."

We called on the schoolmistress next. This being Saturday, Molly Larcombe was at home in the school-house, which was on the bend of the picturesque stone and slate terrace that formed the village 'street' and which was connected to the school by its garden, where the parish flagstaff stood. I had been surprised, when I first came to Tyneham, at the extent to which Mrs Larcombe involved herself in her pupils' lives. Having been born and brought up in a town, I was unprepared for the close-knit community spirit that existed here in the country and for the care and concern exhibited by all and sundry toward those in pain, or in need, or with any kind of worry. Apparently in keeping with standards set by Tyneham's past schoolma'ams, Mrs Larcombe raised money to equip her pupils with warm slippers for wear in school while their boots and stockings were drying by the stove. She would also buy potatoes, which she roasted to supplement the children's dinners, and would keep an eagle-eye on their outfits, helping mothers where necessary to clothe their families. All this and more she did, in addition to her teaching duties and to her work as church organist.

She seemed pleased to see us and made us as welcome as the Hoddens had. Jeremy was worried afterwards that she had looked rather gaunt, but I could reassure him on this score, since she appeared healthier than when I had last seen her.

No flag flew from the flagstaff, for today was not an ecclesiastical, national nor local 'occasion'. Maybe the next flag to fly there would be the one that was raised at the end of this war.

We paused after leaving Mrs Larcombe to exchange pleasantries with, among others we met while out and about, Mary Meader, wife of Joseph, the shepherd. The Meaders lived in the end cottage, by the village pond, and Mary's hair, of a paler gold than mine, had been passed on to all her four children, two of whom clung to her skirt as we spoke. This set me pondering about the baby that Jeremy and I hoped we had made last night. Would it be dark or fair, boy or girl? I rather hoped that it would be a boy in his father's mould.

Before returning home, we went where we always went prior to Jeremy rejoining his ship at Portsmouth – to church. We entered the churchyard via a short flight of stone steps wordlessly. Why speak, when words were superfluous, as they often were, with us? There's no need for speech, when each knows the other's thoughts. In fact, our feet took us to St Mary's as a matter of course.

Some of Jeremy's ancestors were near as we approached the church door, while others were not far, being buried beneath the south transept in the family vault. The stones on certain graves were so old that they had sunk in to the earth until only their tips showed. These, I supposed, belonged to the Tudors and the Elizabethans. Just one Tice gravestone from those early days was not sunken. Dating back to the sixteenth century, its engraving had understandably worn almost smooth – but I had succeeded in deciphering the name 'KATHARINE'. And I had wondered about my namesake, who lived so long ago in the House that I now lived in. Like me, she had married a Tice son and had come upon marriage to Tyneham. Or such was my conclusion, right or wrong. I wished there were some way in which I could erase the centuries between us and find out for certain how life had been for Katharine.

Jeremy and I sat in the family pew in the south transept and absorbed the timeless atmosphere, together with the pervading smell of mould and leather, old books and bindings, candle wax, lamp oil and hassocks made of straw. Then, side-by-side, we said a silent prayer for peace and for an early end to all the slaughter. I also, of course, said a prayer for Jeremy, that he might be spared for me.

This done, I opened my eyes and raised them.

Above me sat the Virgin Mary, with Jesus on her knee, beneath a weeping willow tree. To either side of her there were, in miniature, local scenes – Tyneham's fishermen busy at sea and farmers tilling the fields – while through the clear glass surrounds could be seen our actual hills and trees. There were, too, painted butterflies that looked so real they might have just flown in from outside. In particular I noticed a Camberwell Beauty with outspread wings reposing on Mary's robe.

While noticing this, I brought to mind how Jeremy had seen in me a likeness to Mary, and how he had spoken so tenderly of making a mother of me. Ever I would remember his words and his expression, no matter what the years might bring. There was no question of not remembering, both because of him and because I could never again enter this church without a reminder from Mary of the love my husband felt for me.

After lunching with William, Jeremy and I set out again – this time in a different direction. We crossed Hole Field, where the reservoir was that supplied the House with water, and then, walking briskly against the wind, reached Rookery Wood. Here ivy grew knee-deep and we were towered over by the tall trees that the rooks nested in, repairing and reinhabiting their old nests each spring. How noisy rooks were! Tyneham mornings always began in the hour before dawn with the gulls clamouring as they flew inland to feed. Their screams began the birds' chorus, which the rooks soon joined in with their loud caw-cawing.

On our way to where we were going we ascended a rise smothered with snowdrops and aconites. These were early this year, growing there in the shelter of sycamores and beeches, and Jeremy picked a small bunch, offering this to me with some ceremony.

Further on, there were cascades of harts'-tongue ferns near the dipping well of cold spring water that was set in a deep stone-roofed recess, behind a small wicket gate. The air here, in Nature's green shade, was cool at all times of year and sweet with the scent of moss and fern.

Our calves began to ache as we crossed the Eweleaze and West Plantation, for we were not currently accustomed to the steep gradient. Reaching the Eweleaze's upper portion and the Twelve Acres bridle gate, we paused to inhale deeply of the first tangy breath of the sea. There were stone steps in the wall beside the gate and, indicating these, Jeremy told me: "They are part of the old church path from South Egliston, which was frequented long before this gate had being. It was the route dear old Louis Stickland always took to church each Sunday morning, wearing his dark frock coat and square-top hat. He could do anything with his hands, coming as he did from a long line of fishermen and boatbuilders, and walked everywhere, even as a very old man. He preferred the difficult path round Tyneham Cap to the one through Egliston Gwyle, Parson's Mead and Shoemaker's Lane, which he used solely on exceptionally stormy days. His like won't come again."

"What about his son?"

"Will's a good man." Jeremy frowned. "But Louis in his frock coat, and the world that he stood for, belonged to an era that has gone with the war."

"How sad that sounds! Are you sure it has gone, never to return?"

"Fairly sure. Wars bring change in their wake and I can't see this war proving an exception. Can't you feel the wind of change blowing, even as we stand surveying a scene that has remained unchanged, virtually for centuries?"

There was a wind on my face, but I was loath to acknowledge it as a wind of change. "I want everything to stay the same," I said, "And you've just admitted that this valley of ours had hardly been altered by previous wars. So why are you expecting it to be affected by this one?"

"It isn't an expectation – just some instinct that could be wrong. I wasn't talking so much about Tyneham as about the whole of Britain. I believe that victory won't come cheaply."

"I'll pay any price, make any sacrifice . . . just as long as you return safely to me. You will return, won't you, Jeremy?"

There, close to the cliff-top, with all Tyneham spread like patchwork beneath us, my husband took me in his arms and said: "I, too, have tried to bargain with God. But He won't be bargained with! And I've come to the conclusion that that is for the best. Where would everybody be, if we could direct our own and others' destinies? I find comfort in the fact that we can't – and that the future isn't in our incompetent hands. There's comfort for me, too, in the knowledge that everything will work out right for us. It might not work out according to our prayers and preconceptions – but it will all happen according to a Perfect Plan. This said, I SHALL return. I hope to be back bodily, so that you will instantly recognise me. Should I not be . . . "

"No," I interrupted him, kissing him fiercely, "no, Jeremy, please!"

"I must say it, Catherine, – and it's because of what you said this morning that I can find the strength and the words with which to speak. Death, as we're aware, does not separate. The separation that we feel is caused by our own shortsightedness and not by the act of dying. Which brings us to things unseen. The dead are no less alive than we are, if you see what I mean. But because we can't see them . . . because they have gone beyond the limits of our poor vision, we mourn them, and miss them and feel bereaved. I'm certain we shouldn't. I'm certain, too, that should my body perish, my soul would rush straight to you, staying close to you till you were ready to join me on the next phase of our journey. You would simply need to adjust your sight until you could see me. Or maybe it wouldn't be your sight needing adjustment. Maybe my soul would reach out to your soul until you perceived me from within. Whatever the means, between us we would find it, my darling."

"I know we would," I said, clinging to him. "But why are we having these conversations? Have you had some premonition?"

He grinned. "No – nothing so dramatic. It's just that in wartime we have to be prepared for every contingency, haven't we?"

I agreed, and we proceeded upward toward Ocean Seat, Jeremy needing one stride for every two of mine. Surmounting Gad Cliff – so named because of its shape, a 'gad' being a quarryman's wedge – and heading for Tyneham Cap, we were nearly blown from our feet by the wind, which was whipping the sea to a frenzy below us in Brandy Bay. My hand secure in Jeremy's, we reached the Seat, which was sheltered on all sides save the south by high mortared walls of undressed stone. In peacetime, there was shipping to watch from here as it passed up and down, and the local fishermen were to be seen netting in their mackerel-shoals, with much oar-threshing to keep the fish within bounds. Now there was no shipping and nor were Worbarrow's fishermen out in their boats, but the birds were up to their usual antics. War had neither clipped their wings nor dampened their spirits. So concealed were we by the Ocean Seat's walls that the ravens and peregrines were unaware of our presence until they had flown within a few feet of us – and even then they remained less concerned with Jeremy and me than with their skirmishes. They feuded overhead, outmanoeuvring each other and flying higher, ever higher, while squawking and screaming discordantly. The gulls, too, tuned their shrieks to the falcons' and we were soon wishing that for a while at least the birds would join the Channel shipping and fishermen in obsolescence.

For we had not come to see them, but to be where we first met and to see the sea that united Jeremy and me while he was away, serving in the Royal Navy.

I would come here from time to time without him and from this seat would gaze beyond Long Ebb to the horizon, trying to conquer space. I could cross the dipping land and the sea to my husband, if only I could discard my body and will the essence of me to find Jeremy. Bodilessly, I could be with him in an instant on the strength of my will and of my belief. But with my body constraining me, I could solely look out to sea and think of Jeremy, somewhere there on the ocean, sweeping for mines and for freedom.

Today, though, with him still beside me, I could look at him as well as the sea, believing briefly that space had been conquered and that we were free. I snuggled against him, saying: "We're fortunate, aren't we, to have this secret access to the clifftop?"

"We certainly are, although of course we mustn't abuse our

privilege and get in the army's way. This is their territory, not ours, pro tem, just as that," he pointed, "used to be the coastguard's path – right at the cliff-edge in parts. When father was young, all the coast stations were still manned and each one contacted its neighbour twice every twenty-four hours using this path, which is marked as you see with heavy, whitewashed stones. These helped the coastguards when it was foggy and reflected the light of their lanterns at night. I've sometimes fancied that I could see their lighted lanterns still, moving after dark along the cliff. It has seemed to me that those men whose feet trod this path so regularly haven't entirely gone . . . that maybe their hants linger on."

'Hants' was dialect for ghosts and their haunts and it was strange to hear him use a Dorset word. I wondered whether he had used it to avoid the word 'ghost', which somehow seemed the wrong term.

I observed: "I've often had that feeling – almost as if past lives continue somewhere in time and as if, given the right conditions, we could find them. Perhaps, even, we do stumble over them periodically. The trouble is, in stumbling, we're inclined to think something outside our understanding is our fancy, rather than fact. We should try to change that."

"We should," he agreed, his mouth on mine now effectively silencing me. I was happy to be silent within the warmth of his arms and his kiss. I soared with the birds in my mind, becoming one with Jeremy, the wind and the sea.

# Four

We had a tradition, my love and I, that we observed each time he was home on leave. At sundown on the eve of his departure from Tyneham, we returned to the place where he had made his marriage proposal. He had proposed in early autumn, just as the harvest moon rose to fill the gap over Shoemaker's Lane. We were surrounded by sheep at the time, but were oblivious to them and to everything save the sight of that amazing moon and the feeling we shared of absolute belonging. I belonged not just to Jeremy and he to me, but also to the universe and all its galaxies. I knew then what belonging meant and knew happiness as I had never known it.

So we went back, each leave, to Cowleaze Knap as the sun sank over the sea, and we re-lived our memory.

That February evening, we were again blessed as we had so often been, with a clear sky and a huge sun that shone red on the horizon. And there were Dorset Horn sheep on the Knap as we climbed, chewing nonchalantly. Except that it was not autumn, but approaching spring, everything was just as it had been.

There was the same slight wind, the same awed feeling. Instead of now, it could so easily have been then, were it not for one thing. At that time, no war was raging and there was no ship waiting to take Jeremy from me. Peace reigned and, though there was an unpleasant German dictator, we had just been assured by our Prime Minister, following his third meeting with Adolf Hitler, that for the second time in our history there had come back from Germany to Downing Street peace with honour. Neville Chamberlain had then, as he waved the joint declaration that he and Hitler had signed, uttered the noteworthy words: 'I believe it is peace for our time'.

We did not doubt him – not then. The doubts had come later. So we were secure in our love and in our future when Jeremy asked me to marry him.

We were still secure in our love – more secure, even. But, while we climbed in the fading light, other words of Chamberlain's sprang unsolicited to my mind. 'From this nettle danger,' he had said, 'we pluck this flower safety.' He had not plucked the flower, however. He had instead misinterpreted Hitler's character and we had been plunged headlong in to the very danger that he thought he had averted.

And from tomorrow Jeremy would be back in the thick of that danger. Cold fear gripped me as against my will I considered the possibility he had earlier asked me to consider – that of him not returning physically to me. It was one thing to theorise about death, quite another to confront its actualities. I did not see how I could confront these, should Jeremy fail to return.

Oh, I believed him when he said that in death he would come straight to me, just as I had meant all I said after we left the Hoddens. We both had faith that dying did not divide and this faith remained unshaken. So it did not need testing. I was far from ready, yet, to put it to the test.

Resting my head against Jeremy's heart a little later as we stood embracing in the moon's silvery glow, I said: "Come back just as you are. Give me time to adjust my sight. I need more time, my darling!"

"So do I," he whispered. "So do I. And I'll try. Whether or not I succeed, remember this closeness. For this is how close I'll always be to you, no matter where I am, no matter how far. Cowleaze Knap is ours and our love will endure. Whatever happens, this is by no means the last time that we'll be here watching the sun sink and the moon rise."

Though I tried not to, I cried. This leave of Jeremy's differed from his previous leaves. A feeling of isolation filled me and I wanted to scream at war's futility. Young men who should have had their whole lives ahead of them were being sent to their deaths and my beloved husband was preparing me for something that he – consciously or subconsciously – sensed. War was terribly wrong. There had to be some saner solution to the world's problems. There had to be a future for Jeremy and me . . there just had to be!

Fear of no future threatened to engulf me. But, as Jeremy kissed my tear-wet cheeks and whispered words of love while holding me tightly, his strength flowed in to me almost like a tangible thing, making me stronger than I had been.

By the time that we descended from the Knap to the House I was able to face his departure bravely.

Next morning, at dawn, I drove him to Wareham station. In his officer's uniform, with two gold rings on his sleeve, he looked unbelievably handsome. I could hardly bear to look at him, while at the same time wanting to feast my eyes. Nor did I like to recall William's lost expression as he and Jeremy had said their 'goodbyes'. How hard, these partings . . . how they numbed the heart.

As our Wolseley climbed the hill that wound steeply between fields and neat hedgerows from the House to the Lulworth road, neither of us looked back across the Knap to see the north gable and the last of the chimneys disappear among the trees. We kept our gaze fixed ahead, instead, to where the hills of Corfe formed a ridge between sea and valley and to the dip where, in the morning mist, the grey face of Smedmore could be seen beyond Steeple's church, snug in its green coppice.

Far below us to our left, as we rode the ridge, were the protected waters of Poole Harbour, with all its islets, fusing with the mist.

Our road now wound and dropped down dramatically, through hanging woods, toward Creech. As I changed gear, Jeremy asked me: "What will you do today, after seeing off my train?"

"Perhaps, later, I'll start your portrait."

"And sooner?"

"There's the garden, which I've neglected rather."

"What –or who – could have caused your neglect, I wonder! Darling, don't just WORK in the garden. Pick some of that winter jessamine growing in the southern courtyard and arrange it indoors. Its scent is so glorious. Have it near you  as you reproduce my face. Then I'll be able to visualise you in a scented room working on your canvas. It helps, to have a specific mind-picture, doesn't it?"

Our little fingers linked of their own accord on the gear-lever as I answered: "Yes . . . it helps a bit."

But there was no help for us when we reached the station and saw his train – the train that would take him from Tyneham, ultimately to some unknown and distant destination. Ever conscious of the fact that, as we were constantly reminded, careless talk cost lives, Jeremy never discussed his destinations, even with me, if indeed he knew where he was destined. It was a feature of war-time that such secrecy was observed, even with wives. And I was glad of this in the respect that through not knowing where Jeremy was going, I could try to minimise the dangers in my mind.

Now his train, puffing steam over the platform, was waiting.

"I love you!" my husband said, gazing at me as if to imprint my every feature on his memory. "Aren't those words inadequate?"

"Yes." My throat constricted. "And yet they say everything that needs saying. I love you, body and soul, too, and I'll . . . I'll be waiting."

A final embrace and then he was aboard the train. It eased from the station. There was one last wave.

After buying some supplies in town, I returned to Tyneham. It was as if I were returning in a vacuum.

But there was work to be done. Once I had spoken with William, whom I found with his favourite, black, labrador, Hector, in the Porch Room, I headed straight for the garden. It was soothing, to turn the earth and to plant things. I had much digging to do, and some sweet pea seeds to sow in a trough that I had prepared previously. They liked a rich diet, which they rewarded with a long succession of blooms, sweetly perfumed. My state of mind had benefited from my gardening by the time that I went in to start sketching.

Before going in, I acted on Jeremy's suggestion and cut some winter jessamine. This grew close to the old magnolia that, facing the sun, was trained up a gable-end and a cydonia that in summer bloomed brilliant red. The entire south wing was given over to a creamy Banksia rose that had been growing there for more than a hundred years. As I cut the jessamine, breathing its fragrance in, I could hear the faint splashing of the fountain from the circular stone basin between the Terraces. William had constructed this to take the overflow from the reservoir in Hole Field, and it now accommodated newts, water boatmen and other pond-life. All kinds of species lived in Tyneham, side-by-side.

Some had died, and been immortalised. As I entered the House through its 'new' north entrance I saw again the mounted heads of a huge moose, a 'royal' stag and a sable antelope. These – from beyond Dorset – I disliked. It seemed most unkind, to kill something and then keep its head as a prize. Nor was the hall's camphory smell to my liking, reminding me as it did of medicine.

The north porch was thought of as new inasmuch as it had been added as recently as 1862. Above this was the L-shaped Porch Room, where the House was run from. All household correspondence was dealt with at the writing-desk by the big mullioned window, and there was a telephone extension so that calls could be made without the long haul to the downstairs telephone. There were also finches and canaries chirping and singing in window cages, bringing cheer to the room's occupier.

Jeremy had shown me his boyhood writing table, which was positioned in the Porch Room in a considerable draught. His father, John, had been a believer in hardship for his only son, never permitting any form of heating in Jeremy's bedroom, nor a hot-water bottle – nor even, for outdoor wear, a winter coat or gloves. I wondered whether he subconsciously blamed Jeremy for the loss of his much-loved Geraldine. Not that I had anything against the implanting in a child of self-discipline. And William had told me that the Tices had long considered the spending of funds on personal comfort to be an unnecessary indulgence. So maybe I was being hard on John. Maybe he was just doing for Jeremy as had been done for him – and, certainly, I could find no fault with the outcome of that upbringing.

After a late lunch with William, I set a canvas on my easel in what was once the footman's room, and in a vase nearby I re-arranged the winter jessamine. I had first arranged this down in the store room, but in carrying the vase up two flights of stairs I had upset my arrangement. And until it was totally to my liking I could not begin sketching. My surroundings had to be satisfactory in order for me to function artistically.

The footman's room, along with the butler's, was approached through a small sunken doorway and passage above the west wing. It was a long, low room, housing at one end brass-nail-studded boxes for travelling carriages and a big leather box which went away to school with one of Jeremy's ancestors in the seventeenth century. Wig boxes, also, were stacked against a wall, and there were several trunks containing clothes worn by long-dead Tices, as well as an oblong box brimming with rapiers and dress swords.

I liked to work in here, among the belongings of Jeremy's forebears, because the room had a particular atmosphere. It had, too, a north-window. This was less important, though, than its sense of presence, which caused me to doubt that I was surrounded solely by BELONGINGS from past centuries. For I seemed to feel the gaze on me of actual persons. Those that had gone before had not gone anywhere, but had stayed here, in my estimation. Were they watching me, these ancestors of Jeremy's, and if they were, why could I not see them in return? It irked me, that I could not see, for I regarded this as a failing. But soon such thoughts were forgotten, in the process of creation.

There were some intrusions, though, on my concentration. These came from the rats in the roof-space. Hordes of them inhabited the vast areas beneath the peaks and valleys formed by our roof. Their scamperings had been, when I first encountered them, somewhat disquieting, but by now my disquiet had eased. I ensured, all the same, that the low door which led in to the roof was kept locked. This did not guarantee freedom from rats in our living quarters, but it lessened the likelihood of them patrolling the passages as they used to when William was young, and gnawing doors and panelling.

With gentle strokes of my pencil I began to recreate Jeremy's face. I did this without any aids, for it was as if he were in front of me. I could see him almost as clearly in my imagination as if he had been. It began to be as though I were not imagining. He was standing, wasn't he, there by my winter jessamine?

I knew that this was not so, and yet I was no longer alone. As his face took form, I felt him close and did not feel that he had gone.

As day succeeded day, and as I started to paint his portrait, this feeling strengthened. With Jeremy's eyes looking at me from my canvas, there was no loneliness. There was a yearning, perhaps, for his arms around me and his mouth on mine. But I could cope with that yearning, until he came home. It was vital for me to cling to the belief that he WOULD come home.

I would wander the House sometimes, when the day's work was done, familiarising myself with my husband's heirdom, and I found it fascinating to reconstruct in my mind the life that had gone on.

The landing where the grandfather clock stood was situated at the third turning of the central staircase, and the clock faced a high south window with heraldic glass in memory of an ancestor. The family crest was featured there, in bright colour, together with a phoenix's wing and a gold visor, and there was an inscription honouring Jeremy's great-great-grandfather. From that landing, the square-cored stairway rose in four further sections to the top floors, with deal substituting there for the solid stone of the lower steps.

At the head of the staircase that led to the footman's and butler's old rooms was a little bedroom known as the Throne Room. So named by past children, this chamber contained a great many steps surmounted by a platform just able to accommodate the bed. How often, I wondered, had the scullery-maid, whose room this was in the old days, lost her footing on a floor that shelved in so surprising a manner – and where had she stood to dress and to comb her hair? There was nowhere, unless she stood on the bed or on a step.

There were rooms, too, for the cook, kitchenmaid, under and upper housemaids and another that had been the domain of Jeremy's grandmother's and mother's maid. Earlier on it had been the nursery and I had considered putting it to that use again some day. From its high window-seat there was a wonderful view of the lawn and avenue and, suspended from its ceiling, was an empty coconut husk recalling long-distant nursery days, along with a fragrance of tallow dip and of seaweed brought back from Worbarrow Bay by William's generation. This section of the attic was known as the Coconut Room and there was no surveying that ancient husk without seeing the room enlivened with children.

There was a room, though, that I favoured still more than this one as a nursery for Jeremy's and my future offspring. It was the room mid-way between the Porch Room and our bedroom which once rejoiced in the occupation of Sarah Mintern, my husband's nurse. Stories about her were legion, for she was a sterling character of strong opinion and great resilience, with black hair worn in a chignon and with a nose for naughtiness that meant no misdemeanors went unrewarded with a hairbrush. She would sit by the window, I had heard, humming to herself while her hands were at work with knitting, darning or sewing. It was the view from her window which more than anything influenced me in wanting her room for my babies' nursery. South-facing, it overlooked the kitchen yard and the House's oldest wing, which was ablaze every autumn with the glory of the Virginia Creeper that clambered not only over the walls but also over the roof and chimneys. I loved looking across to our medieval origin and imagining how life must have been when the Tices first found Tyneham. How far the outside world would have seemed, by brougham, and how self-sufficient those Tices would have needed to be. We still were, but to a lesser degree. Cook still baked bread in the brick oven within the old hall's great open fireplace and, forming the western end of these earliest buildings, was the dairy where our cows had been housed prior to the farm undertaking to supply us with milk, since when their area had been left free for hanging game and poultry. Finally, facing the Tudor entrance was the door to the dark vault used as a beer cellar until quite recently. Pre-war, its key was held by the butler, who rewarded with mugs of beer brewed on the premises those whose business brought them to the kitchen-yard. An azarool thorn tree grew outside the brewhouse, a seeming guardian to the brew within.

Times were changing, but the buildings remained, and it was interesting to contrast their current functions with those of the past. I dared not contemplate, though, how the old homestead's former inhabitants would react to their rooms' current usage, as a store for lumber and onions, apples and potatoes. And not only that, for they served, too, as cat-nurseries, where mothers could rear their young safely and undisturbed. Were the inhabitants of yesteryear aware of our treatment of their territory and, if they were, why did they not make their awareness known?

It seemed to me that I would have done, in their position, were the doing within my power. Were they powerless to acquaint living beings with their existence? It would appear that they were.

On the last day of February William, frowning as he browsed through THE TIMES, said to me: "Shouldn't we have heard by now from Jeremy?"

We were seated in the library and had just been watching foxes at play in front of the yuccas and the old walnut tree. These were young cubs, down from the cliffs, and we were amused by their antics. Less amusing were the grown foxes' and the rogue badgers' night-raids on our fowl houses.

"There's been a letter from him."

"Yes, but that was written from Portsmouth, before sailing."

"He's only been gone two weeks. While that's an age in terms of missing him, it isn't long in terms of hearing. We've waited more than a month, haven't we, periodically?"

"We have indeed! I don't know what's the matter with me."

"I hope I haven't been neglecting you, William."

"Oh," he smiled, "you mean since starting Jeremy's portrait? No, you haven't Catherine, And I, too, have been busy, so time has hardly hung on my hands. I should be adjusted by now to his absences, and shouldn't be bothering you with an old man's meanderings."

"Who is this old man? Do I know him?"

His grin gave him youth again. "You're good for me, Catherine. You seem never to see any age-discrepancy. You'd have me believe that I'm your contemporary!"

"You ARE, but for having been born slightly before me."

"Ah, the varying degrees of 'slightly'!" he sighed. "My creaking body tells me that I've been around for quite a time."

"I haven't heard any creaks. How do you feel inside?"

"Extraordinarily youthful, talking like this to you. You've banished my misgivings, Catherine, and done wonders for my equilibrium."

So he had been suffering – uncharacteristically – from misgivings, not meanderings. I pondered this as he retreated behind his newspaper again. But I told myself that it did not mean anything. We would hear from Jeremy soon. And there would come a day when he would be back home. I took up the knitting which had lain in my lap since the start of our conversation and persevered with the pullover I was making for my husband.

Daylight was fading. I especially liked the library around this time. It was a particularly peaceful room, with books cramming the many shelves and with the distinctive scent synonymous with old bindings. The northerly view from the mullioned window was over the shrubberies to William Woadden's Avenue, which came into being because of an illness afflicting Jeremy's great-grandfather. William Woadden, who was butler then, suggested felling some trees so that the invalid could see across the valley to the hill. His suggestion was acted on, and a gap was formed, then grassed over. And in the grassy gap had been planted poetaz narcissi in their thousands, while between the trees, looking eastwards, there grew in the mossy turf periwinkles and cyclamen, primroses, anemones, dogstooth violets and strawberries. All these contributed to a spectacular spring and summer, while over by the kitchen garden wall were pecan trees, escallonia, callicarpa and a fan palm which, despite our winds, had over the years grown tall and strong.

It suddenly struck me that every flower and shrub and tree growing in the grounds had its roots in Jeremy's ancestry. His ancestors had planted and planned for us, just as we tried to plant and to plan for our succesors. What a beneficial arrangement this was, with each generation augmenting the beauty of Tyneham.

"Where have you gone?" asked William.

"I was thinking of William Woadden."

"But you never knew him."

"No, I know of him, though, and have come to know his Avenue, which says quite a bit both about him and about the Tices. Not every family would listen to their butler's advice."

"We believe in listening, and in treating staff as friends rather than servants – if they're worthy of our friendship, that is, as they mostly have been. And I know you and Jeremy will continue in that tradition, for you have both already made a beginning." He sniffed the air and glanced around him before observing: "There's a storm brewing. The atmosphere has closed in – and just look at that ring around the moon!"

With surprising speed, the last light of day had withdrawn and, rising to pull down the blind, I looked to where William was pointing.

The moon was full and was encircled with the biggest ring I had ever seen, bringing to mind Dorset's saying: 'The larger the wheäl, the nearer the geäle'.

The storm broke while we were dining.

# Five

By the time that I went up to bed the gale had gathered strength. The south-west wind was no longer whining, as it had been, but roaring and tearing at the trees in West Plantation. I had seen outpost sycamores and elms bent sideways and permanently maimed from past buffetings. Hard now to believe it was just the wind and the rain I was hearing, and not the sea surging in. Torrents of rain against my window-pane, driven in by the tempest, had me fearing at times that the tide had forgotten to turn and that Tyneham would soon disappear forever beneath the sea.

At least our walls were four feet thick! I lay in my bed feeling profoundly thankful for this. No modern wall, surely, could withstand such ferocious gusts. I dreaded to think what might be happening to the Nissen huts, further down the valley, which were by their very nature temporary. Corrugated steel could be tossed in the air like a leaf by this wind. The thought did not bear the thinking.

Like repeated thunderblasts the tempest butted us, sending shudders through the House and shaking the frail old casements as the gale gained still further momentum.

I felt the wind within, as if I were a part of it. There was no question of sleeping, for I was the wind, with all my senses tuned to the anguish in me and to the need to vent this. Why was I anguished? Because man was killing himself unnecessarily . . . and because . . . because Jeremy was out there, somewhere, on the turbulent sea . . .

The wind that was part of me must be whipping the waves to a frenzy. Where was Jeremy? Was he currently at sea, or safely in harbour far, far from here? Wherever he was, he was not safe.

There was no safety, in war . . . there was nowhere for him . . . no anchorage.

I tried not to think of this, tried to separate myself from the wind. I felt feverish, tossing and turning and trying with all my might to shut out the storm. But there was no shutting it out – no escape from its merciless onslaught.

I must go to him. Solely through going could I help Jeremy . . . and he needed my help, badly. His need drew me.

As the wind I could go where no man went, for I was free, unfettered by a body, filled with vital energy.

A silken skirt swished. I heard this despite the roar of the wind, despite being the wind, and I saw that a woman from some bygone age was walking our passageways. I would have walked with her, but had no choice in the matter, for I was wanted elsewhere.

Where was I? The air was still suddenly and the moon was rising to fill the gap over Shoemaker's Lane. I was high on our hill, searching . . . searching for Jeremy.

He would come to me. I had thought to go to him, but he must have thought differently. And it was appropriate that we should meet on Cowleaze Knap, for this more than anywhere was ours. Jeremy had said so. He had also said that our love would endure and that we would often be here, watching the sun sink and the moon rise.

There we were! As if I were a mere onlooker, I saw the two of us – phantoms both – clasped in each other's arms, an echo from that moment when we were last so clasped.

What did this mean? Was it because I was the wind that I could see Jeremy and me as if I stood outside Catherine? It must be. So I must revert to being me in order to find Jeremy.

His voice was calling me. I tried to answer . . . tried to tell him that I was within the wind, but could not speak. Speech as I had known it was not given to the wind, so I was trapped by my new identity. And I knew that unless I spoke Jeremy would go.

I awoke.

There by my bed, in the half-light preceding dawn, stood my husband in full uniform. He stood mutely, gazing at me. "Jeremy," I gasped. "My darling Jeremy!"

"Hello, Catherine."

I opened my arms to him, but his remained at his sides and his face registered no pleasure at being home. Puzzled by this and by the fact that he remained standing, I asked: "Why are you back so soon? We weren't expecting you."

"I wasn't expecting to be back yet, either," he said, not moving. "I had no leave due to me. It has all been . . . very sudden. There was no warning, except for the storm which swept us off-course. I had thought one would be forewarned. But I came straight to you, just as I promised to."

These words chilled me for some reason. I didn't allow myself to dwell on why I felt such a chill. "Before you woke me, I was dreaming of you . . . of us, I mean. We were up on the Knap. I'm glad that this isn't a dream."

"In retrospect, you'll come to question whether you dreamed. That's how it has to be. You will remember the storm, but you won't be entirely sure whether . . . "

"Oh, yes, the storm!" I interrupted, sitting up. "Thank goodness that's over! It was quite the worst one I've ever known. I was filled with the weirdest imaginings. Aren't you going to kiss me, Jeremy?"

"No," he said slowly, seeming perplexed by having to refuse me. "I don't think so. I have news for you . . . news for us both."

"Oh?"

"I'm not sure where this news comes from . . . but we are soon to have a son."

"So we DID make a baby!"

"We did." Jeremy managed a little grin. "And we'll both be so proud of him. Remember that 'both', Catherine, whatever you might forget. It's most vital you should remember that I'll be as proud of him as you are."

"Of course you will! You're his father."

"I am, and shall continue to be, actively. I'll be like a guardian angel to him, and to you, as you go through . . . all that has to be gone through. Some of the thoughts you'll think will come straight from me and my strength will be your strength from now on, Catherine. So stay serene, beloved. Don't grieve. There's no cause for grief. Try to see, and understand, that – please."

"You're frightening me, Jeremy! Why aren't you holding me?"

"Don't be frightened . . . and think back to what we said, about bodies. I don't need to hold you, to be close to you. We can be closer, now, than we've ever been. And we shall be. So no doubts, my sweet Catherine."

I must have drifted off to sleep. When I next looked to where he had stood there was no sign of Jeremy.

I lay for a few minutes luxuriating in the knowledge of his early return. To have him back so quickly was like being given a beautiful, unexpected gift. I must make the most of it!

As I left our bed and padded on bare feet over to the window to draw back the curtains, I was struck quite forcibly by the degree of stillness that had settled over everything. After that storm, this was almost eerie. It was as if the whole world had stopped breathing. And it seemed, strangely, to me that the atmosphere was due somehow to Jeremy. Where was he?

He had probably gone to tell William he was home. He would not be breakfasting without me. I glanced at my watch. It was past eight o'clock. My men would be waiting for me to join them.

William would be as surprised as I had been to see Jeremy. It was especially surprising that Jeremy had succeeded in making the journey through such a storm.

I let the blind up and blinked at the scene of devastation that greeted me. At least a dozen trees had been torn down and now lay haphazardly, their roots above the ground. Poor trees, to be uprooted so suddenly! There had been no time for them, yet, to adjust to death. They would need time, just as we would to accustom ourselves to the changes in our landscape. So much had changed. My view had never looked so desolate. I turned from it, feeling horribly afraid.

All was not as it seemed. There was something . . . something that I was not grasping. Whatever it was, I did not want to grasp it. I knew, though, from the knot that was tightening in me that it had to do with Jeremy.

I would go to him. He would tell me that my fears were unfounded. He would hold me and all would be well again.

But he hadn't held me, while I was in bed. He had said . . . Frantically, I searched my memory. There was no remembering his words, though. I was too taut, to remember . . . too scared.

Heading for the dining-room, once I had washed and dressed, I met Annie, a village-girl who came in daily to help me with the housework. Times being hard, we had to make do with a minimum of staff. "Have you seen Mr Tice?" I asked.

"I seed 'un," she answered, bobbing in a kind of curtsey, "eatin' brikfast."

So Jeremy had been so hungry after his journey that he HAD begun breakfast without me! Thanking Annie, I ran along the corridor from the hall and took the six steps up to the dining-room two at a time. Then I burst in, breathlessly.

"Good heavens!" William said, rising to his feet. "Whatever's wrong, Catherine?"

He was alone in the room. Registering this, I blurted out to him: "I can't find Jeremy."

Looking perturbed, he asked me: "Why the search? Jeremy won't be back for weeks . . . will he?"

"He came home in the night. That is," I bit my lip, "I THINK he did. Oh dear, now I don't know what to think!"

I was swaying on my feet when William, who could be

surprisingly nimble when he needed to be, caught hold of me. "Come and sit down, my dear," he advised, guiding me, his arm round my shoulders, to the chair next to his. "I expect it was the storm, causing you to . . . to imagine things."

"I wasn't imagining it. I can't have been." My legs were so weak that I was glad of the chair beneath me and of the table to hold on to. "Jeremy was with me. And . . . and Annie has seen him. She . . . " I knew suddenly that it was William she was saying she had seen. The knowledge made my eyes brim.

"She meant me, didn't she?" William suggested gently. "Could you perhaps have dreamed of his homecoming, Catherine?"

"No," I told him, as he poured me a cup of tea, "it wasn't a dream. I know that it wasn't, because I WAS dreaming, when Jeremy woke me. He was definitely in our bedroom, telling me that . . . that . . . "

"Drink some tea. It's good for the memory. Incidentally, there's a letter for you from Jeremy."

"Is there?" I did my best to pull myself together. It was awful of me to worry William, who was looking at me with such concern. I looked at the letter lying on the leather wallet our mail arrived in, under lock and key, but could not consider reading it yet. "So the postman got through to us, despite the effects of the storm," I said.

"Yes." I could see that William was choosing his next words carefully: "You're thinking that if Percy got through, Jeremy could have done so, too. He didn't, though, Catherine – at least, not physically. If he had, he'd be breakfasting with us, wouldn't he?"

William was right. He must be. Reflecting on everything, I sipped some tea. So Jeremy had not come to me physically. He had come without his body – achieving a feat that we had both known could be achieved. And he had come to tell me something. If I could just calm down, I would remember what that something was – and, remembering, might make sense of all this. Taking a deep breath, I then took another . . . and another, slowing my breathing right down. Peace now began filtering in to where chaos had so recently reigned. And, slowly, with the peace came knowledge. I smiled as I told William: "Jeremy came for a reason. He and I . . . we are to have a son. That's what he came to tell me."

William's eyebrows lifted. "He did? Heavens above! I hardly know how to react to that, except perhaps to say that I hope with all my heart that Jeremy is correct. It would be good to have a baby's presence in the House again. Would a congratulatory kiss be in order, Catherine?"

Whether it would or would not, William kissed my forehead then and we continued with breakfast. As we did so, I could not escape the feeling that there was something else – something I had not remembered. And every so often I noticed William looking at me as if he, too, believed I had not told the whole story. There was a vague unease in us both that went unspoken as we talked about the storm and about how to deal with its aftermath. Knowing William was hoping I would open Jeremy's letter and read bits of it to him, I did so. But I did not read it fully until I was alone.

In the Porch Room, after breakfast, I read:

'Beloved,

It might seem to the ship's company that I am with them at sea, but in truth I have remained with my woman in Tyneham. Can you sense my presence? It should be almost a tangible thing and I trust that it is, since I want you never to feel far from me.

I wonder when you'll be writing to tell me that we made a baby! Not that I doubt we did. I'll never forget that night, my darling, nor indeed any of the nights and days we've shared. They are all part of me now, as you are, and go with me wherever I go.

How are you and William? I feel bad at not doing the lion's share of all the work that needs doing in Tyneham. Come to that, I'm not even doing a mouse's portion! Please tell grandfather that I'll make it up to him when this war grinds finally to a halt. He'll be able to relax a little at last. Not that I can imagine him relaxing while there are still seeds to sow and trees to plant and umpteen things needing organising . . .

Loving you, Catherine, has made a new and better man of me. I can now see so much that I was blind to previously. Our love enhances everything, somehow, heightening awareness of this world of ours . . . and of the unseen world, around and within, which colours things according to how we think. Beautiful thoughts, I have come to see, bring us beauty . . . and it's wise never to think thoughts of the darker variety. It's so true, that we reap as we sow. Even Hitler's going to know the truth of that, by the time we're through!

The war does drag on, but can't for much longer. It's said that good things come to an end. Well, bad things must, too – and as soon as they do, I'll be winging my way home to you. Meanwhile, we'll try to meet bodilessly, won't we? That must be within our capability. Love, I firmly believe, is the key to life's every mystery.

Thank you for your letter, incidentally, and for sending in such measure Tyneham's tranquillity. This reached me and restored some sanity to the troubled world I have to inhabit while at sea. Oh, for an end to man's insanity and inhumanity, so that the world can revert to some sort of normality!

I was glad to learn that you'd made a start on my portrait. Knowing how hard you work, and how fast, I don't doubt that it will be framed and hung well in advance of my next return.

How I yearn to see it, and to hold you again in my arms!

Consider yourself held there, please.

Forever your Jeremy '

As I read, and re-read, the letter, my feeling of unease decreased. There was nothing wrong, nothing forgotten. Jeremy's written words had supplanted his spoken ones and, holding the letter that he had so recently held, I felt strong again. Writing back to him, I told of last night's storm and of our meeting, and of how he had succeeded in removing any need for me to tell him we had made a baby. My response was in the box in the hall well before three, which was when our odd man emptied it, taking its contents to Tyneham post office on his way to the farm to collect the milk for tea.

The following morning, I took time from my painting and from my chores to visit Jessie Richards and her new daughter. Jessie was married to George, a hedger, and their stone cottage was quite close to the shore. One of a terrace of four, it stood along the Worbarrow road and from its rear windows was an unrivalled outlook over Flower's Barrow, and the spectacular sweep of coloured cliffs as far as Arish Mell. The road between the farm and the Bay had been built by the Admiralty back in the days when access to the coastguard station was vital. We knew this as the Lower Road and it bordered the gwyle, curving with the bends of the stream. Before its construction, the path to the sea lay between the top edge of the Corn Grounds and the wall of Gold Down. Now known as the Upper Road, I preferred it to its more modern (and more even!) counterpart and, en route for Jessie's, started along it from West Plantation.

Thirty silver firs growing there had fallen victim to the storm. They were either down or split in two, and an ancient yew on the north-east side of the House had also been uprooted, along with trees of other varieties. What a storm it had been! One night of such ferocity had been quite enough for me. I would not have wanted to experience the December, 1929, five-day gale, which succeeded in blowing the village hall and piano away and which was still, understandably, a local topic of conversation.

I was wearing wellingtons, which proved a wise precaution after all the rain. With Hector at heel I walked through thick mud on to grass that was spongy, stepping over branches and often over trees. I passed the place where stunted sycamores, oaks and maples grew slanting towards the east, blown to this shape by a succession of sea-winds. Pheasants liked to nest in the reedy foliage of the montbretias and day lilies that thrived in the shelter of these poor distortions. I had not eaten pheasant since seeing them nesting there, and mutton had not much tempted me since I had lived in the vicinity of sheep. The day was approaching, I had come to think, when I would altogether avoid flesh-eating.

I breathed deeply. Tyneham valley air was like no other air I had ever breathed and my lungs could never tire of it. Salty, it consisted also of seaweed, storm-tossed leaves, garlic, cow parsley and all the many ingredients brought by the changing seasons and left to linger on the breeze. No perfumer could ever capture this fragrance of nature. It was good, to be breathing here.

From the front of Jessie's and George's house, one could see the Tout. This was an elongated hill jutting out to sea between Worbarrow Bay and Pondfield Cove in the mode of a small narrow-necked peninsula. William Lisle Bowles had written, early in the nineteenth century, that most of the hills of the sea-coast and through Dorsetshire were still pronounced Teuts by the common people. Teut had now turned to Tout and ours put me in mind of a slumbering dinosaur almost entirely surrounded with water. Jeremy and I had sat on its summit, before the war, while he told me the story of the smuggler who was stoned to death at Cow Corner, which was at the western end of Worbarrow Bay and which faced us as Jeremy told his tale. It seemed that the smuggler, when chased by revenue men, ran away from them unaware that at the beach's far end the cliff rose like a precipice, cutting off his escape. So, having no other option, he then ran in to the sea, where he was stoned mercilessly to death. According to Jeremy, whenever the moon waned the smuggler's screams and his attackers' shouts were to be heard echoing in the still of night. So I had listened, at the appropriate times, for echoes of that strife, and periodically these had reached me from wherever they had gone. They were stored in some dimension other than this one, along with every event that had ever been. All that had gone before would come again, and again, in circular motion, with events recurring endlessly.

This notion struck me still more forcefully when I first saw Jessie's baby. That wee girl, held so lovingly by her proud mother in the tiny bedroom she had been born in, had come from somewhere beyond the womb. Conception might seem to be the beginning, but it could not be, because there was no beginning to existence, just as there was no ending. Where, then, had this infant come from, and where would she go, upon death? She would go where we all went – back to the source of creation. But before then she had ahead of her her little lifespan.

"How sweet she is!" I said, looking with wonder at the brand new, cherubic face belonging to baby Beatrice. "And how small! The things I've knitted might be a bit big for her, just yet."

"That's best," said fresh-faced Jessie, who was propped up on pillows in bed. "Thanks most kindly for knittin' them."

Just then, the child opened her eyes, which were blue and somehow knowing. Her face might be new, but those eyes, for sure, mirrored a soul that had seen this earth before. I asked: "She was born during the storm?"

Jessie nodded. "The wind was makin' me leary. Then she started birthin'. I won' be fergittin' her birthday."

Nor, for different reasons, would I. Perhaps certain storms brought their own phenomena. This one had brought Beatrice, along with news of my son. There was no knowing what else it had brought, nor what other wonders were being constantly wrought. There was, though, knowledge that we were in the hands of a restorative Providence.

When Beatrice started crying for her next feed I left, feeling awed by the miracle of birth and by the fact that Jessie's and George's love had helped bring another life in to the world.

Hector was waiting patiently for me on their doorstep and wagged his tail as I emerged. We crossed the gwyle and took a long route home via Baltington, passing one of the withy-beds that were a local feature and that reflected the redness of the bracken. Withies were the willow stocks grown as osiers for lobster pots. I had also used some, from our enclosure in Rook Grove, as canes for supporting my carnations. Hector and I were tired by the time that we had crossed Three Acres and West Mead and arrived home, and I would not hazard a guess as to which of us was hungriest. But I had by virtue of my roundabout route seen for myself that the storm had, amazingly, spared the Nissen huts – which must, I concluded, owe their salvation to their very sheltered position. I had, too, spoken to David Maynard, an RAF officer from the rectory, who had told me that he had seen a primrose-throated shore-lark this morning. This seemed to me a sure sign of spring, and I paid news of the lark more attention than the news that within the past week the 5th Schnellboot Flotilla had sunk four British ships off Dorset's coast. It did not do to dwell on ships sinking, nor indeed on any bad news. Our path to victory did not lie in brooding over defeats, but in the optimism of a lark's song and of unswerving faith and firm resolve. I admit, though, that I could solely be optimistic after checking that Jeremy's ship was not among the casualties.

Keen to finish his portrait, I virtually closeted myself in the footman's old room for the next week.

Over tea at the end of this period, William asked me: "How is the work progressing?"

We were relaxing in Oak Hall, which faced east with an entrance from the terrace and which was a big, square room. William was warming his hands in the heat thrown from the 'tortoise' stove. "I'm pleased with progress," I told him. "That is, I think I'm pleased."

"There speaks the perfectionist! No artist has ever grown great through complacence. The road to greatness is steep and paved with doubt as well as with dedication. That's how it has to be, if new heights are to be achieved, Catherine."

"You're right!" I sighed, gazing through the window to where the grassy slope of the avenue seemed to touch the sky. "But who's to say whether there's any greatness in me? There might easily not be."

"I agree. Greatness isn't given to all and sundry. Is it given at all, I wonder, or does it have to be earned through endeavour? Whichever, I suspect that its seeds have been sown in you, my dear, and that you will nurture them as they need to be nurtured. If you will let me see Jeremy's portrait I shall, of course, be still better equipped to proffer an opinion."

"You mean, see it now? But it's unfinished!"

"As is our Gainsborough in the dining-room," William said with a boyish grin, "which nonetheless avoids amateurishness, don't you think?"

"I shan't allow you near it, if you intend comparing me with him!"

"The comparison is already made, and my verdict is that you're prettier than he was," laughed William. "So now do I qualify for a peep at your portrait? I've shown remarkable restraint, I think, in not stealing a peep before this."

I could not resist his boyishness, for he was so reminiscent of Jeremy. But I was in no hurry to finish tea.

How catastrophic it would be, to see sympathy in his eyes, instead of esteem, or to have to face the fact that my best would be a real artist's reject. Could there be a worse catastrophe?

After entering my 'studio', William stood staring at his grandson. He stared for so long that I hardly knew what to do, nor how to deal with the silence that filled the room.

Then, still surveying my canvas, he said: "I wasn't altogether sure what to expect. You were so adamant, to start with, that your speciality is landscapes. That may or may not be the case.

But this portrait . . . takes my breath away. It is, indisputably, Jeremy to a 'T'. You have breathed life in to him . . . given him immortality."

The telephone rang then, snatching William from me.

# Six

I had wondered arrogantly whether there could be any worse catastrophe for me than to fail as an artist. There could, I saw instantly, as William returned from the telephone. His face was ashen, his tread heavy. There was no need for him to speak. I knew without speech that something had happened to Jeremy.

We faced each other, wordlessly, there in front of my husband's portrait, for the longest moments I had ever known. Then, trance-like, William clasped both my hands strongly in his and spoke: "That was James Collis, from the Admiralty . . ringing as a friend, not officially . . . to tell me . . . that Jeremy's ship . . . "

He could not finish. I felt frozen. "Is there any hope?"

"No."

One word – just one: how like William, to be absolutely honest with me and not to pretend that the information received might be wrong. No sense in false hopes, no sense in . . . anything. I was gripped by a feeling of such futility that it did not occur to me how HE must be suffering. I was the sufferer, I alone, and my pain could not be borne. A cry emitted from me: "He can't be dead . . . he CAN'T be . . . not my Jeremy!"

I heard the cry as if it issued from someone else entirely. I also, in that moment, saw William's face and was ashamed. Jeremy was not mine exclusively. He might seem to be, because of what we were to each other, but this was a fallacy. I had been forgetting completely that he was William's cherished grandson and also heir to Tyneham. Poor William! How could I even begin to help him?

"There is no death," William suddenly said, his arms now

around me. "There's just a . . . transition to a different level of being. This, I believe completely. So we won't be without Jeremy. We . . ."

". . . mustn't grieve. There's no cause for grief . . . and Jeremy doesn't need to hold me, to be close to me. He said so. He . . . "

In a rush, it all came back to me and I was gradually able to share Jeremy's visit with William. It comforted us both to know that he had visited and that he would be a guardian to us and his son from now on. And it came as no surprise, ultimately, to learn that his ship had been blown up on the night of our storm. Because this had happened in shark-infested waters, I was almost relieved to learn that it had been blown up, fast, rather than just sunk. Bodies might be unimportant, but better for Jeremy's not to have been torn apart by sharks. William and I wished, though, that we could have brought his body home to Tyneham.

This would have helped, somehow, for with a burial and a gravestone we would have had a focus for our feelings. However, knowing ours was a wish without hope of fulfilment, we wasted little time on wishing.

We kept busy, instead, working all the hours God sent and channelling all our energies in to the thousand things that needed doing. Being busy left less time to think.

Both William and I tried to take Jeremy's advice not to grieve, but this was by no means easy. However close to us Jeremy might be, we could not SEE him and at times our faith was tested sorely. Was he here, as he had said he would be, or was he elsewhere doing whatever souls did when first freed from their bodies? We concluded eventually that he was everywhere, and in the very air we breathed, but we did not reach this conclusion easily.

Those were dark days, through which occasionally a little light filtered in. I don't know where we would have been without Lily who, bustling about in the background of our lives while

70

mourning silently, helped convey some sense of normality. And she brought us many messages from villagers who wanted us to know that we were not alone in our tragedy.

It was hard not to feel alone, hard not to feel isolated by our misfortune, though with this war on we were of course only too conscious of how commonplace it had become to have sacrificed a husband, father or son. Yes, everyone was making sacrifices. Ours was not large, compared with some. But it SEEMED the worst thing ever to have happened to anyone.

We sat at mealtimes surrounded by Jeremy's ancestors. Seeing them there, on the dining-room walls, reminded me of saying to him on his last leave that I would wait to paint his portrait until his face looked more lived in. Well, I had not waited, and now his face would never age. He would remain as young always as he had been when I painted him. Not that I had finished the painting. I was too burdened by my unbearable sense of loss even to think of finishing it.

And William had told me, on that fateful evening just as the telephone began ringing, that I had breathed life in to Jeremy – giving him immortality. Oh, the irony of those words . . . oh, the anguish!

Perhaps the worst pain came when I took up my knitting. I took it up unthinkingly, seeking I suppose some kind of therapy. Then, registering the wool's texture and shade, and the size of the garment I was making, it flooded back to me that the jumper was for Jeremy. Without knitting a single stitch, I flung the work from me.

William commented: "I saw that coming, Catherine, but couldn't think how to avert it."

We were in Oak Hall, having had tea, Horus and Hector at our feet. "It's hard, isn't it," I said, composing myself with difficulty, "to come to terms with Jeremy no longer needing any of his things?"

"It certainly is. While we live, we surround ourselves with

belongings, which assume an importance of sorts. In fact, to some they are all-important. Yet we leave this world, as we enter it, with nothing." He frowned, leaning back in his big armchair and closing his eyes momentarily. Opening them again, he smiled wryly at me and said: "We are rich or poor, my dear, according to how much love we give and receive. Jeremy was rich, and is still, in your love, as you are in his. I hope that helps to put the jersey in perspective?"

"Yes, it does." I felt humbled by his summing up. "Love lives on, doesn't it – love and spirit? I never doubted that, before Jeremy died, but recently doubts have crept in at times."

"They're bound to, Catherine, while we're still reeling from the shock of his passing. Theory is easy, practice quite another thing. As the shock wears off, though, I KNOW we'll feel him close. You will, especially, for I suspect no woman has ever been loved more than he loves you. If he could come to you on the night of the storm, he could again – and will, I'm sure, whenever your need is at its most acute. I'm talking, of course, of him coming in a form whereby you'll see him. Until we're practised in feeling, seeing really IS believing."

"The fact that I saw him then should suffice," I said, "and it does, in a sense. It's the missing, isn't it, that's our undoing? If it weren't for missing him so much, I could be more as Jeremy might expect me to be. I'm not at all proud of myself, for failing miserably to practise as I preached!"

"I'm proud of you, Catherine," William told me, "so you've no need to be."

I was deeply touched by his words – indeed by all those he had spoken since the knitting incident. Retrieving Jeremy's part-finished jumper from the floor, I said, strongly: "I shall finish this. It should just fit someone who means a great deal to me."

William smiled. In his smile I saw Jeremy.

Mother rang that evening. I had been hoping that she would not ring just yet, suggesting a visit.

"You're so much on my mind, dear," she said, "that I think I should come to Tyneham. I could arrange things, I find, on checking my diary, to be with you by the weekend."

"I'd like that," I told her, "except that . . . that William and I . . . we're fine . . . but really not quite up to socialising. So would you very much mind deferring your visit, just for a short while?"

She took exception to this, as I had feared she might. "Socialise, indeed! You seem to be forgetting that I'm your mother, not some casual visitor. No, I don't mind postponing my trip, or abandoning it altogether – if that's what you'd prefer."

"Of course it isn't, Mother! Please try to see that I'd just be bad company. I'd feel uneasy about you coming all the way from Bournemouth to have a miserable time with me, whereas in a few weeks . . . "

Mother could not seem to see and nor would she, now, consider visiting me. I turned in that night feeling guilty. My guilt turned in time to a fresh surge of grief. Eventually, I cried myself to sleep.

It was still dark when I awakened. Something seemed to have woken me and I lay wondering what this could be, for the House was silent. My feeling persisted that I had not awoken of my own accord, but I was given no immediate grounds for feeling as I did.

Then I heard a sound that was indistinct and that for a few moments I could not identify. I lay listening, my senses strained, in an attempt at identification. Except that I was the sole woman in the House, I would have said after a while that the sound I could hear was of a woman crying.

But both Lily and Annie went home at night – and I felt certain that it was not William I was hearing. A man cries differently from a woman – and, besides, the crying came from far off, whereas William's room was quite close to mine. I was struck by the notion that someone was crying in some other time.

I dismissed this idea as capricious – or, rather, tried to dismiss it. But the crying continued and I could make no sense of its continuance.

In an attempt to establish its source, I left the warmth of my bed and, lighting a lamp, stepped out in to the corridor.

My shadow went with me as I explored. It merged with all the other shadows that the lamplight brought.

I paused outside William's door. It was as I thought. There was no sound from within. It was not him crying. But who, if not him?

Floorboards creaked protestingly beneath my bare feet as I followed the faint sound to the farthest room in the west wing. This was an attic that had belonged in earlier days to the parlourman and head-housemaid. I pushed the door open and went in, holding my lamp high in front of me. The crying ceased abruptly.

It did not occur to me to feel afraid as I shone the lamp around the room seeking the woman who had disturbed my sleep. I even searched for her beneath the big bed, but there was no sign of anyone, and no crying now to lead me in any specific direction.

So I went back to bed. No need to disturb William. I had not felt threatened by the intrusion. Far from threatening me, it had simply aroused my curiosity. And, I realised as I snuggled back down between the sheets, the exercise had taken my mind off Jeremy. For the very first time since he died, I had stopped thinking of him for a short while. So it was possible to think thoughts other than of him. I tried again to think who could have been crying.

And I came quickly to the conclusion that it could not have been a living person. Who, then, and why? I slept again without finding an answer to my question.

Next morning, I questioned William, who had heard nothing. "I must have slept unusually soundly," he said, "unless . . . "

"Yes?"

"I'd intended saying unless your imagination was playing tricks." He grinned. "But I've since thought better of it."

"It's as well for you that you did," I said, smiling back at him. "For I truly believe that some woman, somewhere, was crying."

William eyed me quizzically. "I take it we aren't speaking of someone alive?"

"That's right! Do you know of any ancestress who had an unhappy life?"

"I know of no-one specific, although of course there has been unhappiness in Tyneham – of the kind we are experiencing now and, I'm sure, of other kinds. On the whole, though, this valley has tended to protect its own – insulating its inhabitants in a very real sense against the disillusionments and heartaches that often prevail in a less restorative environment. So I would venture the opinion that there's been less unhappiness here, pro rata, than there's been elsewhere. Which isn't of too much help to you, I'm afraid!"

"Oh, but it is! It narrows the field, doesn't it? The less unhappiness there's been, the less difficulty I should have in establishing who was crying."

"Don't overlook the fact that the wind can sigh – and that its sigh can sound at times like a human cry."

"I'll try not to overlook anything. But I bet it wasn't the wind!"

"I wonder whether we'll ever know what it was – or who. I've also been wondering about Jeremy's son. How soon can I expect news of him?"

"Quite soon. Do we, though, need a medical opinion?"

"Hardly," agreed William, reaching for my hand and adding: "I don't doubt any more than you do that Jeremy has left us his son and that a new era has begun."

This brought tears to my eyes, for Jeremy had spoken, by the Twelve Acres bridle gate en route for Ocean Seat, of the era that had gone and of a new era after the war. I had not known, then, that I would have to face the post-war years without him, although he had wanted me to be prepared for that contingency. Dearest Jeremy! How concerned he always was for me – how concerned he still was, from where he had gone. I would bear his son and would become so receptive to things unseen that the three of us would be as much a family as we would have been, were Jeremy still here physically. In addition, I would achieve, artistically, all that was within my widened capability. Maybe I had had to lose Jeremy in order to become a woman worthy of him. Not that I had lost him – that was just an expression. Love was never lost. It was simply processed in to a different form of energy.

I said to William: "We still have plenty to look forward to, haven't we?"

"Yes, we have – and as far as we can we must look forward, not back."

Spring evenings in Tyneham began with the ring doves calling from the lime trees as the sun went down, and as springtime wore on we grew accustomed to the songs of blackbirds and thrushes from the Hole Field thickets and the garden shrubberies. There were, too, in the orchard and avenue, nuthatches, tits, willow warblers, chiff-chaffs and woodpeckers, while a pair of buzzards lived in a silver fir behind the orchard. Hollow sycamores in the terrace garden housed barn and tawny owls, and there was always a cuckoo to be heard, at this regenerative time of year.

Leaves were unfurling on the trees and the valley was bright with primroses. The huge horse chestnut tree planted by Jeremy's great-grandfather last century was always first in to leaf – and how it graced the lawn, there outside Oak Hall, with its majesty and its wide, sweeping branches.

Our son would play in the 'room' formed by the lower branches, which swept the ground in places, just as his father had played there yesterday. Or would it be Jeremy playing again, reborn in his son, now growing in my womb? It would be both of them, and their forefathers, for in each of us there lived on those that had gone before, while we were the founders of those yet to come.

So went my thinking that spring, as sudden mists rolled in from the sea, obscuring everything and giving their gift of heightened colour to nature. Within such a mist, so surprising in its suddenness and in its chill, I could easily believe that time was indeed without significance and that yesterday, today and tomorrow were one. There was no time other than this, and through the mist I would see, if my sight permitted, the world that the dead and the unborn inhabited. But I had seen, so far, no more than swirling vapour, while hearing just the distant lowing of the Shambles lightship.

I was hoping, naturally, to see Jeremy, and hear him, as I had seen and heard him on the night of the storm. I heard instead, one month from when I had first heard it, the sound of crying.

I was not in bed this time, for it was early evening.

I had just been to look at Jeremy's portrait, which I had not touched since the news of his death. In fact, this was the first time that I had even looked at it since then. I had progressed inasmuch as I could look at it. Soon, I would progress to the point of finishing it – or so I promised myself.

The crying was coming from the direction of the Chintz Room, which was two flights up from the Porch Room, on the House's eastern front, and which still retained its Tudor panelling. Determined, now, to know who was crying, I proceeded softly along the little landing from the top of the narrow staircase and stood awhile outside the Chintz Room door before pushing it open. Beyond question, the sound of crying was coming from within. Someone was deeply distressed, just as I had been over Jeremy. Had been? Yes. Calm had come, from my distress, and I now accepted his death.

Scarcely breathing, I went in. There was no need for a lamp, now that the days were lengthening. I glanced round the room. It appeared to be empty. Light filtered through the old mullioned windows, of which there were two – one each in the north and east walls – containing ancient stained glass roundels. Beside the chimney breast was the built-in cupboard that was kept well stocked with first aid equipment and medical stores, the nearest doctor living at Corfe and a village messenger often appearing at our door – especially pre-war – asking for help in some emergency or other. By the cupboard were two chintz-covered easy chairs and between these and the dimity-curtained windows was a large four-poster, its curtains closed.

There were other chairs in the room, and wardrobes and a Regency dressing-table, but nowhere could I see a person. I could still, though, hear crying. This was little louder than it had been from the foot of the stairs leading up to this wing and yet there was no doubt in my mind but that it was coming from here.

If I was right, it could solely be coming from the four-poster. I tiptoed over and prepared to peep between the curtains.

I was about to peep when – as before – the crying ceased.

There was silence and then, from a different direction, I distinctly heard laughter. Someone was laughing, over by the door.

I turned in time to see a woman wearing a long, green silken dress with a boned bodice and high collar. I saw her clearly. She had her back to me. Then, as I watched with awed eyes, she became fainter before simply evaporating.

# Seven

That was the first of several sightings of the woman in green. Each time I saw her, though, her face was turned from me. I found this exceedingly frustrating and grew more and more resolute to see what she looked like. I was equally resolved to find out why she cried.

Rather strangely, William still had not heard her crying. I wondered at this, since on one occasion we were both in the Porch Room when I heard her – yet he heard nothing. Most men would have ridiculed me and my hearing, but William didn't, just as Jeremy wouldn't have done. William even volunteered the explanation that such sounds were perceived through the mind rather than through the ear, and that therefore one could conclude that my mind was more attuned than his was. He also said it was logical in a sense that our home would be haunted, having been the scene over the centuries of so many comings and goings.

I supposed him to mean births and deaths, rather than everyday to-ings and fro-ings, and this set me thinking about the birth that, next autumn, I would be very much involved in. I had now seen our dear old doctor who, after examining me, had nodded wisely and confirmed that I was to be a mother in November. Then, with tears in his eyes for Jeremy, whom he had delivered, Doctor Cotterrell had said: "You'll need to be both mother and father to the infant. This is a happy and a sad day, indeed. Thanks be to heaven that you are strong." I did not always feel strong. There were times when I felt frighteningly weak. But then, at my weakest, there would come to me some sense of Jeremy's proximity – and his love subsequently flowed through me, strengthening me beyond worldly means. I was greatly blessed, having him watching over me so lovingly. I grew ever more conscious of his presence. And he would be beside me when his son entered the world. At birth, our baby would almost certainly retain some memory of his existence prior to that entry. What would his existence have been – and had he chosen to be born to Jeremy and me? I had as yet no answer to these questions, but this I believed – though children's memories of pre-existence faded after time spent on the physical plane, deep within them their soul's secrets must remain. And I was locating mine again, with Jeremy's help and additionally with the help of the woman in green. Who was she? Presumably, a Tice from some past century who could not bring herself to leave. I could well understand her attachment to Tyneham, but imagined that it must be lonely for her, still to be tied here so long after her life. Was it because she was tied that she was crying? I resolved to ask her this, and other questions, at the very first opportunity.

I saw her again at the beginning of May, when the poetaz narcissi were in bloom and the air sweet with their perfume. I had found that whenever I was about to see her there was an exceptional stillness on the air, almost as though time were held in a state of suspension. I was in my room preparing for bed when this stillness settled over me. I turned from my toilet expectantly.

And there, standing near the window in a shaft of silvery light, was the woman in green. For the first time, she was facing me – a young woman, with hair of a reddish colour and with a sadness about her that I could feel. Her face was somehow familiar and it seemed to me that her dress dated from the Tudor era. It was very elaborate, with a ruff and with encrusted jewellery. But it was her face that most interested me. Where and when had I seen it previously? I tried to remember – and, in trying, forgot all the questions I had wanted to ask her. We faced each other in silent appraisal, she from her century, I from mine, and she faded even as I faced her, withdrawing somewhere beyond my horizon.

I went to bed feeling elated. I had seen her face, so could now identify her from among all the portraits. That must be where I had already seen her – downstairs, amidst Jeremy's ancestry! In order, therefore, to know her name and her life-span, I had merely to find her again. I fell asleep eager for morning and for my search to begin.

By the time that William appeared for breakfast, I was half-way round the dining-room and had not yet found my girl in green. She was more girl than woman and her face was vivid in my memory. But the faces on the walls were not arranged in any order and I had not so far chanced upon a face or costume at all like hers.

"What are you looking for, Catherine?" asked grandfather. "Or should I ask who you are looking for?"

"I've seen my woman again," I answered him excitedly, "and she's from Tudor times, I think. She came to my room last evening. I seemed to recognise her face, so must at some time have seen her portrait. Where would I have seen it, in your opinion?"

"I doubt it's in the dining-room. If she's from so long ago, she's more likely to be in the fourteenth century wing."

"But that's where the cats breed and the lumber's stored – which would explain why I'd forgotten that there are a few pictures on the walls."

"One or two of our portraits are of particularly poor quality – besides which, that wing is in part where she'd have lived. It's better for her to be there, isn't it, than on a wall which wasn't even built in her time?"

I had to agree that this might be best, and made short work of my breakfast. "Do you want to help me in my search?" I asked William afterwards.

"I would help, gladly, if I weren't so busy this morning," he answered me. Then, smiling: "And I've formed the opinion that you've no intention of waiting until this afternoon? I thought not – and strongly doubt that you'll need any help from me. But I'll be keen to examine your findings – and we could look together, later, if you like, at our family tree."

"I never knew that one existed."

"It exists, in fact, thanks to me. Genealogy is one of my hobbies."

"I never knew that!" I said happily. "Between us, then, we'll establish all there is to be established about the girl in green."

"You've never once, I've noticed, referred to her as a ghost. Why's that, Catherine?"

"Because I don't think of her as one. The word is wrong for her, somehow, and open to misinterpretation. A so-called 'ghost' is a sort of shadow, isn't it – a mirror-image of a body that once existed? The girl in green has no substance, certainly, but that renders her no less real than you or me. We, too, are insubstantial, though on another level. Bodies are transient things. Only our souls are eternal."

"Yes, indeed. You've given me good reason for not calling her a ghost. So we'll continue calling her the girl in green, shall we?"

"Just until we know her name."

"Which I suspect we'll know before too long, given your determination. Well, don't let me stand in your way."

I hugged him before setting out for the House's oldest wing and then took the route that led through the walled kitchen garden, past the fig and peach trees, the currants and the gooseberries. After these came the hothouses and the sunny corner, within the angle of the north and east walls, where the carnation bed and violet frames were, together with a stone-lined tank of spring water. A water hawthorn grew in the tank and shed its flowers to shade the large goldfish that swam there and that had been brought as babies by Jeremy from the Woodbury Hill Fair.

Reminders of him were everywhere, even in the fragrant Tyneham air that he had breathed until so recently. It would have been all too easy for these reminders to sadden me, and sometimes they did, but more often I absorbed them and thought of him close by, thus nullifying any sadness. There was more to this than thinking of him there. I seemed to receive from him his new understanding, for answers to my many mind-questions came as if from nowhere. I would wonder and would soon not need to wonder any more. Could it be, that from his enlightened environment he was conveying comprehension to me? I believed – strongly – that it could, such was my experience and my faith in Jeremy.

There was a wrought-iron gate between the two walled gardens and by this gate on the kitchen side grew a catawba vine, basking in the sunshine. Fruit and vegetables were grown in the second garden, to supply the House and much of the village, and peaches and nectarines were already forming on branches that had been trained along the walls. Pears, plums, cherries and melons also did well in the clayey soil and celandines and white violets were the first flowers each spring to peep out from beneath the quickset hedge between this garden and Shoemaker's Lane.

I passed the ice-cold spring that bubbled up in a small spring house positioned just short of the herb garden and thought back to the time I'd been told of, when footmen fetched its drinking water in great earthen pitchers. Did they do that in the girl in green's day? Was this spring bubbling then, already?

I did not loiter in the warm enclosure, hastening instead along the wooded walk bordered by bluebells and tulips that brought me, finally, to the dog-yard formed by the coach-, cart- and wood-houses, House and Old House.

There were four stone steps up to the door and as I climbed

these I could hear the sighing of the blade being drawn through wood in the sawpit. This sound, undoubtedly, had echoed through Tyneham for centuries. How peaceful the sighs, how melodic!

I entered the old homestead and facing me was the huge open fireplace and brick oven where cook baked bread weekly after the odd man had heated it with faggots of dry furze. These bakings kept the building aired, so that no damage should have occurred through damp to the girl in green's portrait. Where was it?

I spotted a small painting near the foot of the worn, winding stairway and crossed quickly to it, weaving between mounds of garden nets. But it was not the painting that I was looking for. In a plain wooden frame I found the face of a man aged about forty, with a flat velvet hat on his head and with a chin that sagged slightly. There was no name and no date – nothing, indeed, to suggest his identity. And the same applied to the other portraits on the ground floor. Whereas those in the dining-room had engraved metal plates at the foot of their frames, these had no means of identification. This did not much matter yet, for I had not found my girl in green. I could only hope that when I found her I would find some way to identify her.

She was not down here. Having explored every inch of wall and every dark corner, I started up the spiral stairs. In the upper room to the right of the stairhead, where an assortment of old furniture and articles was stored, I found a portrait that caused me to catch my breath. It was a woman's face with such similarities to the woman I sought that for a moment I thought my search was over. But her hair was dark, not red, and her eyes and mouth were wrong. She also seemed to be of a more recent century than my girl in green. Could she be her granddaughter, maybe, or even her great-granddaughter? I saw suddenly that there was a name beneath this face, and that there were also dates: 'JANE KATHARINE TICE, 1651 - 1703'.

A sound from above distracted me. Glancing up, I saw that a kitten had climbed among the roof timbers and that it was frightened. It began mewing piteously and pleading with its big eyes for me to rescue it. "If you climbed up, you can also climb down," I said, attempting to sound stern. "You could do that far more easily than I could rescue you, and that's the truth."

Truth notwithstanding, the kitten disbelieved me and continued to plead. When, after a few minutes, I had not succeeded in persuading it to move from its beam, I went in search of a ladder, none too confident of finding one up there. However, I found some steps almost immediately in the neighbouring room, which was used as an apple loft and potato store. They were propped against a wall and as I removed them I saw with a sense of shock that they had been concealing the very portrait I was looking for.

Forgetting the kitten . . . forgetting everything in my excitement, I set the steps down on the floor and stared at the face in the portrait. It was badly painted, but there was no mistaking that forehead, those eyes that had a slight slant to them and the mouth with its enigmatic smile. Her dress was green, even, and her hair reddish. Concerned in case there wasn't one, I looked for a name.

There was no cause for concern. Pinned to the lower edge of the frame was a tarnished plate with the faint engraving: 'KATHARINE, 1519 - 1576'.

After excitedly removing the portrait from the wall and redistributing its dust with a series of energetic puffs, I would have run with my namesake straight to William had not the kitten reminded me of its plight with a loud miaow. Putting the portrait down, I manoeuvred the steps in to position and had soon retrieved the kitten, which clung to me until I reunited it with its mother downstairs in the cat-nursery.

Then, clutching Katharine, I made straight for the Porch Room, where I found William immersed in correspondence. I saw him in profile before he saw me and I noticed how hunched he was, compared with how he had been prior to the news of Jeremy. Poor William, who for so long had had so much responsibility, and who now had no hope of releasing the reins to anyone in his lifetime, unless he released them to me. My heart went out to him, because he would not deem it fair to hand over in toto to a woman and he would have too long a wait for his great-grandson to come of age and succeed him in managing the estate. Was it William's destiny to shoulder great responsibility to the end of his days? And what then? I, presumably, would need to be trained to bridge any gap between his death and my son's succession, which would necessitate still more work for William.

Feeling a great wave of sympathy for him I said: "Please forgive this interruption – but I've found her, and found out her name."

"Both of which finds were a foregone conclusion," he smiled, setting down his pen. "Let me see her, then."

As I handed him the portrait, a canary started singing in its window cage. His song set the finches off and then the other canaries. "Will she be on your family tree," I asked William to the birds' accompaniment, "or was she too early?"

"So her name, too, is Katharine," he said, seeming not to have heard me. "Imagine that, out of all the names she might have had! My tree starts in 1543, with the first Tices to live in Tyneham. I used that as my base for building on – the family's discovery of this valley. And, if I remember rightly, it was Arthur Tice who brought his bride here, to the original homestead, in December of that year, from Yorkshire. Judging by the dates on the portrait, Katharine must have been Arthur's bride. We'll take a look after lunch, shall we, and see if that's right?"

I could hardly contain my curiosity, but had to contain it, of course, until William was ready to study the family tree with me.

I busied myself in the garden until lunch-time, hoeing and weeding – also planting out tubers, now that the threat of frost was past. While working, my thoughts were with Katharine as she arrived in Tyneham four hundred years ago from her Yorkshire home. What was life like, back in those days, and how did Dorset compare, for her, with Yorkshire? Was she homesick for the moors and for the life she had led there, or did she so love her bridegroom and Tyneham that there was no room in her heart for homesickness? There was room for some sadness, or I would not hear her crying echoing over the years. I MUST ascertain from Katharine just why she cried.

Lunch over, I settled down with William in the library and he rather proudly produced the Tice tree. This covered a great area of paper and he made careful folds while spreading it out, so that we could concentrate our study on the sixteenth century.

And there, before me, was Katharine's name together with the information that she married Arthur Henry Tice in 1543. The dates of his life were given as 1510 - 1544.

"Oh, poor Katharine!" I said. "That could be why she's crying."

"What could?" asked William.

"Arthur died the year after they were married. She had hardly any time at all with him, the poor thing. Oh, and her son, James was born in 1544. I wonder whether that was before or after Arthur died."

"After, I should think," William said pensively. "On parallel lines, perhaps, with you and Jeremy."

I shivered at this, involuntarily. "Are you saying that her life could be repeating itself in me?"

"I'm not quite certain what I'm saying. I don't consider myself well equipped to cast light on life's complexities. But I can possibly prove whether James was born before or after Arthur's death."

"You can?" I said. "How?"

He rose to his feet and crossed eagerly to a shelf that contained sheaf upon sheaf of paper. William appeared to know precisely what he was looking for and where to look. He returned to me bearing a partially singed paper bundle and saying: "During my boyhood, there was a fire that started in my governess's room when she knocked over a candle, and that could all too easily have destroyed the family records kept in a cupboard close by. But thanks to her presence of mind, and swift action, the records were saved except for some slight scorching. I have that fire to thank for my interest in genealogy. Our family history could have been wiped out without a trace, you see, which would have been a calamity. So I resolved there and then to keep the records safe and to collate every scrap of information for future generations. Now, let me see." He turned over papers, carefully, telling me that although these dealt with the sixteenth and seventeenth centuries they did not date from then. An ancestor had begun the work that William had now finished. "It's a pity," he observed, "that in many instances my tree only gives years, when we need days and months for our purpose. But in the case of our earlier ancestors, I had often to work with a minimum of information – and, regrettably, never found the time to dig more thoroughly. Time's non-existence could explain why it's so elusive! I am just hoping that in the case of Arthur and Katharine I possess a few facts that might answer our question." He paused awhile, scrutinising a particular paper with care. Then, he looked up and stated: "I'm afraid there's no answer here. But the fact is recorded that Arthur died in Boulogne, having fought in France for his king."

"So he, too, died fighting! Which king would that have been – one of the Henrys?" I felt ashamed for the first time of my apathy at school toward history. "Henry VIII," William told me.

"Katharine must be crying for Arthur, musn't she – just as I've cried for Jeremy?"

"I imagine that she must be."

# Eight

That evening, as I was falling asleep, I remembered something. This came to me as through a mist, swirling in my memory. There had been a time when I, in trying to trace Jeremy's ancestry, had examined every gravestone in St Mary's churchyard. And most of those that were very old had sunk so deep in to the earth that there was no hope of knowing who was buried beneath them. But I had found one (how could I have forgotten?) that was not too sunken and, through the mist that was swirling, I could see now, as I had seen then, the name 'KATHARINE'.

So that had been my first acquaintance with the girl in green. Quite clearly, we were meant to be acquainted. I drifted off in to a dream.

In my dream, we were contemporaries, both living in Tyneham House, both brides of Tices. But Katharine kept saying to me: "You're the last bride that there'll be."

"You're wrong!" I protested again and again. "There'll be others after me. There'll be your son's bride, and mine, and then there'll be their sons' brides."

She answered strangely: "My son's bride has already been, and your son won't bring his bride to Tyneham."

I awoke wondering what she could mean. Then, as I lay looking round my room, I realised with relief that I had just dreamed. And dreams did not mean anything. I need have no fear for my son, as yet unborn.

I feared for my mother later in the month, when William learned from a squadron-leader friend who lived there that Bournemouth had suffered its worst air raid to date. Sixteen

Focke-Wulf 190s had bombed the two main shopping areas at lunchtime the previous day. Buildings were erased and there were many casualties. Anxiously, I dialled mother's telephone number. She did not answer.

"That isn't cause for concern," said William. "Your mother's hardly ever in during the day-time. No doubt she's busy with the W.V.S., or with another of her preoccupations. I'm sure she won't have been in town when the raid was on. Why should she have been, on a Sunday? She'll be home this evening, so stop worrying and ring her then."

"You don't think I should go to Bournemouth and make certain she's unhurt and that her house is still standing?"

"Not unless you've petrol coupons to burn," he said, smiling. "Anyway, what good would that do?"

"It might ease my conscience. I've neglected mother, rather, since Jeremy's death, and since . . . "

"Katharine's advent? You're no more guilty of neglect than your mother is. You and she aren't as close as a mother and daughter might be, but that isn't your fault – it's just the way that it is. The bond between a mother and her children isn't there by right, but by having been earned. Your mother has always had prior concerns. If you were a priority, she would think of you, wouldn't she, and telephone to say she's fine?"

"Not if she isn't fine, nor if she's feeling resentful toward me for having been a bit unwelcoming when she wanted to come and stay. As for mother always having been . . . preoccupied – I've been wondering whether that dates back to when my father died. His death was so sudden, and such a shock, that I think she threw herself in to all her activities in an attempt to come to terms with his absence."

"But he's been absent for a good many years now."

"I know. It could be, though, that her extreme busyness began as an antidote for grief and then became a way of life. It could also be that after all these years – since I was fifteen – she still

90

misses him. There isn't necessarily any end to missing."

"I agree wholeheartedly! And my apology. It had long been my impression that your mother put her committees and so on before her children from the beginning, virtually, and not just from the time of your father's demise."

I could not bring myself to tell him that he was right and that I was misleading us both in wishing otherwise, so I simply said: "I'll 'phone mother again tonight."

I telephoned her before dinner. This time, she answered and told me: "I can't stop now, for a chat, Catherine. I've just come in and have to go straight out again. I'm all behind through attending a concert at the Pavilion yesterday afternoon. With Sir Adrian Boult conducting, the Bournemouth Municipal Orchestra were playing part of Elgar's Enigma Variations. This should have been in celebration of the Orchestra's fiftieth anniversary, but instead the 'Nimrod' passage was played in memory of all the deaths here at midday. Were you aware Bournemouth had been bombed? It's because of the bombing that I've no time to talk. I'm overdue at the W.V.S., where we're doing all we can to help the homeless. Why were you ringing, incidentally?"

"Because I was worried about you, mother. But now I see that I needn't have been."

"Worried about me? Oh, so you HAD heard about our disaster! Don't waste your worry on me. Save it for the injured and the bereaved." There was a deep intake of breath and then: "I'm sorry, my dear. I know you've been bereaved − but you seem to be coping well without Jeremy. And now I really must fly."

We said our 'goodbyes' then and, joining him in the dining-room, I told William: "You were right. Mother's fine."

"And so will you be, when you've eaten. You're eating for two now, don't forget − for you and for the son you'll start and stay close to. That closeness is up to you, Catherine, not up to him."

I was so appreciative of his understanding that I could have cried. But instead of crying I ate with a hearty appetite.

I had not eaten so heartily for quite a while. I tended to be sick most mornings, or in any event to feel sick, and this sick-feeling had been persisting all day, every day. I dismissed it as best I could, being firmly of the belief that pregnancy was synonymous with health and not with malaise. At times, though, there was no dismissing my nauseousness.

Was Katharine similarly afflicted, with James? This numbered among my many wonderings, and I wished that we were the contemporaries we had been in my dream. If only we were, I could question her so much more simply than from my century. I had still had no opportunity to ask her why she was crying, nor whether Arthur died before or after James arrived. For she had not returned since my portrait-find, although from time to time I still heard her cry.

William had had a suggestion to make, about Katharine's portrait. "It's poor," he had said, in agreement with me, following my discovery. "So why don't you paint a new one of her, from memory, just as you painted Jeremy's?"

I had answered that I still hadn't finished his and that, besides, I was rather better acquainted with his face than with hers. Whereupon, William had advised me to hurry and finish Jeremy's, so that I was ready to commence Katharine's on closer acquaintanceship.

I had acted on his advice, putting the finishing touches to Jeremy's portrait with less pain than expectation. Katharine had helped ease my pain.

I stood again by her grave the following Sunday, on my way in to St Mary's. "What are you thinking, Catherine?" asked William, who was standing beside me.

"That she isn't beneath this earth, and never has been. Her bones are buried, but her inner self is as alive as yours or mine. Why do you suppose she is still tied to Tyneham?"

"There could be any number of reasons. Wickedness could

have tied her here, though I doubt that that's true of her. She hasn't a wicked face, has she? Katharine could be tied too, I imagine, by the idea that this is her heaven."

"Do you mean that heaven is our conception of it?"

"I mean that it might be. Who am I, to say with any certainty? Then again, Katharine might be tied by the belief that she is still alive."

It was this idea of his that most intrigued me and I turned it over in my mind during the service. We sat in the Tice pew in the south transept, which afforded me a clear view of the stained glass window. I could face this now with considerably less torment than I had faced it on the first Sunday ensuing the news of Jeremy's death. That attendance had been hard for me, both because of all the sympathy from the rector and the villagers and because of the Virgin Mary. She stirred so many memories of my man in me that I had felt intolerably empty. Now, though, my torment and emptiness were all but past, thanks in large part to Katharine, who these days dominated my thinking. Could it be that she believed she was still living? The more I deliberated William's suggestion, the more fascinating it became. Did death sometimes claim us without our knowing and, if so, why didn't we know? I could only conclude that this was because dying was a good deal simpler than we tended to think. Humans preferred complicating things to simplifying – and death seemed a complication to our minds. Yet Jeremy had spoken, on the night that he died, of there having been no warning of dying, and of his having thought there would be some warning. So was death, truly, just a door that we passed through? If so, many must pass through unknowingly – especially if they died very suddenly – and it could well be that Katharine was one of these. I could even believe that she still did not know, time being so illusory.

Having come to this conclusion, I turned my attention to the hymns, the psalms and the sermon, though it tried to stray again to Katharine.

Her pull was powerful and that day and the next I thought back to my dream. I had dismissed this as of no consequence, but was I right in doing so? For it had been such a lifelike dream with a somewhat disturbing ending. Why might my son not bring his bride to Tyneham? I tried to imagine why, even while trying not to imagine. It would be foolish of me, to believe a dream. But I longed to question Katharine.

In the event, she questioned me!

I was preparing for bed the next evening when the still quality that preceded Katharine infused my room. I felt the atmosphere change and experienced a tingling sensation. Seldom had I known such a degree of expectancy.

She appeared near the window again. I could see her as being similar to me while also seeing through her to the curtains. I wondered how she saw me – whether in her view I had as little substance as she.

I stopped brushing my hair and searched my mind frantically for the questions I had been so eager to ask her. But before I could put form to these, Katharine asked me: "Be you a ghoulie?"

This so surprised me that my queries were forgotten completely. "No!" I replied indignantly. "How could I be? I live here. This is my home."

I saw puzzlement cloud her expression. Then, after a short interval, she said: "T'is mine. I am Katharine Tice."

"So am I, except that I spell my name differently. We seem to live in different centuries."

She looked pityingly at me. "That is an impossibility!"

In other circumstances, I would have agreed. But here we were, by some means conversing across the years, I from my century, she from hers. Could our centuries be unfolding simultaneously, causing us in a manner of speaking to be the contemporaries we had been in my dream? I didn't quite see how they could be, since her century was already history while mine

94

was in part uncharted territory. Nor did I see how I could be haunting Katharine, yet this was her belief.

"How we have met," I said, "is a mystery also to me. But our meeting seems to show that the impossible can at times be achieved. Maybe we should not question why, or how. All I know is, I'm glad to be here with you, because I had grown curious about you."

"I have caused your curiosity?"

"Yes. You see, your unhappiness has . . . conveyed itself to me. Why are you so unhappy?"

She frowned before answering: "T'would be my husband. He is in France . . . and . . . I fear for him."

"What is your husband's name?"

Her prompt answer came: "Arthur Tice. He fights for our King, and for England."

"Which king is on the throne?"

She said haughtily: "You would mock me?"

"No! I'm not given to mocking. But I have a suspicion that we might not share the same king. My King's name is George."

"Mine is Henry," she said with scorn, "the eighth to take the throne. There has been no George ruling over us."

"There will be," I said involuntarily, "and long before my century. Ours is the sixth George to be ruling."

"I do not believe you. You jest with me!"

"I would not jest, so please try to believe. I want us to trust each other and be friends, Katharine. Can we?"

"If you do not jest, tell me when this is."

"The year, by my understanding, is 1943."

"It cannot be! I have not forsaken my century. You deceive me!"

"I could as easily accuse you of deception, but we would both be accusing wrongly." I thought it wise to try a new tactic. "Tell me about James. He's your son, isn't he?"

"T'is curious, that you should know this. He is . . . but I

cannot find him. He has not been to see his mama recently."

"So he has been born?" I questioned lamely. "I mean, unlike my son, whom I am still carrying."

She seemed weary of our conversation, saying: "James is a knave. I care not that he neglects me."

"Does he also neglect his father?"

This confused her. "Arthur is James's father . . . and Arthur is . . . in France."

Katharine, clearly, was not stationary in time, but free to move back and forth. I asked her: "Did Arthur leave for France before or after James was born?"

"Before, o'course! He had fallen, ere . . . "

Her sentence stopped there. I was disturbing her. "Ere the birth?" I prompted.

But Katharine had gone.

She faded even as she faced me, withdrawing I know not where. I knew, though, that I could not follow her there. I could solely hope that she would return before long, so that we could continue our conversation.

Next morning, while breakfasting, I told William of Katharine's visit. "It looks, then, as if we were correct in thinking the death preceded the birth," he commented, "and from her question as to whether you were a 'ghoulie' we can conclude that she doesn't know she's dead."

"In other words," I said, "you were right about that as well. I'm impressed. Have you always been so . . . so . . . "

"Impressive?" he said with a big grin. "Age has its advantages, one being that your guesswork improves with the years."

"I don't believe you. Oh dear – I sound like Katharine, who disbelieved me when I told her which king is currently on the throne! But I doubt you're just good at guessing. It seems to me, you've quietly acquired a whole wealth of wisdom."

"Then don't let me disillusion you. I'm not averse to being

thought wise. Katharine thought Henry was still on the throne, did she? How very perplexed she must be! Not that she's alone in her perplexity. This whole business is beginning to bewilder me. Clearly, man hasn't even begun to fathom time's idiosyncracies. If Katharine can move freely in time, maybe we all can – or could, if we knew how to. Maybe, unknowingly, we do move, if only forward. We're brought up to believe it's time that moves, but I'm beginning to question that concept, which could perhaps owe its existence to the movement of the planets and the illusion thus produced. How very complex it all is!"

"Unless it's too simple to comprehend."

"True. How ironic, if through seeking intricate solutions we've blinded ourselves to straightforward truths! There's one truth, though, that I'm not blind to and that I acknowledge as of immense value: with the birth of your son, the Tice name and estates will triumph over tragedy and be perpetuated."

I felt a qualm as William said this, for I had not told him of my dream-conversation with Katharine. It was time to tell him – time to air my misgiving.

When I had told him, he observed: "Dreams are not prophecies. Surely you aren't worrying about something said in a dream?"

"Not consciously – but Katharine kept repeating that I was the last bride there would be and that my son wouldn't bring his bride to Tyneham. By her very repetition, the words seem to have stuck in my mind."

Frowning he advised: "Live in the present, not ahead. Your son is young yet, to be thinking in terms of a bride for him and fretting. And, in or out of dreams, Katharine can't know everything."

"My poor unborn babe," I giggled. "He is rather young, isn't he, for me to be concerned with his wedding? I agree that I should shelve that concern – at least for the time being!"

Katharine came again that evening, appearing by my bed

more or less as I entered the room. She seemed agitated.

"Is something troubling you?" I asked her, only slightly startled by the suddenness of her appearance. And as I asked this, I realised that I was asking within my mind. I had not spoken in the accepted sense. There was no need to speak. Thoughts could be seen. We communicated mentally. "Let me help, if you're troubled."

"It cannot be," she said vexedly, "that you live after me. You must have lived, and died, verily, and must now be haunting me. No other truth than this can I believe."

"But that would not be the truth," I protested. "The truth, as I perceive it, is that you are dead. Do you not remember dying?"

Vigorously, she shook her head: "We perceive differently. I did NOT die! I would know if I did."

"Not necessarily. Death and life seem to share many similarities . . . and we die without noticing, sometimes, or so I have come to think. It might be that when death is totally unexpected a soul leaves its body quite effortlessly, without any memory of leaving."

"Then you might have died, without remembering!"

"Yes, I might. We might both be dead, or both be alive, you in your time and I in mine. I cannot say for sure, Katharine, any more than you can. All that is certain is that we are communicating, and in a manner of speaking, co-habiting, here in our home."

"This is MY home – mine and Arthur's. It became ours on our marriage. Yet you would speak falsely, and say that it is yours?"

"That is not what I said. I spoke of our home, not mine. Can we not share this House? It is large enough for sharing, and we are not under each other's feet, are we?"

"That's as maybe. But upon Arthur's return to me, he . . . "

"Has Arthur not fallen, then?" I asked, when she failed to finish her sentence.

"He . . . is fighting for King Henry. He . . . "

"Is he, truly, still fighting, Katharine?" I took courage in both hands and went on: "I'm asking because you told me he had fallen ere James was born. Did I misunderstand the meaning of 'fallen'? Please stay. Please answer my question. Don't disappear again."

"I . . . I cannot answer," she said, an appeal in her eyes. "For I have seen Arthur . . . sometimes."

Her appeal touched me deeply and I would have left her there with Arthur alive, had I not felt compelled to question her further. "Can it be," I asked her, "that you have freedom of movement, both backward and forward, between events, instead of being . . . less free, like me?"

"I feel . . . freer than I did. Does this mean that I must be dead?"

The idea of death seemed to upset her and so I said: "In itself, it doesn't. It is best if you seek the facts for yourself, just as I am seeking them for myself." Remembering my dream and curious as to whether Katharine had knowledge of it, I queried: "Have you ever spoken to me in my sleep? I mean, we spoke one day when I was dreaming, lying here on my bed, and you mentioned my son. Can you recall mentioning him?"

Her expression showed that she had no recollection. "I seldom sleep", she said, "and have no need of a bed. Nor have we conversed while you were sleeping. How could we?"

She seemed to drift off in to some sort of reverie. In an endeavour to bring her back to me I asked: "Is your war almost over? I'm hoping that ours is."

"We have suffered at the hands of the French privateers, who harm our fishermen, thanks to the Turk and his strategies. I hate the French. We will vanquish them, and then . . . Arthur will come home."

Deciding to leave Arthur alone for the moment I asked: "Who is the Turk?"

"Why", she tossed her head in contempt, "the French king!

They call him François, but we have our own name for him – just as the Frenchies sing: 'Weh! que sait-il faire – le Roi d'Angleterre?' They love us no more than we love them."

And now our hatred was toward the Germans. All that had changed in four hundred years was the identity of our aggressors. Katharine had sung the short verse in a high mellifluous voice that I had heard, as with all her utterances, in my head. "When will your war end?" I asked. "Or has it already ended?"

This threw her, and her discomposure caused me to plead inwardly with her not to disappear, but to stay and try to answer. My pleas were heard (and seen, I imagine) for she stayed and said: "It ends, and then . . . it begins again. T'is, I oft times think, never-ending."

Was she caught in some sort of time-warp, from which she could not extricate herself? If she was, I wanted to help her escape . . . help free her from her century so that she could join Arthur in his heaven, wherever that may be. But I had no idea how this might be achieved, unless escape could come through conversing with me.

"Your war did end," I said.

"When?"

I could not answer her, I realised with shame, until I had studied the history of her time. Instead of answering, I hedged: "Long before I was born. Tell me, Katharine, why were you crying when I, too, cried?"

"We were both crying for the same reason," she answered, after momentary hesitation. "We both have husbands who have died."

# Nine

It seemed from subsequent conversations that my grief over Jeremy had drawn Katharine and her grief to me. It also seemed that she had several realms of reality, triggered by her travel between centuries. Depending upon where she was in time, events were often out of sequence and this played tricks on her memory. How I felt for her, in her certainties and uncertainties!

I had been doing some reading, initially to determine the date when Katharine's war ended. And I had learned that the peace treaty between England and France had been signed on Monday, 7 June, 1546, at Campagne-les-Guisnes, as it was now known. This was on the frontier just south of the Field of Cloth-of-Gold. Within six days of the signing, peace was proclaimed in London.

In the course of my reading I made the discovery that in May, 1543 – four hundred years earlier exactly – there took place the publication of a tome entitled: 'A necessary doctrine and erudition for any Christian man set forth by the King's Majesty of England'. This was part of Henry VIII's Reformation and his subjects were told to read it instead of the Bible, bearing in mind that 'it containeth a perfect and sufficient doctrine'.

"Do you read your Bible?" I asked Katharine early in June, again in my bedroom.

"T'is forbidden," she told me, glancing over her shoulder anxiously as if afraid of eavesdroppers. "We are commanded to read the King's Book and to abide by its doctrines. Bad things are happening. There is word here in Dorsetshire, and in Somersetshire, that on the King's orders priests' houses must be searched."

"To what purpose?"

"Thus will they unearth enemy spies, or such is their intent. No priest's house hereabouts is sacrosanct. King Henry will change Protestantism, if he can."

"Are you a Catholic?"

"I am not. Arthur and I are Protestant."

"Are you in danger, then?"

"They have tortured and burned Anne."

"Was she a friend of yours – a Protestant friend?"

"An acquaintance – Protestant, and but twenty-five years on this earth when the King's men stretched her on the rack and then, when she was too pained and weak to stand, bound her to the stake in her chair before burning her."

I investigated this later and found that on 17 July, 1546, a Protestant by the name of Anne Askew was tortured on the rack and burned at Smithfield for her beliefs. Was this the same Anne?

It was, according to Katharine who, when I found occasion to ask her, answered: "They are one and the same. Have I not told you she was an Askew?"

She spoke impatiently, as though I should already have known the answer to my question.

I strove to increase my knowledge, reading at every opportunity about Katharine's century. I read of Henry's devaluation of the currency and of his creation of new coins with lower gold and silver content than the old coinage. He introduced the sovereign, which was worth twenty shillings, and the half-sovereign. But inflation still had to be reckoned with, in a kingdom where it had been unknown for centuries. And this caused widespread unrest.

I read next of the public burning of heretical books at Paul's Cross, which was seen as the culmination of Protestant persecution; and of the invasion of Scotland in September 1545, with Hertford taking the offensive and setting out to capture Kelso. Despite the exceptional cold, and heavy flooding, he succeeded in doing so, burning two hundred and eighty-seven places along his way, seven of which were monasteries.

Meanwhile, Henry had suppressed the chantries – a move which pleased the Protestants, since prayers were said there for the souls in Purgatory of those who bequeathed appropriate sums of money, and since Henry seized these funds to help finance the war.

Reading history began to be like reading a newspaper. Past kings and past actions had never seemed real to me before. School-taught history had, in fact, bored me unbelievably because of my sense of unreality. But now I could see that those populating history's pages had lived and breathed just as we were living and breathing. History had actually happened – was still happening, according to Katharine – which made it endlessly fascinating.

I spent so much of my spare time investigating the sixteenth century that it would have been all too easy to shelve the painting of Katharine's portrait. But William had now had Jeremy's as yet unvarnished portrait framed and had hung it in pride of place above the Sheraton sideboard – rearranging other portraits to accommodate it. So my hands were idle, creatively speaking, and this was bad for them, as well as for my equilibrium. Talent of any kind needed nourishing if it were not to wither and die. Thomas Edison never spoke a truer word than when he said that genius was ninety-nine per cent perspiration and one per cent inspiration. Genius or not, there must never be any rest for me, artistically, but ever a striving toward higher accomplishment.

It was not that I wanted to rest – just that so many of my hours each day were accounted for. Self-discipline was essential in order to do all that needed doing and then to progress with my artistic work. I started strictly disciplining myself.

And I was soon setting a new canvas on my easel in the footman's room. For guidance, I had beside me the old portrait of Katharine, but I would mainly be working from my own memory of the girl in green – which was how I still thought of her, even now that I knew her name. In the background of my concentration as I began sketching came the distant sound of gunfire. The guns being fired on the Lulworth ranges were ever increasing in power because of this war, and on occasion over-shooting had taken place, putting Tyneham in danger. Was the gunfire that I heard confined to the practice-ground at Lulworth, or did there also linger on the air warfare from French privateers?

I had thought to have to work in part from memory, and I did have to, but I benefited, too, from Katharine's curiosity.

Hardly had I begun my task than she appeared in front of me. It was daylight, which she did not seem to mind, although she materialised chiefly at night, and I could see her less distinctly than against a dimmer background. She stood between me and the leather box that had gone off to school with Jeremy's forebear in 1640 – almost a hundred years on from Katharine's arrival in this House as a bride. So that box belonged to a descendant of hers and to an ancestor-in-law of mine! How close Katharine and I were, save for the concept known as time. We seemed to me more like sisters-in-law than like Tice wives separated by four centuries. If only I could interpret and simplify Time!

"Why are you here?" Katharine demanded. "What is your intent?"

Assuming she was not speaking in general terms, but in regard to my being in the footman's room, I answered: "I am here to draw and paint. There's inspiration for me in these surroundings, with all this bric-a-brac from . . . former years. The past is brought in to the present and I'm made to realise that they are not, after all, far apart, but unified – just as we are, you and I."

"Are we?" she said, uncertainly.

104

"Yes, we are. And you also are part of Arthur, as I am part of Jeremy."

"But where are they?"

"They're waiting somewhere for us," I answered. "We will know where later. If we were entitled to know now, we would, wouldn't we? Before your King banned it, did you ever read in your Bible: 'In my Father's House are many mansions. If it were not so, I would have told you. I go to prepare a place for you'? Our places have been prepared in one of God's many mansions with our husbands, Katharine, because we are bound by love to them, and we will follow on at the right time. The time is wrong, just for the moment, and I think I know why it's wrong. I am yet young and have work to do here on earth – artistic work that I believe I was born to do, along with the function of bringing up my son. Only when my tasks are behind me can I join Jeremy. And as for you – you, too, are here for a purpose. It wouldn't be my place to state what that purpose is, even if I knew."

"Yet you surely do know."

"Not your purpose, assuming that you have one – which is, I feel, a fair assumption. Jeremy's grandfather and I have wondered, though, whether you possibly see Tyneham as your heaven. If you do, your viewpoint could be keeping you from Arthur, who will have gone to some higher sphere."

"Heaven is not here," she said immediately. "It is somewhere ... far from this shore, though you in your sapience might opine it near. You and he are wrong, in your wondering."

Discouraged from discussing William's and my ideas about her (and the possibility of her having been wicked was in any event unworthy of discussion), I questioned: "How happy have you been, in Tyneham, Katharine?"

"Happy enough. I seemed ... forsaken, though ... until I found you."

"I'm pleased you don't feel forsaken, now that you have found me. I, too, have profited from our meeting. We need each other, don't we, as we journey toward Arthur and Jeremy?"

The barest hesitation and then: "Yes, that's as may be. Who will be on your board?"

I saw from the direction of her gaze that she was referring to my canvas and answered: "You will – if you are agreeable?"

Like a child, she clasped her hands together in delight, saying: "Now I KNOW that you are my kin, since I am to be in your painting! Most willingly, I agree . . . and can see my portrait's great destiny."

"Which is to be . . . ?"

"You will see. First, you must finish it. And you have barely begun. I shall remain, to further your progress."

Remain she did, and I was helped by her presence once we stopped conversing and I started concentrating.

Katharine was an ideal subject. She kept perfectly still, almost as if transfixed in the pose that we had agreed on, and perfectly poised somewhere between our centuries. When was it that we rendezvoused, Katharine and I? This was not now, not then, but somewhen which did not as yet quite make sense. We were privileged, though, in our arrangement.

When I had worked on the portrait for several days, William asked me, in the library: "How's Katharine shaping?"

"Extraordinarily," I told him. "It's almost as if some other hand than mine were wielding my paintbrush. I don't feel at all responsible for the results I'm obtaining. There's a force at work within me which can claim responsibility. And, according to Katharine, her portrait is destined for great things."

"That wouldn't be surprising," William said mildly. "Have you gained any further information from Katharine?"

"None that you're unacquainted with, except that . . . because of my dream, I've started thinking that Katharine could possibly be tied to Tyneham for another reason than those we've discussed so far."

"You mean that she might be lingering here because of

something in the future, not the past?"

"How perceptive you are! That IS what I mean – and I just hope that the 'something' will be a good, not bad, thing. I know it was 'only' a dream but, though I've tried, I can't seem to escape the feeling that Katharine was warning me."

"If she was and if, as you believe, she's here to safeguard the future, why not leave the safeguarding to her? After all, she's in a position to know what's to come, whereas we aren't – and her role would appear to be a protective one. Let's live, then, unworried, within her protection!"

"Yes, let's," I said, smiling.

Talk turned then to other matters – namely the day-to-day running of the estate and the progress that was being made with the war effort. A sizeable number of German mines and barrage protection floats had been laid just recently off the coast of Dorset and the Isle of Wight by various Schnellboot flotillas, and these could not be cleared by the Royal Navy mine sweeping service until resources and the weather permitted, which seemed poor progress locally. But farther afield, Tunis had fallen the previous month to the Eighth Army under the command of General Montgomery and now a number of Axis forces in North Africa had surrendered or were in William's view due to surrender. And while early in the year the Germans had succeeded in sinking ninety-six of our ships in three weeks, the United States had since then stepped up their launching programme so that far more tonnage was being launched than the U-boats could sink – and Germany was falling behind, too, in replacing her losses. These were but two indications that our efforts were at last paying off and that victory would be ours one day. That day would dawn too late for Jeremy and me and for the many families that had suffered losses, but it would spare others a similar fate – and Britain would again be free.

When William had finished discussing the war with me, I suggested looking again at the family tree. I wanted to see the relationship between the boy sent away to school with the leather-bound box in 1640 and Katharine and Jeremy.

William readily acted on my suggestion and soon the tree was spread on the table before us. We saw that Katharine's son, James, married Mary Wriothesley in 1569 and that they had two children – a girl, Jane, born in 1571, and a son, Thomas, born in 1575. Jane died in 1580, but Thomas survived and married Maria d'Ortega in 1601. This union produced four children – three daughters and a son, Philip, who was their last-born, in 1628. So the box now in the footman's room had belonged to Katharine's great-grandson, who was sent off to Eton two hundred years on from its founding in 1440 by King Henry VI.

William knew who its founder was,. because he, too, following the family tradition, went to Eton for his education. And he had known without recourse to the tree that the box was Philip's property. But he could not tell me without calculation how many 'greats' there were between Philip and Jeremy, so proposed: "Let's count them, shall we?"

This we did, counting twelve between Jeremy and Katharine's great-grandson. "So many people came and went before my advent," I said then, "yet Katharine complains of having felt forsaken until she found me. How can that be?"

"Easily! There were no recorded sightings of Katharine until you came along. Certainly I've never seen her, despite having lived here somewhat longer than you have. It follows, I imagine, that I haven't been seen by her."

"So you are saying that she couldn't see the House's earlier inhabitants, either? Poor, solitary Katharine – how frightening the years must have been for her, all alone here! That is, she thought she was alone – just as we've tended to think we were, in terms of companions from other eras. Things are not as we think. It seems we must constantly amend our ideas in keeping with our discoveries. The actuality of existence is obviously very different from our awareness of it."

"Yes, it is – and you, with your artistic gift, can create a new awareness for art-lovers everywhere. When the world sees Katharine through your eyes it will realise that the dead are undoubtedly alive."

At this ambivalence we both smiled. "When I see her again," I said, "I intend asking just how long the years since her death have seemed to her. They shouldn't have seemed long, should they, if Time is man-made?"

"Indeed not! You'll find, I think, that for Katharine seclusion is a recent thing."

And so I did, bit by bit, starting with: "Am I the first person to live in your House since you and Arthur, or have there been . . . others living here?"

We were in the footman's room again, and she was posing as I painted. She did not answer my question straight away, but considered it before saying: "There was my son, James, and then his children. Not that Jane lived long. She always was a weakling. After them . . . " a lengthy pause, and then: "I have seen shadows . . . shadows that have come and gone."

"Were these just shadows, or could they have belonged to people – people like me?"

"They did not seem to belong to anyone, but they must have done, because once in a while they took form and I did see them as entities, fleetingly. But . . " another long pause before ". . . they never saw me. So I was lonely, perforce."

"You must have been – you poor thing! How very lonely you must have been. Did your loneliness last long?"

"It has lasted a moment . . . or it may be that it has lasted many moments. But they have flown. There is even the possibility that I have dreamed . . . that I do yet dream. Am I dreaming?"

"I don't think so, although I don't know. For all I know, we might both be dreaming – and might be awoken when we are ready by Arthur and Jeremy."

"Might we?" She clasped her hands happily. "Such a bright awakening, that would be!"

"Yes, it would," I agreed. "Who did you see as a shadow and then as an entity?"

"There was Rosie."

"Who was she?"

Katharine shook her head sadly. "A poorer thing, verily, than me. She suffered a great indignity. And she suffers to this day."

"What form does her suffering take?"

"She is in Purgatory."

"Why is she?"

"Because she did not wait to be taken . . . which is a cardinal sin, paid for over and over again. I feel for Rosie. She had few alternatives to doing as she did. She could not face the disgrace that she found herself in."

"Why was she in disgrace?"

"She did lie with a man to whom she was unwed and did bear his bastard. This was seen as a great wickedness in her day."

"Which was when?"

"T'was after me. T'was in 1750."

I was immediately intrigued. Katharine was, in this connection, admitting her own death – the death that she denied normally. And she seemed so certain of the date just given, though this fell in earth-years almost two centuries on from her life's end – and though she had still believed herself to be in the sixteenth century when she and I met. "Are you sure?" I asked her.

"Perchance I am. My memory now and then betrays me – but yea, verily, Rosie did say t'was 1750."

Just as I had told Katharine in an early conversation that we were currently in 1943. She had spoken to Rosie, and seen her, much as she spoke to and saw me – drawn to each of us, probably, by tragedy. I asked: "Have you any awareness of time's passage, other than being told of its passing?"

"Nay. I remain in my century."

"Despite speaking to Rosie and me in our centuries?"

"Verily, despite this. I am real whereas you and she . . . are less real than me."

"Is Rosie a member of our family?"

"Nay, she is our housemaid."

With that, Katharine faded. I would have to wait, for further information about Rosie and her baby.

# Ten

My own baby was by now beginning to make his presence felt. I had stopped feeling nauseous and had started instead to feel at my healthiest, as a new life stirred in me. How precious, my gift – how great my responsibility!

This child that I would bear Jeremy would look to me for guidance as he grew to be a man. I asked daily for the wisdom with which to guide him and the capacity, ultimately, to set him free. Parents owed freedom to their children. Love freed. It did not bind, nor try to stifle individuality.

Maybe mother had done this for me. Maybe it was love, not indifference, keeping her remote from me and ever busy. I made up my mind to look in to this possibility at the very first opportunity.

Meantime, I told William about Rosie.

He reacted: "There was, come to think of it, a local suicide sometime in the eighteenth century – and the death is documented, if sketchily. When I've time, I'll see if I can find the documentation, if you like."

"Yes, please. That would be interesting. What do you imagine mother would make of Katharine?"

"I'd rather not hazard a guess! You intend telling your mother of her then?"

"Not exactly – but I have it in mind to visit her soon, so might just mention Katharine in the course of conversation."

"If you do, don't be disappointed if she doesn't believe you," warned William.

Deeming a surprise visit to be best, despite mother's busyness, I set out early one morning toward the end of June for

Bournemouth. My route at the start took me over the same ground that I had covered with Jeremy when I drove him that last time to Wareham station. I passed Creech Grange, the stately manor set deep in its protective declivity, where a branch of the family lived, and drove on down to Stoborough. As I drove, I did not seem to be driving alone. A sense of Jeremy filled me until my whole being seemed to be infused with him. He was more a part of me than he had ever been. Far from taking him from me, death had delivered him to me in perpetuity.

There was bliss in our fusion, as we had known there would be. My love for Jeremy and his for me surpassed, today, all loving that we had shared physically. It spread gloriously through me until tears pricked my eyes and I cried with a kind of ecstasy.

So it was not grief making me cry as I passed the station where we had waved 'goodbye'. My feeling was greater than grief, greater than joy. It was a feeling of union, not just with Jeremy, but with all creation.

And it must have shown, for as I stood on her doorstep after my drive through Lytchett Minster, Upton and Wallisdown, mother – a rather fragile figure, with greying skin and hair – opened the door with the greeting: "Good gracious, Catherine – what are you doing here, and looking so radiant?"

"Hoping we can have some time together. Are you free to spend the day with me, mother?"

"I might have been, had you given me warning," she said with a sniff, permitting her cheek to be kissed. "Why didn't you think to warn me, dear?"

"It wasn't that I didn't think," I told her as we went indoors, through the hall and inner hall, to the kitchen, where mother was in the process of clearing her breakfast things. This house, that I had grown up in, was large for just one person and was set in a natural garden on a wide tree-lined avenue a mile or so from the centre of town. The pine trees that were a feature of the area were well represented here and took pleasure, it seemed, in liberally discarding their needles over both the back and front lawns. Squirrels were frequent visitors, and foxes, too, often ventured near from neighbouring woods. Tom and I had had a happy enough childhood in this environment, and I had thought that I liked town-life until I found Tyneham. "I didn't warn you," I went on, "because I came on impulse, wanting to be with you and not wanting to risk being dissuaded from coming."

Mother seemed surprised – and suspicious – at this. "Why the sudden urgency, when it isn't too long since you refused to see me?"

"I refused . . . ?" I began. Then, remembering: "I just wasn't seeing anyone, so soon after Jeremy's ship went down. You'd have hated being stuck with me then, in Tyneham."

"I still would have come, Catherine." She had automatically squeezed us each a cup of tea from her breakfast pot, and we sat to drink these at the table by the window, through which there was a wide view of the back garden. "It was my duty, as your mother, to come."

"No, it wasn't!" I saw her expression, which discouraged me from going on. "That is to say, even if it was, I wouldn't want you to do anything for me out of duty."

"Why ever not?"

"There has to be a better reason for doing things."

"I disagree. There's nothing wrong with duty. I was brought up to be dutiful – and I tried to bring you and Tom up that way, too."

Her tone suggested that her efforts in this respect had not met with success. Seeing no sense in prolonging this particular discussion, I said: "Let's not argue. I haven't come home to argue with you, but to . . . to catch up on news. Your commitments for the day needn't stand in our way, need they?"

"Well . . . " she hesitated, and I noted how careworn her face was, how bleak her expression, "if I'm honest my main

114

commitment today is preparation for tomorrow. The W.V.S. are holding a jumble sale, you see, and I need to . . . "

"I could help you," I interrupted, "I seem to have a surfeit of energy."

Mother stared at me. "There's something strange about you. I noticed it straight away and it's even more noticeable now. You aren't looking, or behaving, like a widow."

"How are widows supposed to look, and behave?"

"Oh, I don't know – grief-stricken, I suppose. But you're looking remarkably happy and healthy, considering."

"Considering my seeming loss of Jeremy, and my pregnant state?"

"Catherine – expectant state, please! And whatever do you mean by 'seeming' loss? Have you heard news of Jeremy – news to suggest he might not be . . . ?"

"Dead," I said, when mother shrank from the word. "No, I've no news to suggest that he survived in the physical sense. But the soul survives, after the body dies and . . . I have proof of it."

"Proof?" Mother's eyes widened. Then her mouth set in a stern line. "There IS no proof. There can't be, because – because death, believe me, is the end."

"Why do you go to church, then, and profess to believe in the Resurrection?"

"That is insulting – and a blasphemous question! I don't 'profess' anything. Our Lord rose again from the dead, but that was because he was God's Son. We can't presume to compare ourselves with Him."

"But we are ALL God's children!" I held mother's gaze across the table before stating: "And I've met a dead person."

"Catherine," she said, outraged, "don't say such things! Your behaviour is worse than strange. I don't know what to make of you today . . . and I can't imagine what your father would say."

"He is probably saying that you should listen to me – listen and believe."

"IS saying? You spoke in the present tense."

"As was my intention. It seems quite likely to me that father is here in this room with us, listening as we speak and longing to join in."

At this, mother's eyes filled with tears. I had seldom seen her close to crying before, except at father's funeral . . . oh, and at grandmother's. I had sometimes, even, thought of her as inhuman. Now she said: "If only that were true! I would give everything that I possess, to believe as you do."

"I don't just believe, mother. I KNOW, from first-hand experience. Don't you want to hear more about the person I've met?"

"Nothing you can say will convince me, I'm afraid, that you've met someone who's dead."

"So your mind is so closed, is it, that though I could help you to believe as I do, you won't even give me a hearing?"

"You can speak," she said wearily. "Just don't expect my belief."

Starting with the name on the gravestone, I told her about Katharine, omitting nothing. Mother kept her face expressionless throughout my monologue and refrained from butting in, so I had no means of knowing what she was thinking. After I finished speaking, she asked me: "Do you realise what this is reminiscent of, Catherine?" When I shook my head, she went on: "You used, as a child, to talk of friends that you played with, out there in the garden and up in your bedroom. I even saw and heard you playing with them. That is, I saw and heard you playing games of pretence all by yourself. Those 'friends' you said you saw and spoke to were invisible to everyone but you, just as this . . . this Katharine presumably is. You were always afflicted with a vivid imagination."

Until her reminder, I had forgotten my childhood friends. Now, remembering them, it occurred to me for the first time that they, too, must have been dead. I also remembered mother's reaction to my claims. Upon mention of my playmates, she had accused me of telling lies and had taken me to see a man who, with hindsight, was probably a psychiatrist. He had found nothing wrong with me, but from then on I had 'buried' my friends very deep, never mentioning them to mother again and in time forgetting them.

"I'm not imagining Katharine," I told mother, "and I'm not – and never have been – a liar. But if you prefer thinking of me as one to facing the truth of this matter, then that's no more than your entitlement."

"I don't think that you're deliberately lying. I think it's more a question of being in a vulnerable state – what with one thing and another – and of looking for answers. You aren't the first, and won't be the last, to find one where none exists. Why, even I might dream up a ghost in that House you now call home. All those dark corners and corridors – not to mention the wind – would prey on anyone's mind."

"They are not preying on mine – and aren't you forgetting something, mother?"

"What's that,dear?"

"When finished, there'll be a portrait, won't there, to prove Katharine's existence?"

"There's already a portrait, you've said. You're copying it. How's William taking all this? Now, if you were to tell me that HE had seen Katharine . . . "

"He hasn't – but he doesn't doubt that she exists."

"He's humouring you! Maybe that's what I should do – with you so recently a widow, and expecting, too."

"He is NOT humouring me. He happens to believe me – and to believe IN me, as well as in Katharine. He doesn't find her presence in Tyneham at all surprising."

"Doesn't he . . . doesn't he, REALLY? I find that quite extraordinary, for a man of his years and integrity. I'll have to have a word with William."

I must have looked stricken for she hastened to add: "It isn't that I'd be swayed by him, while doubting you. But he is – or, rather, was – a J.P., and, well dear, he's a man, isn't he?"

"Yes, he is," I bemusedly agreed, "just as father was – and father wouldn't have doubted me, either."

"I'm sorry, dear," mother said, crying suddenly and dabbing with a corner of her apron at her tears. "I don't mean to be disbelieving. But your tale does stretch belief, and I just can't seem . . . to accept what you're saying."

An apology from mother was rare. I found myself crying with her and assuring her: "You will accept Katharine, in your own good time – there's no doubt of that in my mind."

"There's beginning not to be, in mine."

I felt closer, then, than I had ever felt to mother. We would come still closer, in the future.

The future was already here and the past was not gone. They were within the present and we were the present's pawns.

We spent the entire day together. I helped mother with her W.V.S. work, while also making some purchases in Bournemouth, which I was seeing for the first time since its Sunday midday bombing raid. Beales store had burned down and Richmond Hill, which rose from the Square, had altered beyond recognition with the devastation of the Central Hotel and the Punshon Memorial Church. The Metropole Hotel and West's Cinema, too, were irreparable. They had taken years to build, but were demolished in a moment. How temporal were material things – how fragile, compared with things eternal!

Before leaving mother I said to her: "You'll come to Tyneham, won't you – soon?"

"Yes," she smiled, seeming younger than she had earlier, "I'd like to come and see you and see . . . your proof. I've enjoyed our day, dear, and now have fewer fears, somehow, for your brother, as well as the first kindling of hope of a reunion at some stage with your father and my mother. Although I can't pretend to have been totally won over to your way of thinking, life already feels . . . fuller."

"I'm glad, mother. Don't conclude, though, that I'm trying to make you think as I do. My aim is merely to share a recognised truth with you. Give my love to Tom, please, if you're writing to him imminently. I wrote recently, telling him to win the war and hurry home."

"Let's hope he does as he's told! Oh, and remember me to William."

This I did, on my return to Tyneham. "You look," he observed, "as if you've made some kind of breakthrough."

"I have," I said, "thanks to Katharine and to you. In case you don't know, mother sets great store by your opinion."

"While that's gratifying, it's your opinion she should listen to. It vexes me, that she's so slow to value you."

"Maybe I've been slow, too, to appreciate her point of view and to . . . to understand her. We understand each other better now that I've seen just how frightened she is – how in need of reassurance."

"Frightened . . . your mother?"

"Yes, just as so many humans are – of the unknown. It's the not knowing that is frightening. I wish I could tell everyone about Katharine."

"I imagine that one day you will. You're a most determined girl. When the world sees her portrait and is told its story, then there'll be widespread conviction about the after-life, believe me. Ah, there's the dinner-gong. Let's eat, shall we? All this philosophising makes me hungry!"

While we were dining, I heard – or seemed to hear – a baby's cry. Setting down my knife and fork to listen, I then asked William: "Did you hear something?"

"The ring doves calling," he answered. "But I fancy that isn't what you meant?"

I shook my head, listening intently again. "I could have sworn

I heard a baby crying. Lily hasn't brought a baby here, has she – or Annie?"

William said, eyeing me quizzically: "I was with cook in the kitchen earlier and was struck by the absolute absence of babies."

"You're laughing at me!"

"If I feel any emotion, it's envy that you can hear and see things I can't hear and see. I'd like to share your ability, Catherine, but it quite clearly isn't for sharing. It is to recompense you for Jeremy and to facilitate the painting of Katharine's portrait by someone whose work will one day be prominently displayed. That way, mankind will question its source . . . and as a result be reassured. There's a purpose behind all this and your portrait of Katharine is either the whole purpose or part of it. Is it her baby crying, do you think?"

"It's more likely to be Rosie's."

"Ah, yes – Rosie. I've found the notes on her. They were written by my grandfather and are fuller than I remembered. I'll show them to you, after dinner."

We were about to peruse these together when unexpected visitors – the rector and his wife, who were living in Steeple until they could return to the rectory – arrived, keeping us occupied until bedtime. So I went to bed not having yet seen them. I climbed the stairs thinking of Katharine and hoping it would not be long before she visited me again.

She must have tuned in to my hope, for as I lay reading in bed the stillness stole over my room that I had grown accustomed to as a prelude to Katharine's arrival. So trusting was I in this as a sign she would arrive, that I closed my book and waited. I did not have many moments to wait before becoming conscious of her standing between the white dimity curtains that were undrawn at the foot of my bed.

She seemed to emerge from nowhere and to return there again later, but I knew better. I knew that there was somewhere for her and that her somewhere was here, she in her life's setting and I in mine. We lived side by side, each in our time, and were acclimatising to both being domiciled in Tyneham.

"I heard a baby earlier," I now said to her. "Whose baby could I hear?"

"Why, t'was Rosie's! I did tell you of her."

"Yes, you did – but how is it that her baby is still crying?"

"Still?" Katharine queried. "T'is today Rosie died. He would cry, poor sweet babe. He misses his mother."

"Can't you take him to her?" I said, shivering at the thought of the baby's cries echoing on each anniversary of Rosie's death.

"Nay! She is in the Shadow Lands. I cannot venture there."

"Why – are they far?"

"They are fraught with . . . danger. And they are dark."

She uttered the word 'dark' with awful emphasis. "In what way are they dangerous?" I asked.

"Once you are in, it is no simple thing to leave again, lacking one who is advanced, for protection."

"What would this advanced person need to protect you from?"

"Those who inhabit that domain. The evil they have done lives on with them. They suffer damnation and draw in souls who would pass, wanting them to share their darkness."

I shuddered, saying: "If you haven't been to the Shadow Lands, how do you know all this?"

"I know not how I know. The knowledge . . . seems to be . . . part of me."

"Surely Rosie shouldn't be where she is, just because of what she did?"

"She should, until she repents. It is very wrong, to reduce by our own hand our allotted span. We must pay for wrongdoing, in direct proportion . . . and see where we were wrong. Rosie will not see."

"Why won't she?"

"She has shut her mind, verily."

"Can't she be helped to open it again?"

"There are helpers, helping her – but they cannot proceed far, except by her wish. She is not even aware of them – so absolutely has she shut herself in. Walls surround her of her own making, just as the living at times erect walls around themselves, keeping out the light that would otherwise shine. We must each will our own enlightenment."

I said with feeling: "I shall steer clear of Rosie's Shadow Lands, if I can, and aim for a very different destination."

"You determined your destination before your birth. T'is the land of those who bring light in to the world."

"But I have not brought light in."

"You will, at the right time."

"When will that be?"

Katharine smiled enigmatically . . . and left me.

# Eleven

The following afternoon, in the library, William handed me his grandfather's notes on Rosie. In bold, but now fading, handwriting on a yellowed page was written:

'I have made the discovery that around the mid-eighteenth century (I've tried but failed to determine the date more precisely) a suicide occurred in Tyneham. This is noteworthy since suicides hereabouts are few and far between. Nevertheless, one Rose Grant, spinster of our Parish, is said to have deliberately drowned by throwing herself at high tide from Gad Cliff. Illegitimate motherhood could have been the cause of her anguish. (There is no known record of who the child's father was). Rose Grant's burial conformed with local law and custom, which laid down that bodies of suicides be deposited at night far from the village church, by a crossroads – which in this instance lay on the Parish boundary – with a stake through the heart to prevent the occurence of a ghost. The crossroads chosen is now known as Maiden's Grave Gate and is high on the ridge between East Lulworth and Creech, at the boundary between Steeple and Tyneham parishes. An ancient oak marks the place – this is distinguishable from other trees by two carvings of coffins on its trunk. Would the first coffin be for Rose and the second – smaller one – for her baby, who lasted but a short while after her? The Coffin Tree, as it has come to be called, is the last oak in to leaf each spring and the first to shed its leaves each autumn. Could this be significant? May Rose find respite from her sin.'

I said: "Amen! I find it so disconcerting, that Rosie's still suffering."

"I do too," said William. "But she won't have suffered in vain, if her plight teaches us something."

"To sin less, in order to suffer less? Certainly, Rosie has given us good reason to assess our imperfections!"

"And no doubt Katharine will soon supply the missing information."

"You mean Rosie's lover's name? We already know the date as yesterday's, in 1750. Fancy going to such archaic lengths to bury a poor suicide, so comparatively recently!"

"It doesn't say much, does it, for the 'enlightened' eighteenth century?" William agreed, before proceeding to tell me the location of the Coffin Tree.

It transpired that I in fact passed the Tree and Maiden's Grave Gate whenever I drove from Tyneham on to the Lulworth road preparatory to driving to Wareham, or to Corfe or Steeple. So I had often passed poor Rosie's bones by, blind to her suicide. Well, I would paint the Coffin Tree for posterity so that her circumstance was no longer shrouded in secrecy and so that people could pray, perhaps, for her release from the Shadow Lands.

I waited for a still day and then climbed the hill that led past the new forest and the cuckoo pond, with Limekiln Plantation beyond the neat hedging to my left and with the farm at North Egliston nestling below me in a curve of the valley to my right. Cattle were grazing on the pastureland, and the fields, in their varying shades of green, were spread out around me, lacking symmetry – being broken at haphazard intervals by quick-set hedges and stone walls – but, with their coppices and circles of trees sheltering farms and cottages, having a compensatory quality. This was a peaceful scene, with the sea just out of sight beyond the jagged edge of Rosie's Gad Cliff and with the sun shining brightly from a serene sky. It was a scene that would hardly have changed over the centuries and that by no means reflected the world's current strife and hostilities. I shared this

124

scene with Jeremy, with Katharine and with Rosie and with all who had ever passed through Tyneham, as well as with all those who would ever pass through here. I was at the meeting point of past, present and future. So this was the answer as to whether I was a 'ghost' from Katharine's future, haunting her, or whether she was haunting me from earlier. For we were both here, currently, within our own eras.

The tree in whose shade Rosie was buried grew in the fork between the Tyneham and the Lulworth roads. It was a most majestic oak – and, I reasoned, preferable as a memorial for Rosie to a gravestone. She had died in the sea, dramatically, and now drama reigned over her earthly remains whenever a sea-wind tore and tossed these far-reaching branches. As for the carvings in the trunk – I found them, and touched them, thinking of Rosie's tortured soul as I did so and asking for her mind to be opened, so that her torture might end.

Then, after distancing myself to obtain the right perspective, I settled down and began sketching. Trees are hard to sketch. It is said by some artists that there is nothing harder to reproduce on paper than an egg. This may be true, but I believe that trees equally reveal the shortcomings of Nature's copyists – and for me, ordinarily, a tree is hardest.

Rosie's tree, though, was extraordinary – and I sketched feverishly, like one possessed. A scout car containing four soldiers drove past me, reminiscent of my century, but aside from this slight impingement on my consciousness I could well have been outside 'time' – free of its boundaries. I saw solely the tree that had stood here for hundreds of years. All else ceased to be. I ceased, losing all sense of identity. I became the tree – and sketching myself was easy. For I knew every nuance of me – every twig, every leaf – intimately. I worked from within and, when I was done, the oak tree grew in my pad for all to see.

When, over tea in Oak Hall, William saw it growing there he

said to me: "To say that you must have been inspired would be a gross understatement. You have captured so much more than the tree – its whole essence, it seems to me. Will your sketches become paintings, some day?"

"They will become just one painting," I told him, "once I've put the finishing touches to Katharine, which I should soon have done, assuming my present progress continues. In fact, if Katharine will only come before then for her final sitting, it should be ready for you to see by next weekend."

"I'll be depending on her coming," said William. "I'm keener to see this portrait than you can imagine. There's not a shred of doubt in my mind but that Katharine's right regarding where it's destined. It must hang where it can . . . ".

" . . . bring light in to the world," I quoted, half under my breath, hastening to tell William: "Those were Katharine's words, not mine – and I've no idea whether I'm right in how I've applied them. They just . . . tripped off my tongue."

"You ARE right – I'm certain. And you're altogether a fascinating woman. Jeremy knew a thing or two, when he chose you."

Nonplussed by his sentiments and by the love in his eyes, I replied: "It's kind of you, to say so, William."

"I'm not being kind. I'm being factual. I have . . . envied my grandson his youth and his marriage to you."

It was astounding, to hear William speak in this vein – and yet why was I astounded? There had been a bond between us from the beginning. There would be, because of Jeremy, who was very like William. Maybe, even, William was a little in love with me, and I with him. This was no bad thing, and needed no action. It was a reaction, rather, to Jeremy's departure for a higher plane.

"There's never been need to envy him," I told William, touching his hand. "After Jeremy, I love you more than anyone I've ever known. And don't regret your birth-date. You have

126

qualities that only come with age."

"Bless you," he said, his eyes moistening. "Bless you, my dear Catherine!"

Willing Katharine to accompany me, I went next morning to the footman's room with a view to furthering her portrait. It was raining, which absolved me from having to do any gardening. I was pleased, being eager to see Katharine completed.

I had not been many minutes in front of my canvas when the room's atmosphere changed to proclaim her arrival.

Then she arrived, saying: "I felt your need of me, so did not delay. I came straightway."

"Thank you," I said. "Where were you, when you felt my need?"

"Why, in my kitchen – which is not your kitchen."

"What do you mean?"

"My kitchen is a beauteous room, wherein I look upon a great open fireplace and through a seven-lighted, mullioned window across to Gad Cliff."

I tried to digest this. Our kitchen, nowadays, faced north, while the view that Katharine described was to the south. And while the fourteenth century wing boasted a big open fireplace, its windows were not south-facing. So where was Katharine's kitchen?

I asked this and she answered me: "T'is where you eat. I have watched you eating."

Mystified, I said: "But we eat in our dining-room."

"Which is within my kitchen."

"Really? I've never seen you in there . . . and neither has William."

"Who is he?"

"Jeremy's grandfather. We eat together. If you have watched me eating, you must also have watched him."

"T'is not so! I know of no-one with you, although . . . I have upon occasion seen . . . a shadow."

"If William is just a shadow to you, what am I? I mean, how do you see me?"

She frowned, before answering: "As a ghoulie. You are not solid, as of flesh and blood. I can see through you."

This shook me slightly, though it should not have done. Katharine saw me exactly as I saw her. So she must be seeing my soul, and I hers, without the solidity of a body. I was as much a 'ghoulie' as she. Where, and what, was reality? And why could Katharine see me, yet not see William? This must be for the same reason that I could see Katharine, but he could not see her. Katharine and I had somehow discovered each other – our discovery excluding him. His consciousness was, perhaps, less elastic than ours. I was lucky in my elasticity and in my friendship with Katharine.

I now asked her: "Do you cook, in your kitchen?"

"I have never cooked," she said immediately, "and I have not eaten . . . recently. But I do like the room. T'is bright, therein, with a fine view through the window."

"Your view is of Gad Cliff?"

"I have told you it is."

All this needed analysis. I would speak to William on the subject of Katharine's kitchen.

I had taken up my paintbrush and spontaneously had started painting. The eyes needed some attention, and the hairline. I was concentrating on these areas when Katharine suddenly said: "Hearken! I did hear hooves on the stone. Can this mean my Arthur is home?"

With that she was gone, but not for long. Reappearing after a few minutes, she sadly informed me: "My ears played me falsely. The courtyard is void."

"Don't be sad," I advised. "Trust, instead, in Arthur's eventual homecoming and your reunion with him."

"I try to be trusting . . . but my mind . . . is troubled, at times."

"Your troubles, and mine, are as nothing compared with

Rosie's. Do you know who her baby's father is?"

"Why, t'is common knowledge."

"It hasn't been recorded."

"T'is well it has not been. Rosie would not want it written. She is so ashamed, you see, of her harlotry – though she does dearly love him."

"Who is he?"

"T'is Jeremiah," she said softly, "the youngest son."

"Jeremiah Tice?" I gasped, recalling the name from the family tree because of its similarity to Jeremy. "Are you saying that it was a Tice son who compromised Rosie – and that the family knew this?"

"Yea to the first, nay to the second."

"Yet you said that the baby's paternity is common knowledge."

"Among the servants, it is, below stairs. Not among the family – although Jeremiah is its black sheep. He's the devil in disguise, some think. I have heard whisperings. T'is as well that his baby died and that he fathered no other offspring, else they could have been cursed with his characteristics. He takes and never gives. Hurting others is a game with him. He hurts again and again. In all our family history there has never been another like Jeremiah, praise be. But Rosie – poor, misguided thing – loves him, which is her saving grace, if she would only be saved."

I noted that these observations had been made in the present tense – a further indication, it would seem, that they were part of the present rather than of the past and that Katharine's and Rosie's lives were concurrent with my own. Was my child's life, therefore, already being lived in some other dimension than this one? It appeared that it could be, along with the lives of my grandchildren and great-grandchildren ad infinitum. So William could compile our entire family tree, if only we had the ability to see all that there was to see. Katharine had an intriguing ability, which was increasing, apparently. I had the impression she was becoming better and better informed – as if her mind were opening like a bud in the spring. She had known about the Shadow Lands without knowing how, and she knew much about Jeremiah, considering he had not been 'real' for her – real, that is, as Rosie and I were. Rightly or wrongly, I believed much of this to be recent knowledge which she perhaps absorbed from the very atmosphere. Was such absorption just for the dead, or also for the living who could find the faculty? It must be for both, I suspected – for I was receiving a new understanding from Jeremy.

Wondering whether Katharine's and my minds were opening simultaneously, I asked her belatedly: "Wanting to be saved is in itself sufficient, then?"

"By my estimation. That is the beginning of the journey to the highest plane."

"You make it sound like a long journey."

"It need not be, although for many t'is long . . . and tortuous. They will not admit their wrongs, you see, and without such admission there can be no advancement. Nobody judges us. We judge ourselves – and there is naught to judge, is there, unless we own that we have erred?"

"No, I suppose there isn't," I agreed, pensively. "So is there no Judgement Day?"

"There is, at life's end, when we are shown the errors made along our way."

"Were you shown your errors?"

"I . . . do not remember."

"Do you know, then, who shows them to us?"

"No one shows them. They are . . . there. They have their own existence, our successes and our failures, from when we succeeded and when we failed. We look at these differently, after life, seeing with enlightened eyes and judging where we went wrong, so that later on we can . . . put matters right."

"When will your Judgement Day come?"

"Somewhen. T'will be after I have helped your cause."

"By that, do you mean this portrait?"

"I mean the portrait . . . and more."

I saw as she said this that her painted eyes were finished. They now held the expressiveness that they had lacked before. I had righted these, and her hairline, in the course of our conversation almost without noticing. This would have been amazing, had I not ceased to be amazed by anything connected with Katharine. I asked: "What other cause do I need help with?"

"This is now within my knowledge, but not yet within yours. Something has to happen – something WILL happen, to change Tyneham."

Fear filtered through me at her words, which for some reason resurrected my dream. "What do you mean?" I asked. "Please tell me what you mean."

But Katharine had gone, leaving me to my imaginings.

William noticed nothing amiss, when I reported selectively on my conversation with Katharine and questioned him about her kitchen.

"So for her it still stays as it did, does it?" he said, gazing about him as we sat talking over dinner in the dining-room. "She's right of course. This WAS the original kitchen."

"Was it? I can't see how it could have been."

"Apparently, early in the nineteenth century the roof timbers of the first kitchen were found to be in a dangerous condition. So my great-grandfather's solution was to knock the whole room down and rebuild it as a dining-room – bearing in mind the preference by then for a kitchen to be north-facing. The great open fireplace that now stands in the hall of the medieval wing was taken from the kitchen and over there," he indicated with a gesture the room's north-west corner, "was once a spiral staircase which led up to the Partridge Room. This was in the roof space of the ancient House and so named because partridges were kept there, caught up and fattened among stooks of corn until ready to be eaten."

"Poor unsuspecting things! There's something I find puzzling."

"What's that?" asked William.

"Katharine described her kitchen as being a beautiful room, with a seven-lighted mullioned window and the great open fireplace that you just said was moved long ago to the fourteenth century wing. She spoke, too, of her view across Gad Cliff. So is her view the same as ours, through our south window, or is she still seeing ALL her surroundings from her century, do you think?"

"I imagine she must be," said William. "If the walls which surrounded her still surround her, her landscape won't have changed, either. She has stayed in her time even while straying in to our time. Pursuing that line of reasoning, our home should similarly remain as it is for us, no matter how much it alters for our successors. I like that idea. And I like Katharine's assessment of Jeremiah. Every self-respecting family has a black sheep somewhere in its ancestry, but until now I wasn't aware we had one. What other surprises has she in store for us about our past, I wonder."

"And about our future," I wryly observed; "the future that's already here."

# Twelve

William's reaction to Katharine's portrait was rhapsodic. There is no other word for it. Never before had I seen him so excited – or so in awe. I felt quite embarrassed by his eulogy, although it also pleased me.

"So Katharine has been proved right again," he ended. "You've destined her to rank alongside the Mona Lisa and works of that calibre. How proud I am, and how proud all the Tices would be, to have an artist of your stature in our family! Oh, if only Jeremy . . . "

"Yes," I agreed, "how often there's a new 'if only'. I've lost count of all there have been, and can't imagine how many more there'll be. I'm resigned, now, to the fact that I'll probably miss his physical presence for as long as I live. But he's here, spiritually, isn't he? I'm conscious of him daily and nightly – more so than I could possibly have been in his absences, had he lived. Besides which, if my portrait of Katharine is, as you and she think, important, it might be that he had to be sacrificed for its sake, if you see what I mean."

"Are you saying that but for Jeremy's death you and she might never have met?"

"Yes, I AM saying that – and more than that. Were he still with us physically, there would be less of me to give to my work because part of me – perhaps too large a part, artistically speaking – would be reserved for Jeremy. But now I hold nothing in reserve. I give my all to my work, which maybe is necessary."

"Maybe it is, if one is to succeed with the kind of success that you will achieve," William said, giving my hand a gentle

133

squeeze. "And Jeremy would be first to agree that this work was worth any sacrifice, even that of his life. It must go to London, Catherine. We cannot keep it here, in Tyneham."

"We can for the time being," I told him. "I'm too busy to tout it around London. I plan to make a start soon on the Coffin Tree and on some Tyneham scenes. Katharine would anyway feel lost in a big city. This is where she belongs."

"Just for the moment," William said knowingly. "Just for the moment."

Katharine was soon speaking as William had spoken.

After I had embarked on Rosie's oak tree, she appeared in the footman's room beside me and said: "There is a great gallery, where all the world will come to see me and exclaim over your artistry. But the time for that is not yet. There are more immediate things for you to do than undertake a journey."

"What are they?" I asked, chill unaccountably seeping through me.

"You must proceed as you are proceeding. First, the Tree, and then this whole locality. Tyneham has to be seen by future generations as it is and as it has been – not merely as it will be."

"How will it be, and when will the change that you've spoken of take place? Answer me, and don't disappear," I pleaded, "unless you want me to worry."

She smiled sadly: "I am here to lessen your worry . . . and your grief."

"Is further grief, then, in store for me? Are we to suffer at the hands of the enemy?"

"Be still. Be at peace. Do not dwell ahead, nor behind. Dwell with me, outside Time's idiosyncracies. And do not pre-judge who the enemy is."

"Whatever do you mean?" I asked anxiously.

"Simply that Tyneham's fate is separate from the fate of England. It has its own destiny, its own enemy . . . its own tragedy."

134

"Tell me then, what the tragedy is!"

"I cannot, specifically. This, though, I can say: Tyneham will be taken from within, not from without, which will set it apart – keep it safe, in a strange way."

"Safe?" I said, grasping at the straw she had offered me. "Please explain."

"Things are due to be different. After your war has been won, the world will lose its . . . innocence. Bad things will happen, with the old being scorned by the young and with a new Sodom for Nature to take in to account. Materialism, too, will curse mankind. All this, though, will pass Tyneham by."

"Why?"

"Because our valley is to be preserved - taken out of time and held forever in a state of suspension. But you will not see this, at first, as preservation. So you must needs be brave, in the beginning, and not just for your own sake. William will need your bravery – as he has needed it already."

"You are frightening me! How can our valley be taken out of time?"

"You will see . . . and you will not be frightened. The anticipation of a thing is worse than its advent. Heed me, and be content."

"I'll do my best."

"T'will suffice, if you bear ever in mind that thought is all-important. Thoughts are things. We can create and destroy, in our thinking. Good can turn to bad, or bad to good, depending on the way we think. Our power is omnipotent. Use your power to good effect, when all around you are sad and scared."

"When will that be, Katharine?"

"There will come a warning."

Then I was alone – if indeed, she had gone from the room. She had gone, in any event, beyond my vision.

I could not work at first. My mind would not accommodate the Coffin Tree. It was too busy surmising what was to happen to Tyneham and what would become of William, should there be some catastrophe. He was an old man who had grown up and grown old in Tyneham. His roots went deep – far deeper than mine, for I had no blood-tie to this valley, though I was tied by love and by Jeremy's ancestry.

Gradually, I withdrew from my worries and settled my mind, concentrating on my canvas until all I could think of, all I could see, was Rosie's magnificent oak tree.

William's conversation at dinner that evening centred chiefly to begin with on the tests that had been carried out recently at Studland Bay and at Kimmeridge. He spoke at length about the tests' success and while he was speaking my attention sometimes strayed from him. But I kept bringing it back again from the unknown future to the known present. For William, the present was concerned with the RCL, which was a tank-landing craft that had been modified locally to carry batteries of rocket launchers. In no more than half-a-minute a thousand explosive rockets could be fired on a concentrated area, with the aim of annihilating enemy strongholds – an aim that would now succeed, thanks to the RCL's modification, William said. He then went on to say: "The Dorsetshire Regiment's First Battalion will have sailed in to the Med today, on the STRATHNAVER, bound for Sicily's beaches. It won't be long now before the Allies have landed there – and, when we have, heaven help our enemies."

"Why is it,"I enquired, "that men seem to have an ingrained understanding of war-strategies, while women – if I am at all typical - find them fairly incomprehensible?"

"Probably because of childhood indoctrination," William answered with a grin. "If girls were given soldiers to play with as children, and boys were given dolls, then I imagine you might have needed to reverse your question. Unless, that is, boys are born more belligerent."

"I hope they aren't," I said. "since if they are, I'll be holding a belligerent baby in my arms inside four months – and there are other characteristics I could wish for my son."

"My great-grandson," William marvelled, in a different mood from his earlier one. "I wonder what life will hold for him. To think that he's likely to see the twenty-first century! There'll have been changes by then – changes beyond my imagining."

"And mine," I said, my thoughts turning to Katharine. "I can't quite comprehend that those changes have in some sense already taken place. I mean, they must have done, for the dead and those with inner vision to know of them. Is this within your comprehension?"

"No," responded William. "My mind seems to be self-limiting. I've come to the conclusion that all our limitations are of our own making. Oh, to escape from the narrow path we are on and find infinite horizons! You're well on your way to finding them. With Katharine as your confidante, anything can happen. Have there been . . . further confidences?"

I considered carefully before saying: "She has spoken, just as you have, of change. I gained the impression that something is to happen affecting Tyneham, but that's all it is – a mere impression."

"I take it from your tone that this 'something' is likely to be to Tyneham's detriment?"

"My tone wasn't intended . . . "

"I'm sure it wasn't," William interrupted. "My dear, while I'm pleased to have your protection, I'd be still more pleased to have your absolute trust and confidence. I might be an old man, but I'm strong. Don't forget, I'd survived the Boer War and the Great War before we embarked on this one. So can I know what you're protecting me from?"

"You're too astute for me and my attempts at secrecy," I told him, smiling. "Do remember, though, that Katharine's statements are often open to misinterpretation. She sees Tyneham's fate as separate from England's generally – even speaking of our having our own enemy."

"Some country other than Germany?"

"Unless I'm misinterpreting her totally, she might mean that Britain is in some way to blame for what is to happen. You see, she spoke of the enemy within."

"Good heavens!" He thought awhile and then: "I wonder whether this could have anything to do with requisition. The War Office has requisitioned so many large houses that all along I've been half expecting a move to take over our home pro tempore. It's undeniably large for just two of us – soon to be three – and we could well be called upon, if this war goes on much longer, to make that sacrifice for our country, couldn't we?"

"I suppose we could," I said slowly. "Isn't it, though, rather late in the day? I mean, surely if the Government were going to requisition Tyneham House it would have done so already."

"Not necessarily. Bearing in mind the ever-increasing size of the firing ranges at Lulworth and all the new kinds of guns and gadgetry the army's being given to test, there could yet arise a need for extra housing for locally stationed army personnel – and while I wouldn't enjoy handing over our home, I would do whatever needs to be done to help win this war, as I know you would, too. My theory would account for Katharine's reference to the enemy within, wouldn't it? Yes, I strongly suspect that she was referring to the British Forces taking over our home – and, if she was, we can rest assured that our sacrifice would be just short-term. It's the long-term we must trust in, isn't it, Catherine?"

I agreed, aware that I had not told him everything. Katharine's talk of a tragedy and of Tyneham being taken out of time suggested more than requisitioning, but why worry William? Time enough to worry him if and when there came the warning that Katharine said would come. Until then, all I could do was trust.

I sat on my bedroom's wide window-seat next morning, in my nightgown, gazing out across Cowleaze Knap. If I used my whole concentration, I would see Jeremy and me locked in an embrace that was there for all eternity. Concentrating, I looked across the trees to the place where he proposed to me and where we had returned by tradition on the eve of his every departure from Tyneham. I could see sheep . . . and I could see a black-faced lamb such as I had seen once in a dream. The lamb was gambolling all on its own, slightly apart from the rest of the flock. It seemed to be on the precise spot where I had stood with Jeremy. I fixed my gaze on the lamb, puzzling over its significance.

Without knowing why, I knew that it was significant. I also knew that I was to be shown the reason. Then the lamb began to grow. It grew as itself at first, its legs lengthening, its soulful face turned in my direction. I could see its face clearly, though it was far from me – and its eyes, which all at once were Jeremy's.

There is no knowing what happened then. It is not something that I can explain.

I felt myself being drawn to him. I was drawn through my window as if it were unglazed and as if I had taken wing. And we were together again. He was holding me in complete freedom. For we were free of our bodies – free of those encumbrances that had restricted us previously – free of our sexuality. We had been lovers, and would be, but this love that now bound us transcended the physical plane. We had shed earthly desires and emotions and were one in that moment with the heavenly hosts. This was more than a state of bliss. It was a state of absolute belonging and blessedness.

I belonged and was thus blessed still, back on my window-seat, Cowleaze Knap in front of me.

But for this feeling, there might have been some scope for believing that my experience had been hallucinatory. I knew, though, because of it, that I had not hallucinated. My soul had just met with Jeremy's.

Our meeting left me feeling fearless. Because of him and because of his love for me, I was as protected as I possibly could be – and removed from worldly influences. Whatever happened in life could happen only superficially, and all things were fleeting, however they seemed. My soul stood with Jeremy's and with Katharine's outside strife – outside time.

Katharine shortly confirmed this for me. Later on that day, she observed, as I worked on the Coffin Tree: "T'was a happy sight to see – you and your love, Jeremy."

"You saw us?"

"Indeed – there on the Knap, borne on the breeze like leaves. Your happiness – yours and his – made me happy. You have begun to see life's simplicity."

I HAD been as light as a leaf as Jeremy's love magnetised mine and drew me to him. That was how it had been – a kind of magnetism too strong to defy. Not that I would have tried to defy it. Nor would I have succeeded, had I tried.

"Life IS simpler than ever I realised," I agreed. "I'll try not to complicate it again . . . and try not to be tied by time in my thinking. You're helping me to see how unimportant it is and how free I can be of its boundaries. I'm learning to accept truths that could not have seemed true, until I met you."

"No truth is absolutely true. Each leads to another, truer, truth until we stand, finally, in the full light. T'is useless, to stand there too soon. We would need to shield our eyes, which would defeat our purpose. Not that we could stand in the Light, while we are yet blind. The Plan would not permit us to."

"How much are we permitted to do?"

"We have freedom of will – and most things are permitted, with right on our side. You will fight, when a great wrong is dealt to you."

"Does this great wrong concern Tyneham?"

"It does . . . and the fight will not be won."

"Why fight then?"

"They have to be shown their wrongdoing, and WILL be shown."

"Who are 'they'?"

"People in high places. People who should be better than they are."

"Will they take our home from us for a time?"

I knew her answer before she answered me. It echoed strangely from my dream: "You're the last bride that there'll be. Your son will not bring his bride to Tyneham."

# Thirteen

Trusting in the long-term, as agreed with William, I did not bother him with the imaginings Katharine had stirred in me. And I was not as bothered by these as I might have been, prior to my meeting with Jeremy. William's attention was, in any event, occupied quite soon with news from farther afield than Tyneham.

On 11 July the familiar voice of Alvar Liddell anounced on the wireless that the Allies had landed last night in Sicily, with only a token opposition from the Italians and Germans, whom we had taken by surprise.

"The island will be ours within the month," William estimated over breakfast as the broadcast ended, "and then our invasion of mainland Italy can begin. Mussolini can't last long. Not for nothing is Italy known as the soft underbelly of the Axis. Montgomery will quickly show whose is the superior strength. Good for the Dorsetshire Regiment! They've played their part in our success. Our boys are doing a grand job out there, far from home!" His expression clouded over. "It's to be hoped that most of them will live to be old men, so that they can tell of their exploits to their grandchildren."

He was thinking of Jeremy, who had not lived to be an old man. Poor William: I was sad for him, that he had not known my joy on Cowleaze Knap. I said: "It's funny to think that by then their war will be history, and as unreal to many school-pupils as the Corn Laws and the Industrial Revolution were to me. But that, of course, was long before I met Katharine."

"She has rather changed our thinking," William drily agreed.

I next heard from her the following evening, while in bed

reading. Struck by the feeling that I was being observed, I looked up from my book and there she was, watching me from between my bedposts.

"They are married now," she announced.

"Who are?" I asked her, putting my book down.

"Why, the King and his Kate! They were married today."

"Were they? Which King and which Kate – I take it you mean your Henry and his Catherine of Aragon?"

"How behind-hand you are! T'was his divorce from Catherine which did cause him to break from Rome with such consequence. His new wife is Katharine Parr. They were married this day in the Queen's Privy Chamber."

"Which day are you speaking from . . . and which year?"

"T'is Thursday, the twelfth day of July, and the year, why – t'is 1543."

We were four hundred years apart, exactly. And yet we were not apart. We were here, together, outside time's confines. I no longer questioned how, or why. Trust sufficed – along with faith that I would one day face the full light of Truth, knowing then all that there was to know. There were, though, questions for Katharine meantime.

"Where's the Queen's Privy Chamber?" I asked. "In Buckingham Palace?"

"Buckingham Palace?" she repeated, uncertainly. "No! The Chamber where King Henry married his Queen is in the Palace at Hampton Court. Queen Katharine is bonnier by far than Queen Anne, who did come from Cleves to marry him on Cromwell's suggestion – and whom the King called his Flanders mare, I have heard tell. That marriage boded ill for Cromwell."

"Why did it?"

"Because he had told the King of the beauty of Anne's face and body, whereas Henry found her to be exceeding plain, without cultural attainment but with an appetite like the horse that he mistook her for. So he would not bed her . . . and t'is thought, at Court, that his shock when he saw her helped Cromwell along the road to the scaffold."

"Gracious! If that was Cromwell's fate, what was poor Anne's, for her failure to be a beauty, and to entice her husband in to her bed?"

"Henry did annul their marriage, settling money on her, and lands. She does now live in the fine manor house of Bisham, where the King has oft gone in summer to escape the measles and the smallpox and the plague. He did found an abbey there, so that prayers might be said for the soul of Jane Seymour."

"What happened to her?"

"She died birthing the King's child. And since then Bisham Abbey has been taken by Cromwell's men, along with every monastery in the land. But the Benedictines left little behind them – just some milch kine. The Abbot, t'was thought, had sold the church plate and such in London."

"Was Cromwell acting on Henry's orders, when he took the Abbey?"

"Of course! It had to be confiscated."

"Did confiscation, then, mean in effect delivery in to the King's coffers?"

"Yes! Which displeased the Pole family, who did not condone Henry's differences with Rome. They owned Bisham when the Abbey was taken – and Margaret, who was known as 'my lady of Salisbury', could not silence her tongue. Nor had she silenced it at the time of Henry's marriage to Anne Boleyn – of whom Margaret disapproved. So, on a charge of treason, the King first executed her eldest son and then sent Margaret to the Tower. For two years he did imprison her there, before beheading her. T'was her royal blood saved her from being beheaded in public. But she could not be buried at Bisham. They buried her instead on the corner of Tower Green, in the Chapel of St Peter ad Vincula, poor woman."

"And then Henry took over her home, giving it later in

144

settlement to Anne of Cleves? What a wicked King!"

Katharine sprang to his defence, saying: "He is not wicked! How can you claim such a thing? He is . . . cruel . . . maybe."

"Are you afraid of being tried for treason? Is that the reason for your 'maybe', which seems an unnecessary after-thought to me?"

"Arthur, he did warn me against speaking too freely. Speech can be dangerous. As I have told you, it has been . . . and will be again. Is this not so with your King?"

It was hard to imagine King George confiscating monasteries or beheading subjects whose views did not coincide with his. He and his Queen, Elizabeth, were such peace-loving people who reigned justly, as far as I could see. Dangerous talk, in our time, did cost lives, though, as we were told so often – the difference between my time and Katharine's being that we were not at risk from our own King. "No, it is NOT so!" I retorted, perhaps haughtily. "My King is as kind as yours is cruel. I can speak as I like. Henry can hardly behead me."

"Be not too certain," she said. "He is not above beheading a ghoulie, if need be. And do not count on the kindness of your King."

"What do you mean?"

"My meaning is that George will do to Tyneham as Henry did to Bisham, if for a different reason. There IS bad blood in the monarchy, as you have seen. We have the bond, you and I, of being Tyneham's first and last bride."

"But," I protested, "this war will end and then, if our home has been taken, it will be given back again."

No comment came from Katharine. She had silently withdrawn.

Next day, I headed as soon as I could for the library, where I delved again in to history books.

I read that the spring and summer of 1543 were wet and cold and that it was a dismal time in other ways, too, for English

Protestants. Reading on, I learned that the war in Europe was turning in to a triumph for Henry and for Charles V, of Burgundy, who in 1516 had inherited the Spanish dominions from one grandfather, Ferdinand of Aragon, and who had succeeded his other grandfather, Maximilian, as Holy Roman Emperor in 1519 – entering then in to a lifelong rivalry with the young king, François I of France. I saw that Charles marched against Queen Anne's father, the Duke of Cleves, capturing Düren and killing its inhabitants in August, 1543. Or would Katharine soon be telling me that Charles had yet to march, it still being July? The Duke of Cleves's capitulation left Charles free to turn on François – with the help of Henry, who sent five thousand six hundred troops under Wallop to assist Charles in his besiegement of Landrecies, while also sending twenty thousand crowns to Antwerp toward the cost of Charles's mercenaries. From Landrecies, Wallop wrote in glowing terms to Henry of Charles's new-fangled weapon, the incendiary bomb. These ignited as, fired from twenty-one cannons in to the town, they soared through the air – and they bounced a number of times upon landing, setting fire to the buildings they bounced on or over.

Surprised to see that so long ago there existed bombs as 'modern' as incendiaries, I then turned back a few pages and read of Henry's and Katharine Parr's marriage. On the date Katharine had given, and in the Queen's Privy Chamber at Hampton Court, his new bride took Henry 'for better or worse, for richer for poorer, in sickness and in health', promising in addition to be 'bonny and buxom in bed and at board till death us depart.'

One week on from the wedding, Marbeck, Filmer, Testwood and Pearson were brought to Windsor from their prison in the Marshalsea, Southwark, and tried for heresy. Testwood was too ill to walk without crutches, but was brought nevertheless. The life of a fifth man, Bennet, was saved by the plague – which

146

necessitated that he remain in the Marshalsea. And there was a reprieve for Marbeck. The other three, though, were sentenced to be burned. Before the faggots were lit, in the park below Windsor Castle on 28 July, they each drank a cup of ale to toast the day that they would meet again in heaven. Hilles, recording the incident and remembering the executions at the time of Henry's marriage to Katharine Howard, wrote that Henry had burned three 'godly men' at Windsor 'because he was always wont to celebrate his nuptials by some wickedness of this kind.'

All this and more I found, but I failed to find any reference to Henry's seizure of Bisham and subsequent gift of this to Anne of Cleves.

"That wouldn't necessarily be recorded," William observed. "Quite clearly, his seizure of Bisham was just one among many, and I don't doubt Katharine's account for a moment. She's vivid in her descriptions, isn't she? Flanders mare, indeed! I find myself wondering what her next divulgence will be."

Katharine waited two weeks and two days from the date of Henry's marriage to his Kate before seeking me out again. I was in bed, as on the last occasion, and had been about to extinguish the light and settle down for sleep when she appeared beside me.

"You are again abed?" she said accusingly. "T'is slothful!"

"It isn't! I need to sleep. Don't you ever need to?"

"Not now. And there is no fun in being abed without one's man. I like fun . . . and frolic. There must be more for me, betimes."

"I'm sure there must," I answered, for want of any other answer. "It can't be too long before you find Arthur."

"Would that I could find him – or another. There were others, in Yorkshire. And there is one from Corfe, who has caught my eye."

"Who is he?" When she did not answer me, I approached the question differently. "Does he own the Castle?"

"Nay! That belongs to the King, and has done since the death of Margaret, Countess of Richmond – Henry VII's mother – but for one year, when the demesne was granted to the Duke of Richmond and Somerset, upon whose death it lapsed unto the Crown again."

"It seems," I said, "that half England belongs to the King. Does he come to Corfe, and are you acquainted with him?"

"He does not come to Dorsetshire. T'is far for him, on his legs. They do trouble him sore. T'is said that he has the worst legs in the world and that they'll be the death of him. They have to bear his weight, of course, which is a great burden for them. His eating is become most unseemly. This was told to me by Robert Fitz William, who did come from Court to Corfe and thence fleetingly to Tyneham."

"When did he come, and why?"

"The King sent him, to list the Castle's chattels and report on its repair. T'was his eye that caught mine – but Arthur was here."

"So this was soon after your marriage?"

"T'is so. Yet my eye did rove. T'is to Arthur, though, that I plighted my troth . . . to Arthur that I shall go at the appointed hour. He and I, we each understand the other. I pray right heartily for us to be together. And I pray for the martyrs, who died today."

"Who are they?"

"Their names are Testwood, Pearson and Filmer. They were burned at Windsor on Henry's orders for some slight misdemeanour. Nobody is safe, these troubled days."

"What is today's date?"

"Why, t'is July the twenty-eighth."

Strangely, Katharine remained on a parallel to me, to the very day. "Arthur is alive, still, then, isn't he?" I said, this suddenly occurring to me. "He didn't die, according to our family tree, until the year 1544 – and you must be back in 1543, for that's when the martyrs died."

"Must I? Then I can find him, if I truly try." She said this eagerly. Then, her eagerness evaporating: "But why find him, only to lose him again? T'is better to wait until we are both dead and until the fight for Tyneham has ended. Only then can I rest. Only then can we come in to our own."

"Will the fight last long?"

"By man's measurement of time t'will not be a short fight. But by the proper measurement t'will be as the blinking of an eye."

"How is it that you can move about in time, while I am stationary?"

"You have revealed new vistas to me."

"How have I?"

"By being. Before finding you, I felt . . . confined . . . and I knew nothing of your time. I had imprisoned myself in Tyneham, heedless of all that lay beyond its hills. But since our meeting t'is as if I have been awoken from sleep. I am awake to endless possibilites and am free to be where and when I please. It pleases me, mostly, to be at your behest. For we have become friends, haven't we?"

"Firm friends, Katharine. I'm happy to hear that I've helped you. You've certainly helped me. I wish, though, that I didn't know about the wrong due to be done to Tyneham."

"Do not wish such wishes. Your knowledge must serve its purpose."

"Which is?"

"To put your art to work. Not for nothing was your true talent brought to Tyneham, here to be nurtured. Nor were you given this just for our valley's sake. T'is also for your own sake that you are so talented. By virtue of your work, you will win through, for t'will always sustain you. Fulfilment and attainment will be yours, ere you join Jeremy."

"When will that be?"

"Shortly after your return to Tyneham."

"So I SHALL return! Where shall I be returning from?"

"From your other home, at a time of conflict."

"There won't be another war, will there, after this one?"

"Your conflict will be within – long after your reluctant King is gone from his throne."

"Reluctant?"

"T'is whispered that the throne should be his brother's, but that Edward renounced it for love. T'is well, since George has progeny and since Edward will have none. Edward, too, through misjudgement as King, would have plunged Britain in to a far greater crisis than his abdication. Ignorant of this, though, George – a sickly specimen – resents his brother's action. He feels ill-equipped to be King and is bitter at the task thrust upon him."

Remembering King George's nervous stammer and diffident manner I now saw with clearer vision just how hard it must be for him to reign. I had not thought this through before, despite seeing on newsreels the shock he had sustained when King Edward could not be deterred from marrying Mrs Simpson. But I had a question for Katharine extraneous to Edward abdicating: "How is it," I asked, "that you know of my King without knowing of Buckingham Palace, where he lives?"

"His home is material and therefore a transient thing. T'is not interesting . . . and t'was not built in my day. I heed that which endures, not that which passes. You, too, should heed as I do. The soul evolves, whilst matter decomposes – verily, t'is the soul alone that is of import in the end." A pause, and then: "You will do well to dwell on my words, when robbed of your possessions."

"I am to be robbed of them?"

"In a sense. Pay their loss no attention. You will lack naught of the food of life. Rise above earthly strife. In your every endeavour, seek the eternal. And seek me, if necessary, wherever you are and whenever I am, for if sought I will come to you."

"Where will you come from?"

But she was gone.

# Fourteen

I dreamed that I went with Katharine. I imagine it must have been a dream. We went whither we would, at will, and I saw the other side of the veil.

There was no wall which could bar us, for walls were insubstantial. There was no speech, nor need for it, since all who lived before life and beyond death communicated telepathically, just as Katharine and I did. There was perpetual warmth and light, for the sun never sank in the sky, causing us to think in terms of day and night.

There was truth. Souls cannot lie, having no body to hide behind. We had form, much as in earth-life, but could SEE each and every thought. So a falsehood was seen, immediately, to be a devilish device and was thus rendered profitless.

People were kind – kinder than they had been before dying. They shared everything, Utopia-fashion. There were no currencies and there was no food to eat, neither money nor bodily nourishment being needed. We had left these needs behind us when we died.

All physical needs had been left behind. We had new needs . . . new hungers.

These were more selfless than they had been, for we had seen that we were each but a cog in the great wheel. No-one stood alone. We were all components of a glorious whole.

That is, there was glory potentially. First, mankind must emerge from its suffering. To be born was to suffer, since that was the scheme of things, but it did not have to be. We had created our own indignity through envy and greed, anger and fear, all negativity and the abuse of our bodies. We could, however, re-create.

And we would, for we were well on our way. Souls (except those that chose to regress) were striving higher, ever higher, in their quest for perfection, and those that were advanced helped those that were starting. I caught a glimpse of this Perfect Plan.

My glimpse spurred me on. I now knew a little and longed to know more. I drew knowledge from the very atmosphere.

Katharine beckoned and I followed her to an area filled with colour. We were within some celestial sphere and every rainbow ended here – here, where we were.

I rejoiced in the colour, in the music that suffused the air, and in the freedom of movement that I had not known before. Using just my will, I could be anywhere – wherever I wanted to be, instantaneously. I could be with Jeremy . . .

I could be . . . would be . . . was about to be, for he was ahead, opening his arms to me . . .

He had been. Now, without warning, I was back in my bedroom and he was not with me. Or, if he was, I could not see him. Oh, the defects of my vision!

Had I dreamed, or had I been with Katharine, as it seemed? I could not be certain. Whichever the case, there was momentary disappointment in having found Jeremy, only to 'lose' him again.

But I knew better, now, than to think of him as lost. I felt a surge of faith and of optimism. There was nothing to fear in death – everything to welcome. Life should, rightfully, be enhanced by the prospect of release from the physical body. And at my moment of release Jeremy would be waiting for me.

I had come close to completing the Coffin Tree, but had decided to postpone its completion until early autumn, when the leaves began to turn. Then I would take my easel to the top of the hill and try to capture Nature's colours for my work. Meanwhile, I had taken to racing through my household and gardening duties in order to devote maximum time to sketching

Tyneham's many and varied scenes. I sketched these with a sense of urgency which was in part accounted for by my baby. He was growing fast within my womb and was becoming a person for me, with his own identity. He had taken to kicking with such vim that I could virtually identify a foot or a fist and catch hold of it. He was kicking his way in to the world, where he was due to arrive in just over three months. What did the world hold in store for him? I wanted it to store only good things. But there would be grief, to offset his happiness, and there would be failure, offsetting success. There were, in life, two sides to everything – a dark and a light side to everyone. So instead of hoping that he could be happy all the time, I would wish fulfilment for my son. To be fulfilled was surely to be as happy as a human could be. My art fulfilled me. And, after his birth, my baby would be encroaching on my artistry. I must allow for this, while also allowing for Katharine having urged me to hurry.

For both these reasons, I was hurrying to record as much of Tyneham as possible, never allowing my hands to be idle, nor my mind to be still.

So whenever my other roles and the weather permitted, I set off in to the valley or on to the hills with my sketchbooks – or, occasionally, with my canvas and easel. I painted Stickland's time-worn cottage, nestling snugly in South Egliston's gwyle, and while I was painting old Louis emerged through his front door, dressed in the dark frock-coat and square top hat that Jeremy had described to me. Louis then stood stock-still, a gnarled hand holding his walking-stick, as I proceeded to paint him. Only when I was finished did he disappear in much the manner of Katharine's disappearances. But I did not question where he had come from nor where he had gone, for I had been there.

Below Stickland's cottage was the small, rocky promontory known as Broad Bench. This jutted in to the sea between

Hobarrow Bay and Charnel/Kimmeridge. I should not have ventured so close to the cliffs, on account of the sea-defences. I would not have sat looking across Long Ebb and Brandy Bay to Wagon Rock and Gad Cliff, but for the necessity to sketch all the splendour surrounding me. Beyond Kimmeridge Bay, and the hill on which Clavel's Tower stood, lay Chapman's Pool, where lived the friends of Jeremy's he had wanted to take me to see, after the war's end. We would have walked there, together, across these cliffs that rose and dipped so surgingly. We would still walk there, to visit his friends and make them also my friends. I would walk with him, my unseen companion, everywhere we had planned to walk, once Britain was free again.

I sketched, that August, Sea Cottage at Worbarrow from the east. This is where the Miller family lived. Their men had been fishermen for generations, and smugglers before the Crimean War. I sketched from the east to avoid the anti-invasion barbed wire that would have been in the foreground, had I been sketching from the sea-shore, and also to show the cottage to best advantage – seeming, as it did from there, to rise straight from the sea. Indeed, at high-tide the sea battered the cottage's retaining wall, soaking the roof and seaward windows. Three chimneys topped the roof's ancient slates and immediately beyond these chimneys – so that I sketched them against it – lay the expanse of sea which washed Worbarrow Bay while curving across the horizon to the cliffs of Cockpit Head and Ring's Hill as well as in to the Gap of Arish Mell.

I worked then on the four terraced cottages by the Worbarrow Road, the first of which was inhabited by Jessie Richards and her hedger husband. Their baby, Beatrice, whom I had first seen so soon after her birth, was now five months old – a lovely, gurgling little girl. I included her in my sketch, as she lay on a rug on the Richards's lawn.

The cottage above the gwyle came next, for it was quite the

154

sweetest of cottages, with its curvy thatch and little lattices. Its door and windows were so arranged that they gave the impression of a friendly face. Then came the cottage by the stream, and Sheepleaze – my sketch of which aroused the interest of a soldier stationed there. He asked why I was sketching it and I answered him that there were no certainties, in war. I wanted to be certain that, afterwards, I would have this record.

"But nothing is going to happen here," he said. "Nothing bad, that is. We virtually have the enemy licked."

"I'm sure you're right," I told him, trying not to think of the enemy within. "This is just a precaution – probably a superfluous one."

Even as my words were uttered, sounds exploded on the air from quite near. They came from Lulworth and were increasing in volume – the threatening sounds of gunfire.

I never used to be threatened by them. Pointless, now, to be threatened. So I shut out the sound and the threat from my consciousness.

All around Tyneham I went, sketching the old coastguard station from the north-east so that Worbarrow's Tout could be seen, rising on the skyline just beyond it, and sketching cook's cottage with Mrs Hodden seated in the sunshine by her door among fuchsias so tall that they rather dwarfed her. She had recovered well from her pneumonia and spoke with sadness to me of Jeremy.

"Why couldn' the good Lord ha' taken me, 'stead of him?" she asked, while I was working. "I midden be worth the takin', but I'm a wold 'oman and he had his life ahead o' him."

I responded in vague terms as grasshoppers and crickets made themselves heard, along with some Kittiwakes and a tuneful pair of Meadow Pipits. It was exceptionally sheltered here, which brought butterflies galore. I put a Green Fritillary and a Small Skipper in to my picture, just as Martin Travers had incorporated a Camberwell Beauty in to the stained glass window that he had designed for St Mary's in memory of Mrs Draper. I could never see a butterfly without remembering that one on the Virgin's robe and the look in Jeremy's eyes as he likened me to Mary. I would be forever inspired by this comparison.

I sketched the farms at Tyneham and at Baltington, after which I concentrated on the village itself. Excluding from my sketches all uniformed personnel who came and went, since they had no real role in Tyneham, I recorded Post Office Row with the pond in the foreground and with children fishing for evets or chasing horse tingers. I preferred these Dorset words to their equivalents of newts and dragonflies. They conjured their own images and atmosphere. I wanted my child to immerse himself in Dorsetshire.

I was still recording village scenes when I received a letter from mother, inviting herself to stay for a few days.

William asked: "Who is she coming to see . . . us, or Katharine?"

I answered with a grin: "Katharine, I should think! She's been decidedly curious about her since my Bournemouth trip."

"Curious and somewhat sceptical, if I know your mother as I think I know her. Well, it'll be amusing to watch her scepticism disappear. How fortunate, that Katharine's portrait is framed and ready to be displayed. Ready, that is, but for its varnish. In honour of your mother's visit we should, I feel, hang it, like Jeremy's, ahead of its varnishing. They can be brought down and varnished together, later, can't they?"

Oil paint needed six months at least in order to dry and settle adequately. Varnish that was applied too soon cracked as the paint dried. "Yes, they can," I agreed. "So let's find the right home for Katharine, shall we?"

William then paid me the ultimate compliment, insisting on removing the Gainsborough from its long-held position over the mantlepiece and hanging my portrait in its place. Strangely, though 'The Descent From The Cross' had hung there for as long as even William could remember, Katharine seemed instantly to belong. Her presence dominated the dining-room. I did not need to ask her whether it also dominated her kitchen, for it was the wall of the present that we had hung her portrait on. And the wall was pale green, offsetting the green of her gown perfectly.

"Mother can hardly help noticing her, up there," I drily observed. "But where can we rehouse the Gainsborough?"

At William's suggestion we transported this between us to the drawing-room where, after some rearrangement of wall-space, we succeeded in accommodating it to our mutual satisfaction between the two east-facing long windows. This situation seemed to suit it even better than the one we had taken it from. Without causing any discomfiture, Katharine had come home.

I met mother's train at Wareham station two days later. The weather being warm, we both wore sleeveless frocks. As I kissed her, I was aware of a familiar faint fragrance of lavender water.

"Have you heard from Tom?" she asked as we settled ourselves in to the car. "I received word from him today saying he's been promoted to squadron leader."

"I hadn't heard that," I told her, "but then I left before the post came this morning, having various errands to do in town. How well Tom's doing! Did he give any hints as to when he might next be home?"

"No. He'll just turn up on the doorstep one day, without warning, as is his wont. That is, I hope . . . "

"He'll turn up, mother. And by the end of this war, the way he's going, he'll probably be a wing commander."

"It won't matter to me what he is, just as long as he comes through all this. Didn't we just pass the Tyneham turning?"

"Yes, we did. I drove past deliberately. You won't mind, will you, mother, if – petrol permitting – we make a slight detour?"

This was via Corfe. Since Katharine's mention of it, I had

longed to take a closer look at the Castle, now in ruins, which from its high hilltop dominated our Isle of Purbeck. I knew, because it was common knowledge locally, that Corfe castle had stood on its hundred-and-fifty-foot hill since Anglo-Saxon times. 'Corfe' was, in fact, the Anglo - Saxon word for 'gap'. I knew, too, from discussions with William, that though in the course of the Civil War the brave Lady Bankes – along with her daughters, women and five soldiers – valiantly fought off attackers for more than two years with stones and hot embers, her Royalist home had had then to be surrendered when a traitor admitted disguised Parliamentarians in 1646, after which the House of Commons voted to demolish it. And demolished it had been, very vigorously, so that the buildings of the Norman Keep were too mutilated for there to be left any accurate trace of it in its heyday.

All the same, such was its position in the gap between Challow Hill and Knowle Hill, which were in turn bounded on the north by Poole Harbour and on the east and south by the sea, that it was an imposing part of our geography as well as of our history. Not that there was such a thing as history, according to Katharine. Because of her, I saw this more as current affairs.

The Castle came into view quite quickly, Corfe being not far from Stoborough (where we normally turned off for Tyneham) and being built so high. The whole village was on high ground between the Downs, but the Castle was its highest point. As we approached from below, I could easily imagine the redoubtable Lady Bankes defending this stronghold with stones and hot coals, as those who would overthrow the House of Stuart tried to seize her home.

Her advantage was considerable, there so high on her hill. For as they sought to storm the garrison from beneath, she and her helpers could hurl deterrents most efficaciously from windows and battlements. And, with walls nine feet thick, she was well protected from enemy weapons.

"Why are we here?" mother asked, as – on the opposite side from Corfe village – I parked at the foot of the green hill on which the Castle stood and sat staring up at it. "Or am I somehow supposed to know why?"

"No," I said, facing her. "I'm sorry, mother. I don't mean to be mysterious. We're here because of Katharine."

"Your ghost, you mean?"

"Don't sound so disparaging!"

"I can't help my tone . . . and I can't help worrying. You speak of Katharine as if she were . . . "

"Real? She IS, mother! She's as real as we are."

"How can she be?"

"You'll see! There are many realities – and I have the most illuminating conversations with Katharine. She was speaking, only last evening, of the day George, Duke of Clarence, drowned in a butt of malmsey after being attainted of high treason. His drowning resulted in this Castle, together with the manor of Corfe, becoming the property of the Crown – which it had been periodically since King Edgar lived here in the tenth century. So much has happened here, since Edgar's reign – and since Edward I was murdered by his stepmother, Elfrida, who wanted the throne for her son, Ethelred. And it is still happening, according to Katharine. That's why I wanted to come and look again at the Castle, in the light of her disclosures."

"No wonder I worry! This talk is unhealthy. The more I think about it, the more I . . . "

"Then don't think! Don't pre-suppose anything. Try to clear your mind of all supposition before coming to Tyneham and seeing Katharine."

"SEEing? . . . Oh, you mean her portrait! For one awful moment, I thought you meant . . . "

"There's nothing awful about seeing her in person. 'Wonderful' would be a better word."

"That's a matter of opinion," mother said.

159

We drove home to Tyneham via Knowle and Steeple. These were tiny hamlets set among the hills, each with an ancient church and a cluster of pretty Purbeck-stone cottages. Approaching from this direction, we climbed the hill from Lutton, seeing in the process the gap flanked by Whiteway Hill and Gold Down, wherein nestled the House that I shared with William and Katharine. Our home could not, of course, be seen, so well was it concealed by the curve of the Cowleaze and by the trees. But it gave me a warm feeling, just knowing of its existence and of the welcome that always waited there for me.

William must have been watching for us from the Porch Room, for he appeared through the north porch door as I braked in the gravelled yard. "I was beginning to think I'd be lunching alone," he said, after greeting mother and me. "Where have you been?"

Recognising that anxiety prompted his question I answered him: "Sorry if I worried you, William, but I gave in to a sudden whim to drive home via Corfe."

"And to sit for hours gazing up at the Castle," mother put in, her tone slightly tart, as William took her suitcase from the boot of the car.

"I see," he said mildly, smiling at me. "So Katharine's the cause of your tardiness! I might have guessed."

"It sounds to me," said mother, entering through the north porch door, "as if this . . . this Katharine has become something of a problem."

"On the contrary," William told her. "She's more in the nature of a revelation."

On the rare occasions that mother came to stay, I always gave her the White Room, which had once been used as a study and which had an atmosphere of exceptional calm – exceptional, even, for Tyneham. But for the pale blue panelling, upon which hung some delightful small seascapes and engravings, the entire interior was white and – as mother herself said – very soothing.

160

One window was south-facing and was framed by the shiny tan-lined leaves of the great magnolia whose growth covered that wall. Mother's view gave on to the terraced garden, which was ablaze with colour at this time of year. The White Room was two flights up from my bedroom, and was close to the Chintz Room, where I had first encountered Katharine.

It seemed an age since I had heard her crying but been unable to find her. It WAS an age, in terms of what I had learned. I was appallingly ignorant, in the pre-Katharine era. Knowing her had endowed on me an awareness and a maturity beyond my years.

"We'd better go straight down to lunch," I told mother. "Otherwise, we'll inconvenience Lily. I shouldn't really have delayed us as I did."

"Whatever you do seems to suit William. He has mellowed, that man. He isn't falling for you, is he, Catherine?"

"He feels affection for me, if that's what you mean, as I do for him."

"That isn't what I meant." A pointed pause and then: "Since you aren't to be drawn in that direction, might I know when I'm to see Katharine's much-vaunted portrait?"

"Who has vaunted it? I haven't."

"William, whenever I've rung and he's answered the 'phone."

"To the best of my knowledge, that's happened just once."

"Maybe so, but he was full of praise for you. And a man is never too old to . . . "

"Mother," I interruped her, "that will do. Can we please go down to lunch?"

Down we went, mother slightly huffy with me. William awaited us at the foot of the central staircase and the three of us proceeded then to the dining-room, where we had soon seated ourselves.

Mother started on her soup. In raising her spoon, she raised her eyes, commenting: "Dear heaven – the Gainsborough has gone! I like its successor even better. Who is that girl – and is she another Gainsborough?"

Mother's awe and questions seemed genuine, though I did not see how they could be, nor how she could not know that this was Katharine.

"You're looking at the artist," said William, "and at the ghost you didn't altogether believe in."

# Fifteen

Mother had believed, from that moment. And her belief changed her – gave her faith that she would one day be reunited with grandmother and with father.

She stayed for a week – hoping, I think, to catch a glimpse of Katharine, though she would not admit to this.

Before breakfast, on the morning of her departure, she said to me in her room: "You seem, my dear, to have been singled out for some reason."

"How do you mean?"

"I'm not sure whether I can explain," she said, sitting on the window-seat and looking out across the garden. I kneeled near her feet and waited for her to speak. I seemed to wait quite awhile before mother went on: "That portrait you painted – the one of Katharine, I mean, not of Jeremy, although his was good – is in a class of its own. That's why I didn't dream you were the artist. Oh, don't misunderstand me. I've never under-estimated your talent, even if I'm not the type to enthuse over it. I was brought up to believe that one shouldn't enthuse over one's children and their capabilities. So I've tended to play down your brother's and your achievements rather than praise them, for fear of conceit setting in, or complacence. When I first saw Katharine's portrait, though, not knowing it was your work, I didn't for one moment doubt its importance to the art world – to the world in general, for that matter. I was sure I was seeing another Old Master. Which is why, although we had spoken just moments before of your portrait of Katharine, it was beyond my imagining that this was it. And I've been thinking, since, something slightly bewildering – which is that your portrait

163

seems to me to have already been. I can't believe it has only now come into existence, for it's as if I've long been acquainted with it. In fact, I find myself wanting to risk a rather bizarre question." I smiled my encouragement and, colouring, she asked: "Could it, in some sense, have existed beforehand – and could you have been singled out for the purpose of re-establishing Katharine in people's minds?"

"Quite possibly," I said. "It's interesting, that you should speak of the portrait's pre-existence, because while painting I felt that the structure was already there – in the atmosphere, as it were, and that my function was simply to reproduce a work that had been done before. Not like a copier. It wasn't like that at all, but more as if the first work were mine and I were bringing it back from somewhere. So," I ended, smiling, "neither conceit nor complacence is in danger of setting in. My hand held the paintbrush, but I can't take credit for the inspiration."

Mother touched my shoulder, saying: "I think that perhaps you can. My impression is that some of the achievement, at least, must be your own doing. I'm . . . proud of you, Catherine."

Never had I dreamed to hear mother say such a thing. Incapable of any comment, I kissed her – and she kissed me, instead of merely proffering her cheek. I was soon to hear something still more surprising.

Mother said, a little later: "All this has removed the barrier." Before I could ask which barrier, she enlightened me: "After my mother died, I swore to myself that I wouldn't leave behind such emptiness as she left me with. She and I were close friends, you see, as well as mother and daughter . . . and I couldn't cope with the end of our friendship, when she passed over. Death seemed so final, then, and its finality nearly finished me. Because of this, I never encouraged our closeness – yours and mine. I suppose, even, I actively discouraged it. But now there's no need for such discouragement, because I know you won't view my departure in the same light as I viewed my mother's. Can we be the friends,

Catherine, that thanks to me we've never been?"

I cried as I replied: "We can and WILL be!"

On our way down to breakfast, I asked her: "Are you looking forward to being a grandmother?"

"I certainly am, my dear. I imagine you're hoping for a son and heir?"

"I've no need to hope. I know." Pausing in her descent, she turned toward me and said: "Am I to conclude that Katharine has told you your baby will be a boy?"

"Jeremy told me, on the night that he died."

"You are in touch, then, with him, too?"

There by the grandfather clock at a turn of the staircase I nodded, adding: "But not as often as with Katharine."

"It's said that parents learn from their children. I'm certainly learning! And I'll be knitting small blue garments from now on."

I missed her, after her return to Bournemouth, and I marvelled over the miracle Katharine had wrought. For it was little short of miraculous that my mother should speak as she had spoken. She had seemed, by the end of her visit, a new woman.

This was confirmed by William, who said: "Take the fear from death and we're left with an enhanced appreciation of life and of what's important. I'm glad for your mother . . . and sad for her."

"Sad?"

"Yes – sad for all the wasted years, before she became fully aware of having a daughter. We're most of us guilty of waste. I am, as much as the next person. Just ensure that you're never guilty of it, Catherine. You've been given so much to achieve with your time that any wastage would be a crime."

September came and I took time from sketching and painting to concentrate on preparing the nursery for my baby. He would arrive in two months and must not arrive in a world unprepared for him. Friends from the village had begun bringing gifts they had knitted or sewn. My own gifts must be made ready and his

165

room must be fit for Jeremy's and my son.

He would lie in his forefathers' seventeenth century oak crib which Annie had polished at my request, and would gaze around him during his first days of life at a pale blue room near mine here at the heart of Tyneham. Would he bring memories with him, of where he had come from, or would he have no memory of being somewhere prior to being in my womb? It seemed to me that he would remember, in the earliest years, but that by the time he could tell of these remembrances they would have left him. For by then the world would have intervened, blotting out his vision except in dreams. How well arranged . . . how beneficent. Believing that this earth began and ended his existence, he would not miss his spiritual home, or not specifically. But he would experience undefined yearnings that would in the end, if he heeded them, lift him above materialism and bring him back to the place we call heaven.

I had begun to long to see him. Who would I see? Who was this babe that I carried within me? He was part of me and of Jeremy, yet had his own identity. And while our love had helped in his creation, it had not created him. He was, as we all were, the work of the world's Creator, who would receive us back again when we had ascended our spiritual stairs.

So I would look at my baby and would see a small human on loan to me. He might seem to be mine, but I would be deceiving myself if I believed that he was an outright gift, or possession, for this he could not be. He belonged, as all life did, to the universe and not to his seeming origin. Our belonging brought us union with every living thing.

From the nursery window I could see harvesters in the fields. There was something reassuring about the harvest being gathered in. Man came and went, as did the seasons, which came again, bringing all their benefits with them. I always benefited from autumn – more so, even, than from the spring. Springtime, in fact, often saddened me, whereas I found autumn gladdening.

For its mornings were dewy and it coloured the trees stupendously. Soon, I could complete my Coffin Tree.

And soon the last wagon-load of harvest would rumble home, to the accompaniment of old songs and children cheering. Then there would be furmety for tea in Oak Hall as the evenings drew in. Yes, there was much to be said for autumn.

Katharine disagreed with me.

That is, she complained of the bad harvest of 1543 and of the food shortage thus caused, adding: "Nor will next year's harvest be better."

"Can you move from year to year, both backwards and forwards, at will?" I asked her.

"Why, I have no need to! I need only stay still, while the years come to me."

"Does every year that has ever been and that is yet to be exist somewhere then?"

"Of course it does! That is obvious."

"It might be to you, but isn't to me or I wouldn't have asked the question. Is 1945 as accessible to you as 1545?"

"Not quite. T'is hard to explain, with the words so far made, but t'is farther away than my own time."

"I agree that our existing vocabulary is limiting! So 1945 has already arrived. I find that . . . hard to take in."

"Do not think. Simply sup on my testimony as on the air that you breathe. Then you will believe."

We were speaking in my room at bed-time, which was where – and when – we spoke most often. "I already believe," I said. "Belief is easy. Now I must try to interpret. I'll do as you suggest and sup on your words. The more we talk, the more I can comprehend."

Katharine talked then, at length. Rosie, she told me, had taken the first step toward reunion with her son and release from the Shadow Lands. When asked what this step was, she answered: "Why, Rosie has realised that she is her own captor – that t'is, verily, up to her to be freed from there."

"What made her realise?"

"A higher soul came by – one she recognised – and showed care and concern in conversation with her. Thus she learned that her walls were impermanent and that she could think them hence. She will not remain imprisoned, once she rightly repents."

"Rightly?"

"Yes. Rosie has formed the opinion that she must repent of birthing an infant unwed. But, as we have said, t'is a far more serious sin to end our own suffering. T'is because of this she is where she is. T'is this she must rightly repent of."

"How should she show repentance?"

"Through her thinking. Thought is all-powerful. We are all slow to know its power."

"Once we know," I said pensively, "that our thoughts – in combination, I imagine, with our deeds – create our environment, we have nothing to fear, have we? I mean, it's simply a question of taking responsibility for our own actions."

"T'is a pity that those aboard the MARY ROSE at this moment lack your perspicacity – for they fear greatly. Their ship has capsized, you see, and is sinking."

Slightly disconcerted by this sudden divulgence, I asked: "When is this?"

"T'is Sunday, 19 July, 1545. King Henry was dining aboard in Portsmouth when, while he dined, news arrived that the French fleet had entered the Solent. So the King did depart immediately, sanctioning the sailing of his whole fleet, led by the GREAT HARRY, to meet the enemy."

"It was lucky for him that he did not sail with them."

"T'was a stroke of good fortune," Katharine agreed. "For after their exchange of gunfire and after the French had set sail again, along the Sussex coast this time, the MARY ROSE started sinking. Almost five hundred men are due to drown, along with

168

Sir George Carey, Vice-Admiral of the Fleet."

"Can't anything be done, to prevent their drowning?"

"Nay, for t'is written that they must drown. They will thus avoid the plague which is about to break out again."

"Do people, then, sometimes die by one means in order to avoid dying by some other means?"

"T'is often so. The great compassion shown is oft misinterpreted, with blame falsely apportioned. Dire suffering accompanies the plague. I would not want to die of it. T'is better far for Arthur that he did die of gunshot than that he should die of the bubonic. King Henry will go to any lengths to avoid contagion."

"What will he die of?"

"There will come a cold night – so cold that all the rivers will freeze – and on this night he will die."

"Why?"

"Because of his fondness for the 'good' life and for watching his huntsmen in the worst weather slaughter the deer. He can no longer endure icy temperatures, so beset is he with chills and fevers."

"How are the deer slaughtered?"

"Why, with arrows! How else? The King is most partial to venison. But then, he has a liking for every kind of stomach-lining, and for mead in quantity. He has been slowly poisoning himself in feast and in deed."

"In deed?" I queried.

"We poison our bodies as surely with wrong thoughts and acts as with food and drink. The King's body has been badly abused. Do not abuse your body while t'is yours. Fruit, not flesh, is the proper food."

"I have less and less liking for meat," I said. "Are we, truly, not meant to be meat-eaters?"

"Truly, t'is written that berries answer our needs, not meat. Human beings are not by nature carnivores."

"Then why were we given eyeteeth?"

"These were not given originally. We gave them to ourselves through our mode of eating. They became a necessity."

"I see. Then I shall make mine unnecessary again. What is it? What's wrong?"

Katharine had grown agitated, She started clasping her hands together and unclasping them, while looking anxiously around the room. "T'is happening," she said at last. "That of which I did tell."

With a heavy heart, I asked: "The great wrong is already being dealt to Tyneham?"

"T'is not Tyneham that is suffering," she said impatiently. "T'is the King. He is dying. Cranmer is with him."

"Who is Cranmer?"

"You know nothing! He is the Archbishop of Canterbury, who will burn in the reign of Mary. The roads are icy. They delayed his arrival at the King's bedside. He is telling Henry to give some sign that he puts his trust in the mercy of Christ. Ah, he has given the sign! Now he can die."

At such a time, I hardly liked to say anything. But I could not curb the question: "When?"

"T'is two in the morning. The King is dead. Long live the boy, Edward!"

Katharine withdrew then and I soon slept.

Next day I consulted the history books again and learned that Henry died at two in the morning of 28 January, 1547. Thomas Cranmer, Archbishop of Canterbury, was with him and, before dying, Henry squeezed Cranmer's hand as a sign that he trusted in the mercy of Christ.

Stunned and grief-stricken counsellors kept their King's death secret for three days, until January the thirty-first. Then the heralds proclaimed the nine-year-old Edward VI King of England and Protector of the Faith.

With Katharine, I had in some way seen history being made.

# Sixteen

Gossamer threads, like cobwebs, bind us to each other and, on still days that autumn, the surface of the nearer Eweleaze shimmered beneath a gossamer sea. It was as though the whole pasture were spread with a layer of silver, ethereally. After completing the Coffin Tree, I concentrated on the Eweleaze and on reproducing on canvas its silvery haze.

As I sketched and painted, I was conscious of my baby's impatience. He was nearing the end of his sojourn in my womb and was now anxious to be born. His anxiety was reflected in a feverishness in me – a sudden spurt of activity.

The nursery was ready. A big teddy bear that had belonged to Jeremy sat atop a chest of drawers that was laden with small garments and with Terry towelling napkins. Other toys, too, waited to welcome my son – none of them new, with this war on and new toys few and far between. There was a gaily dressed golliwog that old Mrs Hodden had knitted for him and there was a monkey made from scraps of grey suiting by Mrs Cooper, the postmistress. Would he one day frequent Tyneham's tiny post office and shop, where children loved to linger while choosing how to spend their halfpennies and pennies?

Jeremy had told me how, as a child, he wallowed in the post office's atmosphere. Its smell stayed with him, he said, when he was sent away to school and suffered from homesickness. In his subconscious, he could draw upon the blend of cheese and bacon, liquorice, tea and peppermint. And he could see, as if his schoolboy hand still clutched a ha'penny, the tempting array of buttercreams, bulls' eyes, comfits, chocolate bars, sugared almonds and acid drops, as well, of course, as popcorn. No

171

matter how small the amount a child had to spend, he or she was given the same patient attention as was given to every customer. It could safely be said that as well as revolving around our church, life here revolved around our post office. I cherished the thought that Jeremy's son would follow him along the post office path.

For I wanted him to follow in every respect in his father's footsteps. I would bring him up to be kind and caring, as Jeremy had been, and strong and gentlemanly. It would be as though he had known his father, for I would make Jeremy known to him. And he would not feel deprived of a father's love, since Jeremy's remained in existence. There would be William, too, loving him and providing a masculine presence. The child in my womb would want for nothing.

Toward the end of October, on the day that I celebrated my birthday, Katharine came at an unusual hour – unusual, that is, for her. Dawn had not yet broken when I awoke and saw her bending over me. Despite the darkness, I could see her clearly – or was it her aura that I could see, and that illuminated her? I had come to know auras and know their power. We were each outlined by a light that was coloured according to the kind of person we were and that changed colour as we progressed or regressed. But we could not automatically see each other's auras. I had never seen the aura of a living person. I had, though, for some time now seemed to see Katharine's – hence my knowledge.

"You are abed again?" she admonished me. "You have a quaint capacity for sleep."

"As I expect you once had," I retorted. "And surely I should sleep, while I can? I could be due for some disturbed nights, couldn't I?"

"This is so," she agreed, looking long and hard at me. "Your strength should be conserved. The time draws nigh, you see. There is left little opportunity to be as you have been."

I said happily: "I can well imagine how, once my baby's born, life will be dramatically different."

"You speak of your son? I do not speak of him. I am come to speak of . . . other things. The letter . . . t'is being written."

"Which letter?" I asked her, chilled. "It isn't as if we've discussed one. Who is writing it?"

"Those that would take Tyneham. Their deed is almost done."

This said, she departed. My chill deepened until I felt feverish. I tossed and turned, remaining in bed until the darkness dispersed. Then, my brain still teeming with wild imaginings, I prepared to join William for breakfast.

"You look far from celebratory," he told me, rising to greet me as I entered the dining-room. "Have you forgotten that it's your birthday?"

"I had, as a matter of fact."

"Why's that? Has something happened?"

"According to Katharine," I responded, sitting down, "there's . . . change in the wind." I could not bring myself to be more specific – not to him, not this morning. "And I've no reason to think that the change will be to our liking."

He frowned, then almost immediately brightened, saying: "Whatever it is won't happen today, I take it?"

"I doubt it will," I said, shaking my head.

"How forthcoming was Katharine?"

"She was her usual self – hinting, rather than saying anything."

"Hints mustn't come in to consideration – not on your birthday. We shall celebrate, concerning ourselves with tomorrow only when tomorrow comes. I want nothing to mar our celebration – and Lily has promised a cake, not to mention a special meal this evening. Does that sound as good to you as it does to me?"

Following his lead, I said lightly: "Yes, it does! And maybe tomorrow will never come."

"Quite so," said William. Then he said: "Before we start celebrating, I've just one question – concerning the birth of your son. Are you quite certain that a hospital wouldn't be the best place for you to give birth in? It would be the safest place. We can't risk . . . "

". . . what happened to Geraldine happening again?" I gently intervened. "No of course we can't. I wouldn't put you through that a second time for the world. But my son has to be born here in Tyneham. He just has to be. This is something that I feel deep within me. And Doctor Cotterell says I'm rudely healthy. He sees no reason for me to be hospitalised – and he should know, shouldn't he?"

"While I've no wish to be alarmist, Catherine . . . he didn't know in the case of Geraldine. Maybe we should have changed doctors. Not that we could, without seeming to suggest that her death was his fault, which it wasn't, I'm sure. Maybe . . . "

"That's enough of your 'maybes'. Nothing is going to go wrong. If it were, I'd know, for Katharine would have warned me. So please don't worry. Birth is such a natural thing that I don't believe I need take complex measures to produce my son. I'll produce him here, where he belongs, in Tyneham. I've every confidence in Doctor Cotterrell and in the midwife. I swear that I'll be all right."

He smiled at this and said: "I wasn't aware that you were given to swearing. Just don't pass such habits on to my great-grandson."

I opened my present from him then. He had wrapped it as only a man can – in crumpled brown paper tied round with string. I found this very endearing. And his expression as I undid his gift was one of boyish expectation. Having resolved to react with great enthusiasm to the parcel's contents, no matter what these were (William was not normally the most inspired of givers), I lifted the lid of an old jeweller's box and needed no false words of awe or gratitude.

174

Within the box, on a bed of black velvet, lay the loveliest garnet necklace I had ever seen. I gasped at its beauty and at the seeming impossibility of its being meant for me. For I had seen it before – was seeing it, even as I lifted my gaze to the portrait of William's mother. "Yes," William said, following my gaze's direction. "They were hers . . . and now they are yours."

"They're . . . superb! I feel immensely . . . honoured."

"Let me fasten it for you," William said, scraping back his chair and standing with alacrity. "It has long been my wish to see you wearing this. And it would have been mother's wish, too, had she known you. We shared the opinion that the artist didn't do justice to the gems. What's your view?"

Rising to my feet after he had secured the clasp and surveying myself in the small mirror that hung to the right of the south window, I answered: "An injustice was done. But the artist has my sympathy. Such jewels as these could not be reproduced easily."

"You could reproduce them – enhance them, even. Will you, when time permits, paint your self-portrait wearing the necklace? It would mean a great deal, if you would do that for me."

"I'll do it willingly!" Then, hugging him: "I thank you with my whole heart both for your gift and for your faith in my capability. My portrait should at some stage join Jeremy's."

His expresion clouded as I said this. "Yes, it should," he responded, sighing. "You must hang beside him, just as I hang beside Philomena, his grandmother. But I couldn't bring myself to give the garnets to her. I was keeping them, and part of me, in reserve."

We were still standing, facing each other. He was looking at me almost reverently. I asked: "Did Philomena know that you were?"

"We never spoke about it. And she was not especially . . . sensitive. So I hope she didn't know. It would be a source of chagrin, wouldn't it, for a woman to know her husband was waiting for a girl yet to be born?"

"Yes, it would," I whispered. "Poor Philomena!"

"I couldn't even be sure that she would be born, but I believed she would be . . . and she WAS, but too late for me. Had she been born sooner, I wonder whether she would have fallen unreservedly in love with me, or whether she would have kept part of herself in reserve for Jeremy . . . ?"

There were tears in his eyes, and in mine, as I told him: "She could have loved you wholeheartedly. As things are, she loves you dearly. And you were reborn, in a sense, in your grandson, expressing your love through him as you will again, differently, through your great-grandson. Love is never wasted, nor obsolete, William. It has a life of its own, flowering and growing through new generations ad infinitum. So as well as loving you for your own sake, I've loved you in Jeremy and shall love you in Jeremy's son."

"Thank you, Catherine!" He held me again and kissed my cheeks tenderly. "Your words and wisdom have made me a happy man."

On the night of 9 November there was a terrible storm. This was worse, if anything, than the storm that raged on the night Jeremy died. The wind thrashed the trees in West Plantation with such ferocity that I feared they must all be brought to the ground and that the House, too, would be brought down.

I wondered, as I had wondered previously, whether just the wind and the rain were at work or whether the sea was submerging the whole valley, the tide having forgotten to turn. For tonight it was as if the firmament were venting a wrath that would take toll of all the earth. Were we due to be submerged? The thought began to take form that Tyneham must join Atlantis on the bed of the ocean.

Then, with the elements at their most relentless, there came within my room the curious stillness that invariably preceded

176

Katharine.

I waited for her to arrive, which she did in a short while. Immediately upon arrival, she told me: "T'is time."

As she spoke, I experienced a sharp twinge in my side. This was not where I would have expected it, but I imagined that it must mark labour's onset. And, my baby not being due for a week yet, there was no doctor or midwife standing by. Well, that was fine. First babies, it was commonly known, took their time arriving. Mine would not arrive until the storm had abated and until help was at hand.

Completely calm, I asked Katharine: "How long did your son take to be born?"

"That is naught to go by. James was a lazy baby and then a knave. You had best speak in to that . . . that device I have seen you speak in to. Your son is very different from mine."

She spoke of my son as if she knew him. Did she? I felt slight envy that she should know him ahead of me. No doubt she had already been to the years yet to come, wherein she had become acquainted with my son. Knowing him, and knowing him to be different from James, she was urging use of the telephone. Lighting the lamp and easing in to my dressing-gown, I made with lumbering gait for the Porch Room.

It was 3 a.m. As I padded in slippered feet along the narrow landing, floorboards creaked and shadows surrounded me. Within the shadows were former Tices. They were gathering for the birth of their descendant. Keenly, I felt their presence. I also felt, as I entered the Porch Room, a further twinge.

Far from alarming me, or endowing me with any great sense of urgency, this reassured me that my baby was, truly, on his way. Before long I would see him, hold him, care for him. The miracle of birth would occur, with me and my son part of that miracle. I had never known such anticipation as I knew then.

Calling the doctor's number, I subsequently listened to the ringing tone while also listening to the storm. The wind was tearing at the trees, the rain hammering against the casements. And how the wind moaned, while also whistling down the chimneys. On this replica of the night that Jeremy had left the world, his son would enter it. How well thought out . . . how appropriate!

I was so busy with my musings that Doctor Cotterrell had spoken twice in to the receiver before I responded. Apologising for disturbing him, I then told him: "I believe my baby's coming."

With an intake of breath he said: "Great heavens! What a night to choose, for his advent. Have you alerted Mrs Begg yet?"

"No, I haven't."

"Leave her to me, Catherine." A chuckle, then: "Midwives are my pigeon. And don't fret about a thing. It'll be hours before your baby's along. First offspring are devils for keeping everyone waiting. Storm or no storm, Mrs B and I'll be with you long before you're in any need of us. Go back to bed, I should, and try to sleep between contractions. I imagine they're about half an hour apart?"

"No. Less than that . . . much less. Not that I've timed them."

Another breath intake and then: "I expect they seem more frequent than they actually are. But we'll be with you just as soon as we can. Au revoir, Catherine."

The line went dead.

I knew a moment's panic then. Supposing he and Mrs Begg were delayed by the storm and did not arrive in time? Whatever would I do, in those circumstances? I couldn't give birth alone. I might die, like Geraldine. My son might die, too. But no, I couldn't die, for I had given my word to William.

I had better tell him what was happening. My lamp held aloft, I headed toward his room.

As I approached, he emerged through his door looking sleepy and tousled. "Thought I heard your voice," he said, "Nothing's wrong is it, Catherine?"

178

I felt fine again – strong and confident. "No," I answered him, "nothing. You probably heard me 'phoning the doctor to suggest that he and the midwife pay us a call."

William looked appalled. "You don't mean that on the night of such a storm the baby . . . "

" . . . has decided to be born," I finished for him. "He has quite a sense of timing, hasn't he?"

"Oh, Catherine!" William lifted his hands in a gesture of appeal. "How soon did Archie say he and Mrs Begg can be here?"

"Very soon. And he said I mustn't worry about anything. That goes for you, too. Just think . . . we'll shortly be seeing my son."

"All I care about just now is your safety, Catherine."

"I'll be quite safe. I've sworn, haven't I?"

"Yes, you have," he agreed, attempting to smile. As he spoke, a third twinge caught me in my side and I winced. William took my lamp from me, looking thoroughly alarmed. "What's up?" he asked.

"He's tiring of his darkness. We would be, too, wouldn't we, after nine months of it? The doctor suggested I should go back to bed. If I do, you won't get anxious, will you?"

"I'll try not to. While you're acting on Archie's orders, I'll go downstairs to wait for him and the midwife and let them in. Should I be boiling water, or something?"

"Probably . . . and by the time it has boiled, no doubt they'll be here."

But there was still no sign of them two hours later.

And my contractions were now all too frequent. I went with them, knowing instinctively not to go against them, while outside the storm, unbelievably, still seemed to be gaining momentum. Had trees been brought down across the road from Corfe? It was quite likely, on this night of nights, that they had been. If they had, preventing the doctor getting through by car, he would have to walk, which could take too long.

I could not give birth unattended. Panic set in again and, with the panic, came increased pain. I fought the pain . . . fought Nature. Thrashing about on my bed, fighting for breath and for relief from successive cruel contractions, with barely a gap in between, I wept. My face was wet with tears and my body wet with perspiration when there was a surge of water from between my legs which saturated the bed.

I was absurdly unschooled in the procedure of childbirth, but knew enough from my reading to realise that my waters must have broken. I did not know, though, how long it was likely to be before delivery of my baby. I sensed that this must be imminent.

For the pain that I was experiencing was beyond my endurance. The contractions had all merged into one, which racked my body mercilessly. I could not breathe. Nor could I believe that there existed such agony.

Gasping for air, I also gasped: "Jeremy!"

He was beside me, as he had said he always would be. Saying my name again and again, like an endearment, he lovingly lifted me.

Held in his arms, I was calmed instantly. My pain went as if it had never been. I was utterly at peace.

He asked, his eyes searching mine: "Did you doubt my presence, beloved Catherine? Never doubt me."

"I've no doubts ordinarily. But with our son on his way, I needed more than knowledge of your nearness. I needed this."

"Given faith and trust, all needs are answered – everyone's. It's a perfect design, my darling – a foolproof plan. And it's by design that, together, we should welcome our boy, William."

Freed from fear and from pain, I found presently that I was back on my bed again. Jeremy was gone. That is to say, I could no longer see him. But in my arms, as lovingly as my husband had held me, I held our son.

180

# Seventeen

I had just a hazy recollection of the actual moment of birth and of how I came to be holding my baby. The whole episode had had a dream-like quality. But I had not dreamed and nor did I question what had happened to me. For I had shared my son's birth with Jeremy.

William arrived first on the scene. He had been pacing the landing beyond my bedroom, in between watching and listening from the Porch Room for some sign of the doctor's arrival. Each time he had been tempted to come in, he had hesitated lest I was sleeping. This amused me. Only a man could imagine that there were any possibility, then, of sleep! I was also pleased, for it seemed to mean that I had not indulged my pain to the extent of screaming.

Hearing what had sounded to him like a baby's cry, although he was certain that it couldn't have been, William knocked and came in. His expression as he saw my son was disbelieving, then wondering. "This can't be," he said, tentatively approaching the bed, "and yet my eyes tell me differently. Your baby is born . . . and the storm is dying down. We're told 'as above, so below' . . . and it is so. We're one with the elements and with the galaxies, aren't we?"

I said, as he gazed at me and at his great-grandson: "They're part of us, just as we're part of them. The baby's name, incidentally, is William."

"William? You mean . . . you've named him after me?"

I smiled up at him joyously from Jeremy's side of the bed, which was drier than mine and which was where I had found myself following the birth. "We have indeed!"

"We?" Then, comprehending: "Oh, of course – you and Jeremy! He was here, was he? I should have known that he would be. So it was a joint decision, to call your son William?"

It would have hurt him, had I disclosed that it was Jeremy's alone. He wanted me to have chosen his name for my son. "No other name was considered," I said. "Yours was the obvious – the only one."

As he with some emotion kissed my forehead and his great-grandson's, there came the resonant clanging of the great front-doorbell. William went at once to let the doctor in.

By the time that he reached me, Doctor Cotterrell had been briefed as to events (that is, their outcome only) but he was still incredulous at the sight of my baby. I had removed a pillow-case and wrapped William in this, and he was sleeping in my arms, peacefully.

"In all my years in practice," the doctor asserted, shaking his head in puzzlement, "I've never come across such a phenomenon. The storm delayed me, and has prevented Mrs B being here, but little did I dream of such a find when I arrived. Such speed and such . . . such simplicity. I know birth isn't meant to be a complicated process, but this . . . this goes to the opposite extreme. How on earth did you cope, all alone, Catherine?"

I was slow in responding – so slow that he, having removed his jacket and rolled up his sleeves, was busy, seeing to the after-birth and the umbilical cord, by the time that I answered: "I wasn't alone."

"Oh, you mean that William . . . ? But I thought he told me . . ." His face was a study in perplexity.

"I expect he told you that he wasn't with me . . . and he wasn't."

The doctor stared at me, searchingly. "Yet you just said you weren't alone, and I can see you can't have been. The baby is so clean! Who cleaned him – Lily?"

"I can't recall him being cleaned," I said, feasting my eyes on the child entrusted to me. "But if anyone cleaned him, it must have been Jeremy."

"Jeremy? Did you say Jeremy?"

"I did." His look made me feel giggly. "And, in answer to your next question, I wasn't hallucinating."

"You might not think you were, Catherine."

"I'm not concerned with what I think or don't think, but with what I KNOW. And I'm speaking now from knowledge. Jeremy delivered our son."

"That is very . . . edifying."

"You don't believe me, do you?"

"I can't pretend that I do."

"What, then, is your explanation of the scene that greeted you when you arrived in my room?"

"Women have been known to give birth alone, and to . . . "

". . . clean their babies expertly, and to feel as euphoric as I feel, even in the face of supposed widowhood?"

"No. In those respects, you're most unusual. And, quite clearly, you believe that Jeremy played an active part in your son's delivery. So who am I to argue? I feel humble in the face of such faith, and grateful. For if, due to my unavoidable absence, harm had befallen you as it befell Geraldine, I could never have forgiven myself, regardless of whether I was to blame." A long, pensive pause, and then: "What did you mean, by 'supposed' widowhood?"

It had suddenly occurred to me that I was in need of a cup of tea. I wished William would think to bring one to me. I answered the doctor: "I'm known as a widow. And widows are known to be alone, in the respect of having no husband. But I still have Jeremy. He is absent physically, agreed, but he has stayed beside me spiritually."

"So I see." He said this sincerely, smiling at me. "And you've set me wondering, Catherine."

There was a tap on the door then. It was William, with the tea I had wished for. Did my wish create his thought? Propped up on pillows, I sipped the tea gratefully and told William: "Doctor Archie is hovering on the brink of believing me, about Jeremy."

"Is he?" William looked from me to the doctor, then back to me and said conspiratorially: "I vote, then, that we push him over the brink! When I take him downstairs, I'll introduce him to Katharine."

"Who's she?"

"You'll see," said William. Then, to me: "I've telephoned your mother, incidentally, and she'll be on her way soon to see you and the baby. She sent her love meantime and asked a question that hadn't yet occurred to me. What are his other names going to be?"

Without hesitation, I answered: "Arthur Jeremy."

Gently taking my son from me and settling him in his crib, the doctor said: "The choice of Jeremy is obvious, of course, but why Arthur, Catherine? Is that also a family name?"

Sleepy now, I replied: "Yes. Arthur married my friend, Katharine, and brought her from Yorkshire to Tyneham. She was the first Tice bride to live in this House, and I . . . I shall be the last."

I must have fallen asleep as I finished my sentence, for I remember no reaction. I can remember nothing, in fact, until opening my eyes and finding mother at my bedside.

"When did you arrive?" I asked her, convinced she must have made the journey between her home and mine in record time. "Did you fly? It isn't many minutes since William telephoned . . . is it?"

I learned that it was hours, not minutes, since his telephone call. I also learned from him that he had taken the doctor to see Katharine. And, standing there in front of her, Doctor Cotterrell had observed: "If she's Catherine's friend – and it seems she must be – then I must needs rethink my entire philosophy."

184

I was blessed with a good baby, and with a good mother to help look after him in those earliest days. I was soon breastfeeding William successfully, and soon wondering what life had been like without him. For, though good, he was demanding and it quickly became hard to imagine not having his demands to meet – and not having a tiny person totally dependent on me.

It was an awesome responsibility. As he sucked hungrily at my breast, I was awed both by his existence and by the extent to which I was responsible for him. He was a new being, born of my love for Jeremy and his for me, as well as of mankind's need for re-creation. And it was my duty to protect him for as long as he needed my protection, to nourish him physically, morally, mentally and spiritually, to guide him wisely, while always remembering that the most vital element in his development was love. Loving him, I could do him no great wrong and could not altogether lack wisdom, for love was life's key and no act committed through love could have a bad outcome. So I told myself, marvelling over the babe at my breast.

He had his father's dark hair and something of Jeremy, too, in his expression. Not just of Jeremy – also of William. William senior was father to me, I mother to him – and we were lovers, through Jeremy. So we were everything to one another, without needing to be more than we were. How wonderful the world – how infinite its answers!

Katharine came to see William. He was one week old when she came to be re-acquainted with him. That this was not their first meeting was obvious from the beginning. It was late evening and I was on the point of retiring.

"T'is what he wanted," she said, bending over his crib.

"Please explain, Katharine."

"Why, he did want to be born again and be given new lessons."

"Born again?" I echoed. "Are you saying that he has been

born before?"

"Of course! You did not dream, surely, that this birth was his first? Births recur. That is how we learn . . . how you learned your craft. Did you truly think that you, in your youth, could already be a great artist, without lives of practice and perfecting?"

I stared at her, slow to take this in. "You mean that we're all born again and again? But you haven't been! You're still here from the sixteenth century."

"I had been, previously, and in earth-years to come I shall be. That is the law – the unwritten scheme of things."

"Are you quite certain? This is so contrary to the beliefs I was brought up on."

"They were not beliefs. They were indoctrination. It suits the church to indoctrinate us as it has done, with talk of fire and brimstone, hell and damnation for those who are unchristian. The threat of hell is the worst possible one, they think. But they are blinkered and, since the learned civilisations, they have tried to blindfold us."

"To what purpose?"

"By holding humans in thrall, they keep the church rich and powerful. That is their subconscious aim – through which they have lost sight of certain things. Attending church is not in itself Christian – and nor is the pretence of piety. Why pretend, when our pretence can be seen through? We ourselves see through it. We ourselves know the extent of our virtue. Our sins are forgiven, but not by the churchmen. They cannot forgive them. They are mere men. But every man, and woman, has a higher self which is of God. And through this Self, as we live our many lives, we find how to forgive ourselves. In learning our lessons, we cleanse our own lower selves of sin and enter the heaven so falsely promised by the churchmen."

"Are you saying, then, that attending church is a bad thing?"

"This is not my meaning. It is good, to have a house to

worship in. But we can worship within, or without, and should shut our minds to that which is misleading."

"Where does God fit in?"

"He is in everyone and in everything. And He is waiting. At the threshold of perfection, we meet Him. But I have dallied too long! I was come with a warning. Be of good cheer, and be strong, for the deed is done and naught was ever achieved by bad grace, nor by weakness. But be braced for great change. The moment of which we have spoken is come."

She left me then – my prophet of doom. I sat on my bed, uncertain as to what I ought to do. Then my immediate course of action was decided for me by William, who awakened and, simultaneously, started crying as if his heart would break. It was the first time that he had cried in this way. Had he heard and understood Katharine? Were all our hearts about to be broken?

Mother left for home next morning. Before leaving, she said: "You seem somewhat subdued, Catherine. Am I going too soon? I'll stay on, if you aren't yet feeling strong enough to cope with William alone."

"I'm feeling surprisingly strong. Why, I'd still be in bed, wouldn't I, if I felt at all weak, or were pursuing the usual lying-in routine? It isn't William's birth that's affecting me."

"What is it, then?" she asked sharply.

We were in the nursery, settling William down in his daytime surroundings just prior to mother's departure for her train. "It's . . . it's a slight stirring of unease," I answered. "Katharine came last evening to inform me that some great change is on its way."

"Did you ask her what form this change would take?"

"There was no opportunity. Before I could phrase the question, Katharine had gone. In the past, though, she has hinted along the lines that I am Tyneham's last Tice bride. William thinks she might mean our home is to be requisitioned. I think her meaning might be more . . . long-term."

"I'm sure you're wrong," mother said with a frown. "William's more likely, in this instance, to be right, although that wouldn't make sense of your being the last bride. Katharine couldn't have been referring, could she, to some new threat from Germany?"

"She could have been referring to almost anything."

"Oh, my dear – how distressing! Will it help if I stay and wait with you and William?"

"No mother, but thank you all the same. Whatever it is, I'll face it in my own way. I've begun almost to wish it would happen, so that I know what it is I'm facing."

"Telephone me, please, as soon as it happens. Don't keep me in suspense any longer than necessary, will you, Catherine?"

We were none of us kept very long in suspense, for the following morning the postman brought an official-looking letter from the War Department. Dated 16th November, this read:

'Dear Mr and Mrs Tice

Southern Command Training Area
East Holme, Nr. Lulworth

———

In order to give our troops the fullest opportunity to perfect their training in the use of modern weapons of war, the Army must have an area of land particularly suited to their special needs and in which they can use live shells. For this reason you will realise that the chosen area must be cleared of all civilians.

The most careful search has been made to find an area suitable for the Army's purpose and which, at the same time, will involve the smallest number of persons and property. The area decided on, after the most careful study and consultation between all the Government Authorities concerned, lies roughly inside of the square formed by East Lulworth – East Stoke – East Holme – Kimmeridge Bay.

It is regretted that, in the National Interest, it is necessary to move you from your home, and everything possible will be done to help you, both by payment of compensation, and by finding other accommodation for you, should you require us to.

The date on which the Military will take over this area is the 19th December next, and all civilians must be out of the area by that date.

A special office will be opened at Westport House, Wareham, on Wednesday the 17th November, and you will be able to get advice between the hours of 10 a.m. and 7 p.m. from there on your personal problems and difficulties. Any letters should be sent to that address also for the present.

The Government appreciate that this is no small sacrifice which you are asked to make, but they are sure that you will give this further help towards winning the war with a good heart.

C.H. Miller
Major-General i/c Administration'

William and I read the letter, then looked at each other. His face was as drained as I imagine mine must have been. The thing had happened – this thing that had hung over us for so seemingly long. The letter had come and we were to lose our home. Poor William – both of them! Poor war-torn Tyneham! What would become of all its inhabitants, who had never known any other environs? As for us, we had barely one month to vacate the House that had been ours for four hundred years. Would we return? Not according to this letter, which promised payment of compensation, nor according to Katharine, who had said we would fight but that the fight would be lost. And the loss of the fight would explain her original warning that my son would not bring his bride to Tyneham.

This, though, did not bear contemplation. It was unthinkable that William would grow up anywhere other than here. Where else was there, for Jeremy's son? He must grow up in this House, then tend these lands, loving them as so many Tice men had before him. I would not think otherwise . . . could not think that from nineteenth December on this would cease forever to be our home. I was not given to such self-destruction.

William's arms were around me, suddenly, and I was glad of them. We held each other and there was comfort of a kind in such proximity.

I fought off sentiment. I would try, for William's sake and my own, to keep a sense of proportion – a sense of realism. And reality was that with a war on everyone must sacrifice something. We were being called upon, for the time being, to sacrifice our home. It must be my assumption that this sacrifice was short-term and that when the war ended we would return to Tyneham. I would assume this to stay sane . . . and would resolve not to be proved wrong.

There were practical considerations. Best dwell on them. I began by asking William: "How are we to face all that needs facing?"

"I don't know, Catherine," he said, sounding as heavy-hearted as I had ever heard him. "All I do know is that I can face it, if you can."

I knew then that I would have to, for him and for my son. The knowledge gave me additional strength.

Sixty WAAFs, we learned, were to be accommodated in our home and some RAF officers would be calling by appointment to discuss the housing operation. There was not room, of course, for sixty women, but this did not come into consideration. Room must be made. The fourteen farmers within the allotted area had been given notice to quit and their stock would have to be auctioned. With time so short and with so much on offer, it was not hard to envisage the kind of prices the stock would fetch, despite the auctioneers' promise to do their best to attract potential buyers from far and near. It was to be hoped that the farmers between Lutton and Lulworth would not have to suffer financial hardship along with that of being uprooted, when this last was sufficient hardship. William and I kept postponing consideration of where we would live.

Lily had been badly hit. Her letter had come as a bolt from the blue, whereas ours was awaited, more or less. The whole village was in a state of shock, with its oldest inhabitants barely capable of comprehending what was happening to them. Having lived here for generations, they were rooted so deep in this valley that to uproot them, even temporarily, was to risk that they might wither and die. I prayed that the risk was slight, but believed otherwise. For my roots, compared with theirs, were non-existent and yet I felt that there could be no peace for me anywhere I went, unless I could return to Tyneham at the end.

"Will we return?" I asked Katharine, when she came again.

"You will – you, personally – and, when you do, seek me."

# Eighteen

There was a tree that grew behind the tap of spring water from Madmore, at the top of the village street, and this tree – a great elm – had for at least a century been a notice-board, in a sense, for local events.

Now a notice appeared there that was very different from any notice ever pinned to its pollarded trunk before. This was typewritten, on governmental paper, and read:

> 'When the War Department has no further use for the property and it is handed back, you have every right to return to the property. It should not be assumed by you that because the War Department has turned you out, you lose the right of occupying the premises again.'

The Government Land Agent responsible for the notice's appearance had been willing to answer villagers' questions and had pledged, in the course of his answers, that when hostilities ended Tyneham would without fail be given back to its inhabitants.

So although there was horror at what was happening, mingled with grief, there was also confidence that our evacuation would be of short duration and that, just as soon as the war was won, we would be reinstated in our homes.

There was confidence, at least, that the majority would be – the majority being sufficiently young and strong to withstand this uprooting. Not so some, among then Mrs Hodden. Lily's mother kept insisting that she would stay put in her home until she left in her coffin. Her insistence was less upsetting than her reasoning. Try though Lily might to explain, her mother had in her own mind formed the conclusion that Tyneham had fallen to the Germans. She could not take it in that it was our own army which was invading. As far as she was concerned, Britain had given in to the enemy. But she would not give in. Hitler was not having her home – not while there was breath left in her body. He would have to kill her, before she would concede a German victory.

"Whatever am I goin' to do?" Lily asked me despairingly. "Mother means it, when she says she won't leave – and I'm not having her carried out from our house forcibly."

"It won't come to that," I reassured her. "It's just taking her longer than us to adjust – that's all. Be patient with her, for it could be that this is her way of accepting – by non-acceptance, if you see what I mean. If you stay calm, and keep explaining, she'll come to comprehend which is the true army of invasion."

"I'm not so sure she will. I'm not sure at all this idn' the end for her. I shouldn' say this, as her daughter, but I do wonder whether our upset hasn' sent her . . . off her rocker."

I reasoned to the best of my ability with Lily and then sought out William, who was making telephone call after telephone call from the Porch Room in an endeavour to find somewhere to store our furniture. "No joy so far," he said as I entered. "Every warehouse I've approached is full – and there aren't too many in Dorset left to approach. What will we do if I can't find anywhere?"

"There's the cellar," I answered. "It's dry down there, even if it is full of fungus. As a last resort, that's where we'll have to put our belongings. But I have faith that you'll find a warehouse."

"I wish I had," William sighed. "And I wish we had more time to arrange everything. Not that wishes, in our circumstances, are anywhere near constructive enough. Is that my namesake I can hear, airing his lungs? Oh to be so young that the next meal were one's sole concern! I suppose that's why he's crying?"

"I shouldn't be surprised. What time are the RAF descending on us this afternoon?"

"Around three. Do you remember, Catherine, what their H.Q. envoy from Winchester said to me last summer, after the officers stationed in the rectory tapped the pipe from the reservoir and left the village without water?"

"How could I forget? It isn't every day that an offer's made to pay our Water Rate! I do hope they demonstrate a greater grasp of our situation once sixty of them are installed in our home."

"I share your hope, but have my doubts, I'm afraid. Tyneham conditions are archaic, compared with regulation RAF conditions, and I rather imagine that they will mourn modernity instead of appreciating antiquity. Anyway, we'll see what they have to say, at three."

Four officers – two squadron leaders and two flight lieutenants – arrived promptly in a jeep, screeching to a halt outside the north wing. I admitted them, thinking as I did so that since Tom wore their uniform I should not resent their intrusion but should, rather, be welcoming and accommodating. So, as I showed them through to Oak Hall, where William was waiting, I attempted polite conversation.

They seemed hardly to hear me. Their eyes were busy, assessing everything, and I caught a glance which passed between the two squadron leaders. The glance, it seemed to me, was disparaging. I said on the strength of this: "In return for all we are giving up when we go from here, we want your solemn assurance that our home will be treated with the respect it's entitled to and that it has been shown for four hundred years so far."

"You have my word," said the first officer, who was aged about thirty-five, with pale blue eyes and sandy hair, and who had given the glance that had triggered off my remark. "It's a fine home you have here, even if it is antiquated, and we're aware of the difficulties involved in having to leave at such short notice."

"You are? Have you heard, then, of the effect that even the prospect of evacuation is having on Tyneham's older generation? A few are too confused to take the true facts in – and to remove them from their homes in winter, with Christmas coming, makes the whole process still worse than it need have been. I doubt that some of them will survive the uprooting. Couldn't we have been given more warning . . . and couldn't more compassion have been shown?"

"I regret not, ma'am," the same squadron leader said as we reached William. "The War Cabinet has been as compassionate as it can. But war is war, and we must use every means at our disposal to win the battle Hitler began."

During the course of our ensuing conversation, conducted while the officers were inspecting the House and grounds, William mentioned: "When summer comes, you might find the water-supply something of a problem – as they did at the rectory recently. You see, in summer, water from our spring and reservoir is far from plentiful. In fact, it will scarcely meet the needs of a small family. And it's an inconvenience, even to us, that there's just one tap in the House. With sixty WAAFs here, there's bound to be . . . "

"Don't worry!" the second squadron leader intervened. "Arrangements are already in hand for the provision of more bathrooms and lavatories."

This sentence summed up their visit and depressed William deeply. There was no knowing what the Royal Air Force, in its ignorance, would do to our home. Would we recognise it, after the WAAF's occupation?

Fortunately, there was no time to dwell on such questions. There was no time for anything except the organisation of our departure from Tyneham. By 'ours' I mean everyone's. We were constantly being asked advice by other residents, and we helped where we could in giving transportation to Westport House,

195

Wareham, for discussions on alternative housing and associated issues. Few folk had relatives outside Tyneham who could accommodate them, so they were desperate for some kind of home. And their desperation showed.

Mary and Joseph Meader had their four children to think of, as well as themselves, and the task of finding a roof for all six of them began to seem insoluble. Where would they go, from their cottage home? And what would Joseph do, with all his sheep gone? Mary's face, for the very first time, showed signs of great strain and anxiety. Peace was going from Tyneham – the peace that had characterised this valley for centuries. These were troubled times. Ours were troubled minds.

Maybe mine was the most troubled – or would have been, had I given it rein – because of Katharine. The others believed that we would return, and I sought to share their belief. She had even told me that I would return – I, personally. But those words of hers, far from reassuring me, had seemed alarming. Did they mean that I would return alone? If so, there could be no joy in returning and my return could hardly be permanent. For in what circumstances would I come back on my own? I could not imagine.

So I tried to curb my imaginings . . . tried solely to think in positive terms. I could not have endured that month, thinking we would never all be together again in Tyneham.

I thought, instead, in the present, when the two Williams and I were lucky not to be homeless. As soon as I had telephoned our news through to her, mother had offered to share her roof with us; and Jeremy's cousins, too, at Creech Grange, had said they could accommodate us there. William and I had, after discussion, gratefully accepted the cousins' offer, explaining to mother that our decision was based on a need for simplicity. And it was unquestionably simpler to move over the hill to Creech than it would have been to move the twenty or so miles to Bournemouth. Psychologically, Creech was also better, being near to Tyneham and therefore more like home. We would have less far, too, to move back again, after the war was won. Mother understood our reasoning and was relieved, I think, in the sense that we would have disrupted her household. She had never cared for disruption, nor for dogs – and had specifically questioned whether we would be bringing ours. We would have been, so it was best all round that we went to Creech.

One week from the RAF officers' visit we received a telephone call from the rector, Walter Guest, warning us that he was on his way with 'terrible tidings'. He sounded agitated almost to the point of incoherence and we awaited his arrival with great apprehension.

He arrived by bicycle. "Whatever's up, Walter?" William asked, as the three of us stood in the north hall. "We've been beside ourselves, since your 'phone call."

"Let me get my breath back," the rector panted, his round face even redder than usual. "It's all uphill, from Baltington. I 'phoned first to be certain you were home."

We took him through to Oak Hall, where we all sat down. Then, a requested glass of water in his hand, he began: "It's Molly Larcombe. The postmistress sent for me when the school didn't open this morning and the schoolma'am couldn't be found. I raced round, knowing something must be badly wrong for Molly to let the children down. There was no sign of her at home," he paused and with a large handkerchief mopped beads of sweat from his brow, "and no-one had seen her since yesterday evening when she set out for a walk alone. Joseph Meader saw her head then in the direction of Baltington, so I went to the farm. But nobody there had set eyes on her. So I almost left without looking around. Some sixth sense, though, told me not to. God, it might have been, directing me." He shuddered expressively, and then: "I was led in the direction of Mrs Larcombe."

"Where was she?" asked William.

"Prepare yourselves for this," the rector said, looking at each of us in turn. "It's far from pleasant. I found poor dear Molly in the disused cow-stalls . . . hanging from a beam."

We gaped at him, incredulously. Dreadful things were happening, but this thing was too dreadful to believe. Our minds could not deal with the enormity of Molly Larcombe's action.

And yet, now that I was acquainted with it, I did not find it (except the means of death) so surprising. Tyneham's tiny school was Molly's life. She had always given her everything to her children . . . had always cared far more about their welfare than about her own. But bureaucracy was taking them from her – had taken them, virtually – and, oh, the effect of this robbery on Molly! She had, in addition, been far from robust lately. Jeremy had been shocked by her gauntness, back in February, and her health had on occasion given cause for concern since then. Maybe we should have been still more concerned than we had been – for her state of mind, especially. Maybe we could have done something to save our dearly loved schoolma'am.

As I thought this, I heard William say: "They were taking her life's work away. We can't hold them directly responsible for her life having ended, along with her work, but indirectly we know – don't we? – where to lay the blame."

We knew who to blame, but there was nothing to be gained in blaming anyone or anything. It was important, at this terrible time, to try to view Tyneham's and Molly's plight objectively. Her life had been lost in an endeavour by the Government to save other lives. They were not taking Tyneham mindlessly, but in order to further the cause that we were all, like it or not, involved in – the cause of winning our freedom. And when we won – as we would, in time – Molly's life, and Jeremy's, and all the other lives that had been given, would stand for something. They would stand for hard-won Peace and for Britain being Great again.

When Peace came, and the Government gave back Tyneham,

198

we would all remember our dead and would ensure that they were remembered by our descendants. These, our departed ones, would not have died in vain.

Arrangements needed to be made, for Molly's burial. Thankfully, customs had changed since Rosie threw herself in to the sea, enabling us to bury our devoted schoolteacher in St Mary's churchyard, close to the school-house she had inhabited as wife and as widow for almost thirty years. We were also able, thanks to the rector's and farmer's discretion, to keep from the children the manner of Mrs Larcombe's death. There was no keeping this from everyone, since ours was a small community and since there was no stilling tongues – particularly at a time of tragedy. But at least it was generally agreed that the children's feelings must be spared.

We all gathered in St Mary's to say our farewells.

These were said on a day when the valley glowed with vibrant colour. The year never died here, as it tended to do elsewhere in winter, but even so I had seldom seen it appear quite so warm in December. The weather was not warm. It was bitter, with a wind that pierced all clothing. But the valley's glow gave an impression of warmth, for the pale creamy brown of the rowaty grass against the russets and rusts, cocoas and cinnamons and rich browns of hedges, coppices and plough grounds combined to remove the chill from winter. And, deep within the woods, leaves clung right through till spring on oaks white with lichen. How protected, our valley . . . how favoured its children.

We had been highly favoured, but were here to mourn more than the passing of our schoolma'am. We mourned, within the walls of the church that had seen countless christenings, weddings, burials, Easters, Christmasses, Epiphanies and Harvest Thanksgivings, our passing from Tyneham.

It was this passing that had proved too heavy a cross for Molly Larcombe – sending her in anguish to Baltington and now to rest. That is, I prayed that she might be permitted peace, unlike Rosie, who still roamed Purgatory. There were, surely, extenuating circumstances which would spare her Rosie's fate. I asked this for her in a church filled with mourners and with prayer.

Her coffin was later lowered in to the ground, with all heads bowed. Mrs Hodden, of course, was not there, for she had vowed not to leave her home and would not break her vow, even for an hour. Some others, too, among Tyneham's elderly inhabitants, were absent, having succumbed to sickness of heart or body. But most of us saw Molly buried and many a tear was shed.

William said, as we walked home afterwards: "This is a sad and sorry business – indeed it is. The war has more to answer for than its battlefield and bombing casualties. Were it to end tomorrow, allowing us to remain in Tyneham, what then of Molly's martyrdom? She'd surely still be a war-victim and no more a true suicide than she is today – wouldn't she, Catherine?"

"I'd have thought so," I answered him, linking my arm through his as we strode beneath beech and hazel. "To my mind, the war claimed her, no matter when it ends. I hope that's how her death is viewed in the spiritual spheres. I'd hate to think of her having to suffer more than she has already suffered. War creates exceptional situations worthy of exceptional treatment. If only the war WOULD end tomorrow! Do you remember our discussion with Jeremy on when it would end? There was hope, then, that by now it would be over. It's for our own good that we can't see in to the future."

"Yes, it is. It would have been an intolerable burden to have known in advance that we were to lose both Jeremy and Tyneham."

"But we haven't lost them – either of them! They can't be lost, because they'll always remain. Jeremy is essentially unchanged and, as for Tyneham, we'll hold this within just as it is today. From Creech Grange, or from wherever we are, we'll have only to turn our thoughts inward to reap the rewards that are here. All its beauty, all its tranquility, can be preserved forever, if stored within us – and within all those who have lived overlooking Flower's Barrow and Gad Cliff. We'll take Tyneham on our trip, won't we, and bring it back, intact, at the right time?"

"You will," said William, his eyes perilously bright. "You're the future, Catherine – you and your son. I'm the past – and I'm a very old man."

"If that's so," I told him as we came within sight of home, "you're the youngest old man I've ever known. And we both know from Katharine the facts regarding the past and the future, so no more of your morbidity. Let's tackle the present together, shall we?"

"Very well," he agreed, a mite more happily. "In tackling it, I'll tell you of two items – no, three – that will not be among those consigned to the cellar. When we leave here, we'll have with us Jeremy, Katharine and the Coffin Tree. Agreed?"

"Absolutely!"

# Nineteen

With our houseman's help I had begun preparing the cellar for the storage of our most valuable and fragile furniture. There were rats down there, which would gnaw everything unless we took appropriate precautions. I left their poisoning to Norman. He in turn enlisted the gardener's assistance in disposing of all the resulting bodies. Then the task began of filling the vaults with our possessions.

Fourteen storage firms had been applied to, but in vain. William had been turned away again and again on the grounds that the war had first claim. This we were already aware of. The war had claimed Jeremy and was now claiming Tyneham.

The fungus festooning the cellar closely resembled black cotton wool and was prolific, clearly appreciating dark, cold, subterranean conditions. I did not appreciate them, and hated my underground excursions. Whereas up above, in the House, lamplight was more welcome for me than electricity would have been, down here its limitations seemed sinister. I refused, though, to consider what might lurk behind the stone pillars and in the myriad shadowy nooks and crannies. There was no time to indulge wild – or even mild – fancies. There was time solely for brisk, businesslike behaviour.

As well as the cellar, which would be locked up and sealed once full, we utilised the brewhouse and Museum Cottage for storage. Museum was a dwelling in the grounds that had been home, before the war, for our under-gardener. We were, too, able to take some of our possessions for safe-keeping in the laundry cottage at Grange, and at Winfrith Rectory, where our books were stacked in the new granary.

Where we would have been without friends and relatives I cannot hazard a guess. As it was, we were well blessed.

I cannot imagine, either, how I would have managed all the necessary organisation had William been a less placid baby. It became part of Annie's duties to keep an eye and an ear on the nursery in my enforced absences. But, true to character, William seldom gave her any bother.

She began calling him Billy, maintaining that she could not get her tongue round William. Billy he became, for the time being.

"Were you ever called Billy?" I asked William, over dinner one evening.

"Yes, I was, once upon a time," he answered, with a hint of a grin, "though that was when I was very young."

"It would have been. The name suits youth, but wouldn't suit maturity. I'm glad you went from Billy to William, instead of Bill."

"Why are you?"

"Because Bill is . . . brasher than William, and not in keeping with how I see you, somehow."

"How do you see me, Catherine?"

"As a gentleman, through and through . . . and as a love, perhaps, from long ago."

Setting down his dessert spoon, William looked at me reflectively and observed: "That's an intriguing 'perhaps'. Might I ask what prompted it?"

"My last conversation with Katharine. Since our souls never age, is there a possibility, do you think, that at some stage after a body has perished, the soul it housed might need . . . re-housing?"

"I'm not at all sure I follow your meaning."

"Katharine told me that souls keep being re-born in new bodies. And this makes sense – more sense, to my mind, than the traditional concept of heaven. We return, again and again, in our quest for perfection until through our own actions we've cleansed ourselves of sin. If Katharine is right in this, as she has been right in everything, there's much scope for wondering. I have wondered whether those that we love in this life are sometimes the same souls as we have loved in previous lives."

"I wouldn't be surprised! I no longer find anything surprising. And I find myself liking the idea of having lived – and loved – before. Because that augurs well for the future." He smiled happily. I had not seen him look so happy for weeks. "It should virtually guarantee that our love of today will go with us to tomorrow, if in different form – and that thought holds huge appeal for me, Catherine." Warming to his subject, he went on: "We speak, don't we, of old souls, as though we're aware that there are those among us who've passed this way previously? Re-birth would, too, explain déjà vu . . . and exceptional natural talents. I've questioned how someone as young as you could produce a portrait like Katharine's, and about Mozart's start as a child prodigy and about the genius of such as da Vinci. Much could be explained by reincarnation, even if belief in it is outside our Church's teaching. We have a new teacher now, haven't we, in Katharine? And she herself is proof of much that hadn't hitherto been proved. It'll be interesting to see what Catriona and Graeme make of her doings, should she come up in conversation while we're staying at Grange. I also can't help worrying about Katharine in respect of the WAAFs moving in. Will she stay on with them, in your opinion?"

Strangely, I had not yet considered this. Though it was not so strange, bearing in mind all that had been happening. Since the letter from Southern Command arrived there had – thankfully – hardly been time to consider anything. That Katharine had no intention of disappearing altogether was clear from her remark that when I returned I should seek her. But she might now be freer to find Arthur and to pursue her own quests rather than safeguard our interests. "If she stays," I said, "don't forget that she probably won't be aware of the WAAFs. Why should she be, when through all these centuries she's basically just been aware of Rosie and me? Heavens – hasn't the Tice occupancy lasted for four hundred years exactly?"

"Yes, it has," said William, meditatively. "Katharine and Arthur moved in in 1543. How extraordinary!"

Was this an extraordinary coincidence, or could it be of some significance? I hoped it was not significant – hoped that four centuries was not our full quotient. But I refrained from voicing my hopes. "My feeling," I said, "is that Katharine will stay and that you've no cause for worry. The WAAFs won't bother her, nor she them, and she'll probably be able to be more venturesome than while awaiting Southern Command's letter. That as much as anything seems to have tied her here, watching over us and preparing us for the shock. Now she can look beyond Tyneham, while also standing by for our return."

"Yes, she can," agreed William sadly, not convinced by me, although he tried to be, that we two would return home.

Talk turned then to Lily and to her problem with Mrs Hodden, the confusion of whose mind seemed to be increasing daily. In addition, she was now suffering from a severe chill, which Lily hoped was not the start of another bout of pneumonia, nor of 'flu. There was, in fact, a 'flu epidemic raging in Corfe and Wareham that Tyneham had been free from so far. But Lily had been to Westport House and then to see a tiny, virtually uninhabitable cottage offered to her and her mother in Corfe (an offer that she had of necessity accepted, time being so short), and feared she might have brought germs back. If she had, she had. Fate at times could not be fought.

Now was such a time. Fate had decreed our move from Tyneham and there was no fighting her decree for the moment. This war had to be given priority. It was more important, currently, than individual needs. But when it ended – then we would fight, if necessary. And I would pay no heed to Katharine, who had warned that I must fight a great wrong – a fight that could not be won. She could not always be right. Nobody was – dead or alive. I would win the fight . . . and I would not be Tyneham's last Tice bride.

When the cellar had been filled with furniture and was about to be sealed, Katharine reappeared. We were one week from evacuation and I had not seen her since just prior to receiving Major-General Miller's letter. I might have been feeling neglected by her, had my life not changed so dramatically in recent weeks. She arrived, as was her custom, at my bedtime.

"T'is a mistake," she said, "and one which you will live to regret."

"You are not making sense," I mentioned. "Let me at least know the nature of my mistake."

"There will come a great flood, causing the ruination of your furnishings. Many will disintegrate. Naught will be saved. The bowels of the earth are unsafe."

"You are saying," I asked in alarm, "that we are mistaken in storing things in the cellar?"

"I am. They must be moved, ere the women come."

"Will the women cause the flood?"

"Verily, t'will have been their doing. There is much outside their understanding. T'is vexing, that they are to be brought to Tyneham. Move everything, while there is yet time."

Her words were deeply distressing, for I was powerless to avert the catastrophe she was forecasting, the cellar having been used for storage absolutely as a last resort. It would have been preferable, from the sound of things, to have left the furniture where it had been for so many years, but the RAF had insisted on the House being cleared as far as possible. And now, with time running out and with our every minute, more or less, between today and the eighteenth accounted for, it was quite out of the question again to move our furniture – even given an alternative location where this might be stored. Time did not

206

exist and yet it dominated us. The question was how to evade its domination within one's lifetime. I didn't want to die, just yet, to escape. Before dying, I must bring up my baby.

"You might think there is yet time, but there isn't," I told Katharine. "Could you not have come sooner, with your flood-warning?"

"I could not, because I was with Arthur."

"With Arthur?" I echoed, in surprise.

"He is home from the war. We are together, just as you and Jeremy will be, when you re-discover each other far from time's idiosyncracies. I shall not now be lonely, even after you are gone from here."

This brought me to tears. "I'm happy for you," I said, "even while I'm sad for myself. Is your duty done, then?"

"My duty? This has not been defined for me. We define it for ourselves, evidently, and I am bound yet to Tyneham."

"How glad I am, that you will not be gone! Your presence – and Arthur's – will enhance my homecoming."

"I wish you would listen. If you would, you would learn and be saved from false expectations."

"I can't be saved from them – not if my expectation of coming home again is false. I have to have that hope, Katharine. Without it, I am undone."

"Keep it, then, as a hope and not as an anticipation. You will be better off. T'is my aim to aid you – not to make matters worse than they already are."

A change of topic was called for. I could not at present take any more talk of Tyneham or of its not being home. "Where's Arthur?" I asked her.

"Why, he is here."

"Here in this room? I cannot see him."

"Nor can he see you. T'is an odd phenomenon. Arthur does not even believe me, when I speak of another Catherine from another century, yet he stands quite close to where I am standing. He has asked me if you are a ghoulie! Did I not once ask of you that self-same thing?"

"Yes, you did," I answered, chuckling. "We've come far, since then, haven't we?"

"Verily, we have crossed and re-crossed the centuries. They are there, perforce, for the crossing, if we could but pass on our discovery. It would seem, though, that this is not for them." With a wide gesture of her arms, she encompassed the world at large. "T'is secretly, for thee and me."

We smiled at each other, guardians that we were of our secret, and she departed to be with Arthur in this, their home.

It was more theirs than mine, because they were here first and now were safely outside time, while I was still under its influence. And, with time moving on I, too, must move – onward, ever onward, when all I wanted was to remain stationary, within the embrace of my valley.

Could I somehow remain, like Katharine, outside the confines of time – outside this that was happening to Tyneham? Thus I questioned and, from somewhere within, the answer came: "Only when your work is done can you remain. Till then, you are bound by earth-time and by earthlings."

I could not be sure of the answer's source, but didn't doubt its accuracy, for just then Billy cried for me.

Next morning, I asked William: "How safe is the cellar, as far as our furniture's concerned?"

"The fungus could prove a problem, if that's what you mean. But, having protected most of our possessions with sheets, we've been about as careful as we can be in that connection." A prolonged scrutiny of me and then: "The fungus wasn't what you meant?"

"Not specifically, although it's clearly one of the hazards. I was wondering about . . . water. Has the cellar ever been flooded?"

"No – never. So I doubt that's a danger."

"Could it be? Can you conceive of any circumstances which could cause a flood at that level?"

He thought awhile before answering: "No, I can't – not unless a WAAF was irresponsible enough to leave the tap on until the weight of water caused the floor to cave in. Our floors are too thick, though, for that to be a serious possibility – and the cellar is too far below for there to be any real threat to our furnishings from an overflow. Am I to conclude from all this that you've been talking to Katharine?"

Nodding, I then gave him an edited version of her visit, ending: "I think, maybe, she's developing a tendency to over-dramatise."

"That might well be," he agreed. "Was there any mention of whether she'll still be here after the war?"

"There was . . . and she will be. She had someone with her, incidentally."

"Jeremy?"

"No, Arthur. They're together again, here in Tyneham."

"Could you see him?"

"Not so much as a glimpse. And yet, according to Katharine, he was there, with her, in my room. But beyond my vision. It's as if there were curtains, closing me in. What I'd give, to remove the curtaining and see all that lies on the other side"

"If anyone can remove it, you can."

"Your faith in me is so touching, William. I'll try to be worthy of it."

"You already have been." He smiled at me. "Knowing you, though, as well as I do, I imagine you'll find room for further demonstrations of worth! I'll look forward to them whether in this or in the next world. You're a very special girl."

Blushing at his words and under his prolonged scrutiny, I said: "You aren't thinking, are you, of leaving me?"

"There will dawn a day when I must leave, in a manner of speaking. We both know now, though, don't we, that such partings are just temporary?"

"Yes, we do – and you're giving me all the more reason to open the curtains. Once they're open, there won't be even a temporary parting for me and my loved ones. My feet will be in both worlds, just like Katharine's."

"So you won't grieve for me? I don't want your grief. I want . . . only your happiness."

I could have wept right then, for I sensed that we would not be together in life for long. But I did not weep. Controlling my need, I reached for his hand and assured him: "I shall be happy, William, remembering . . . and anticipating our next meeting."

Clasping my hand in both his, he averred: "I'll find you, Catherine, whatever future guise we are in. I'll look in to your eyes and a memory will stir in me of you and Tyneham. Between us, we'll pin the memory down, until we remember all we are to each other now."

The door opened and then Lily entered the room, which we had emptied of all furniture save for the sideboard, dining table and the two chairs we were seated on. We were surprised to see her, having imagined her to be at home with her mother. She brought a change in atmosphere.

"This House idn' no better than an echo chamber," she grumbled, as her footsteps resounded over the floorboards. "It's a favour I'm come for. Could you accompany me, quickly, Mrs Jeremy? Mother's that leary and queer, I'm beyond knowin' how to handle her."

I accompanied her home, wondering how I would handle Mrs Hodden, who had caught the 'flu and whose mind in addition was 'all scrushed and bumbled', according to her daughter.

I soon saw what Lily meant, for I was welcomed with the words: "We're over-run wi' them. But I'm not budgin'. The first athirt this dreshhold's dead. I'll deaden him meself."

There was no doubting that she meant what she said, since as she spoke she waved her stick about in as menacing a manner as her age and frailty and confinement in bed would allow.

"You're upsetting yourself needlessly," I told her, going over to where she lay, her face flushed and feverish, her long hair as white at the pillow supporting her head, "and you're upsetting Lily, which isn't fair."

"Tidn' me, upsettin' her. T'is them Germans."

Her eyes were wild and were darting in all directions. There was terror in them. My heart went out to this poor, fearful old woman. "It is NOT the Germans, Mrs Hodden," I said, taking firm hold of her free hand and stroking it gently, despite the resistance she showed at first. "They are not after your home. We still have the Channel between us and them."

"We haven'!" Her whole body jerked with the force behind this statement. "That's where you're wrong. They've landed in Dorset . . . and they're takin' Tyneham . . . Hitler and his men."

I could feel the tension in her – feel it through her fingers, which I refused to release, though she kept trying to pull free of me. She was like a taut spring and utterly different from when I visited her with Jeremy. With an inclination of my head, I signalled Lily, who had been hovering nervously, to leave. She left, looking relieved.

I sat on the bed and said: "Do you trust me, Mrs Hodden?" The old lady hardly hesitated before nodding. I went on: "Then listen – after first giving me your stick. If you'll give that to me, I'll give you something in return." Her eyes stilled at this and stayed still, focussed on my face. Having studied me, she meekly unclenched the fist that had clasped the stick. I took this from her, depositing it on the floor beyond her reach. Then, I removed from my huge handbag a sketch, which I held for her inspection. "Do you remember me drawing this?" I asked. In answer, her eyes misted over and she moaned as if injured. "I can see you do remember. It was last summer, wasn't it, when the fuchsias were in bloom and butterflies were everywhere? Can you see yourself, seated here, by your door? I want you to have this picture, which I'll have framed for you, and I want you to believe what I'm about to tell you, for it's the absolute truth. The Germans are no nearer now than they were then. It isn't them, turning you out from your home. It's our own Government, asking your assistance in winning this war. And when it's won, they've given us their word that we can all return to Tyneham. Upon our return, we'll have the satisfaction of knowing that we were instrumental in defeating the Germans. You would want to help defeat them, wouldn't you, Mrs Hodden?"

I had set the sketch down, for she was crying freely now, releasing her tension and holding both my hands as if afraid to let go. "I've bin all of a puxie," she whimpered. "Didn' know where to turn, what to do, nor who to believe . . . but I believe you. And I like your drawin'. Can I keep it, honestly?" she asked, tears cascading down her cheeks.

Managing to extricate a hand and find her a handkerchief, I answered: "Only if you promise to take it with you next week, when the ambulance comes to transport you and Lily to your temporary home in Corfe – and bring it back with you, for your wall, after we've won the war and earned the right to return home. Can I rely on you to do that, for all our sakes, and for your own? It will help Lily so much, to know her mother can be relied upon to do what has to be done."

"She's bin makin' a caddle 'bout nothin'," Mrs Hodden said, with a wicked grin. "This war's for the winnin' . . . and I'll soon be bringin' your drawin' home to Tyneham."

# Twenty

On the day before evacuation I went to church. I went alone, to look one last time at the face of Mary the Virgin and to recall to mind Jeremy's expression as he likened me to her. Did I go to torture myself? No. I went because it seemed that I had to go.

The weather was freezing cold and the depopulation of Tyneham had already begun. The shepherd and his family had gone – to scattered homes, it having proved impossible to secure accommodation for all six of them under the same roof. Joseph and his wife had contrived to keep their youngest two children with them, in one room behind a shop in Wareham. Their older two, though, had had to go, separately, in to relatives' homes in Kingston and in Holme. Well, it was to be hoped that they would be back before long, in the cottage where they belonged.

I fostered hope in my heart as, walking with the biting wind, I approached the church door – and saw, pinned to it, this painstakingly handwritten notice:

'Please treat the church and houses with care; we have given up our homes where many of us have lived for generations to help in this war to keep men free. We shall return one day and thank you for treating the village kindly.'

The notice blurred before me as I read the words someone had penned on bchalf of us all. But I refused to cry, for tears were weakening and I was in need of my maximum strength.

Pushing the door open, I entered the changeless atmosphere of St Mary's. Its changelessness was comforting, for it was as if the area within were untouched by time. Outside, the world moved on, while inside everything remained as it had been from the beginning, untroubled by the unrest of man's creation. All was still – all peaceful, the war far from this holy interior.

Seated in the family pew, I looked up at the window. Quite soon, it was as though light illumined my soul. There were within my realm of vision angelic hosts; I heard sublime music and was raised to a higher plane. The music, some instinct told me, was not played on instruments. It was the harmony of our very existence, borne from a different dimension, sweetly, soothingly. How many dimensions were there, of our universe ... how many mysteries, shielded from our consciousness? There were more than my mind could absorb. I was equipped, at my stage of development, to contemplate a mere fraction of all that there was for our ultimate contemplation.

Lowered again on to the plane of my present habitation, I retained a sense of being above current conditions – removed from them. For they were fleeting, in the all-embracing scheme of things. That which was temporal was unworthy of concern. Just that which was eternal had any true worth.

So I was serene as I surveyed the church which would shortly be barred to me and to all its customary worshippers. Serenity, in fact, filled me and it was as if I could see every event that had ever occurred on these premises. I saw, firstly, Jeremy and me, kneeling together before this altar, with Mary above us, and the Tyneham scenes. We were still here, kneeling. He was still speaking of making a mother of me. And he had made me a mother. There was Billy, his heir and the fruit of our love for each other. Present and future notwithstanding, we were here now, from then and from our every attendance, and would ever so remain. St Mary's housed our presence – and this, evacuation could not change.

Nor could it erase the lingering presence of all our fellow worshippers – Katharine having been among the first – from across the years. Their hymns still rose in praise ... their prayers were still being heard.

214

Not all who had worshipped here were human. Cats had occasionally stalked their owners to church – often to their master's or mistress's chagrin. And bats had from time to time swooped low over the congregation, causing quite a stir. Lambs, too, had come and butted each other between the pews, before eviction by the rector. Had they come in search of their heavenly Father, who was Shepherd to everyone? If they had, I did not doubt that they had found Him – just as I had found the peace that I had come seeking.

To every seeker there came the answer. This was a natural law and did not need to be seen to have religious origin. It was outside religion, but within everyone. Church was not essential to our existence. We could not fully exist, though, without regard for the essence dwelling in our souls.

I prepared to go. As I did so, I declined to consider the warring conditions that would, after tomorrow, have hold on Tyneham. Bullets and bombs could not come in to consideration – not here. They were so alien to this tranquil setting. And alien they would remain. For peace infused our valley to such a degree that any hostility could solely affect it superficially. Of this I was certain . . . and I had better things than superficiality to concern myself with.

I had my art and the upbringing of Billy.

The wind was blowing from the sea. I would have walked to Worbarrow, had there been time, to watch the waves break over the beach. But time was at a premium, despite its meaninglessness. Meaning nothing, it contrived to mean so much. Life was of necessity illusory. Only with death did we shed our time-concept, along with other illusions.

Instead of walking to Worbarrow, and gazing again on the Tout and on magnificent Flower's Barrow as well as on the coloured cliffs that curved round the Bay before their switchback descent at Arish Mell, I drank in my memory of these scenes, holding them securely within me. Ignoring the

NAAFI canteen being assembled by military personnel on Mount Mead, I subsequently memorised the village street, turning by the pond to look back at it; and Shoemaker's Lane and Ocean Seat. I had recorded all these and more in my sketches. Now I was committing them, free of sentiment, to my inner vision. I would look inward, whenever need so dictated, and I would find Tyneham, perfectly preserved. It would always be there for me, no matter where I was destined, and would sustain me, should I seek sustenance.

So we were not leaving Tyneham behind, but taking it unscathed in to the world beyond these hills. Maybe we had needed to learn that it could be taken, rather than being left when we went. And, once we had learned, we could surely come home again.

With the wind behind me, I wafted along. It had been my intention to return immediately to William and Billy and to all the tasks that awaited me, but I was blown in a different direction.

Was I light as a leaf, that I could be blown on a whim of the wind? I must have been, with my human weight removed from me. Weightlessly, I was wafted to the Cowleaze.

It was bereft of sheep. They – poor things – had been auctioned and scattered, just as we were in the process of scattering. I would not dwell on the likeliest destination of the lambs that had gambolled here last spring.

I stood on the Knap . . . waiting.

Though aware of Jeremy in everything, I seldom saw him. I would have liked more sightings, but accepted that I could not necessarily have what I liked. So awareness sufficed.

However, here on the Knap, I could frequently see with superior sight. On this, the eve of a different life, I would see as I had seen. Jeremy would come to me.

In my mind, I said his name. I said it with longing. My longing brought him.

There on this bridge between my environment and his, we kissed. Our kiss was of the spirit, not of the flesh. My spirit fused with Jeremy's.

Within our fusion I heard: "The Knap is where I'll be, whenever you need me. Come physically, spiritually or in your dreams and we'll meet. It will be but an instant till our ultimate meeting. Live, for that instant, and love and sketch and paint, while being both mother and father to our son. You are due to part from William. More of his heart than he's aware is invested in Tyneham and his years on earth are almost done. But he has lived beyond his three-score-and-ten and is content. You have caused his contentment, beloved Catherine. You are all things to all men. Yet it is we who belong. Hold on to our belonging and, at the appointed time, come home."

I would have clung to him, and gone where he was going, except that there was no-one to cling to. I now stood alone.

I stood, buffeted by the wind, and found that through the trees I was facing the mullioned windows of the tall north gable. This had been my first sighting of Tyneham House, before my marriage to Jeremy and before I had any inkling of what lay in store for me. I had surveyed it then, loving him and little caring where in the world I went, just as long as my hand was in his, my heart in his safe keeping. I had not known that the war would take him and that I would come to regard this House and Tyneham as more than home.

Nor could I know, in advance, of Katharine's lingering presence and of the affection I would come to feel for a girl who had lived and died ahead of me. Had I known, I would not have believed. It was the experience that had brought belief. We were leaving, but she was staying. The kings and governments of her day had not seen fit to evict her from Tyneham. So she was safe – but only for the moment. Some day, she would need to leave this safety. It was essential that she left, if her soul were to progress. Earthly attachments stand in the way of progression.

Sooner or later, therefore, she must detach herself totally from her home, and move on. Probably Arthur had come to help her in this detachment. At least I knew that he would not help her too soon. She would not be gone before my return.

I started downhill, back to Billy and to William.

Before Jeremy said so, I had known that William did not have long. Quite apart from our recent conversation – and though he seemed to be bearing the sadness and strain of evacuation – there was about him these days a vulnerability not in evidence prior to receipt of the Major-General's letter. And he cried easily, which was quite uncharacteristic. I had the feeling that he was dying within and that the aftermath of the wrench from Tyneham would probably kill him. Well, the wheels were in motion and there was no slowing, nor halting them. Whatever was to happen would happen, and I must somehow accept that.

I sighed as I entered our drive through the gate from Shoemaker's Lane and saw an unseasonal scarlet bloom on the Smithii rhododendron. There were always flowers to be found, out of season, here in Tyneham. I had never known a Christmas without primroses, an autumn without magnolias, nor a winter without a rose. But they would be blooming from now on for the Military and not for those who had nurtured them, and who appreciated them. I hoped that the WAAFs would show some appreciation, both of our garden and of our home.

William was watching for me, from the Porch Room. I saw him as I drew close to the glorious horse chestnut tree that grew at the edge of the lawn. He waved to me – his last wave, possibly, from within these walls.

I thrust this thought aside. It was not easy. I would have found it easier, just now, to indulge in defeatism – and to avoid, for the moment, facing William.

But there could be no such indulgence, nor avoidance, for as I reached the hallway, he was descending the central staircase towards me. "Catherine!" he said, his steps echoing hollowly from the stone and his face creased in welcome. "How long you were gone! I was growing concerned."

"I'm sorry, William. I didn't mean to be long. I just followed where my feet led me . . . and you know how wayward these feet can be! There've been no problems, have there, with Billy?"

"He's been crying, but Annie now seems to have silenced him."

"How about you? Are you all right?"

"Yes, I'm fine."

Looking hard at him, I said: "That, I think, is open to question. What's wrong?"

"I can't conceal anything from you, can I, Catherine?" Taking my arm and walking with me toward the kitchen, where it was warmest, he went on: "Not that there's anything, really, to conceal – just a feeling." No more was said until we were in Lily's former domain, seated close to the great cooking range. "I shouldn't be telling you this . . . shouldn't be bothering you with it. But I know you'll understand, as you understand everything. While you were gone, and I was here – but for Billy and Annie – on my own, I felt . . . almost like a ghost."

This startled me. I asked: "How do you mean?"

"It was as if I had . . . moved on. Not to Grange. Beyond my lifespan. I was with Katharine. I wasn't just seeing her for the first time. I was of the same substance. Could I have died, without actually dying? I was . . . frightened."

I held him, for he needed holding. We clung together like children – he the younger child. And we both cried. It seemed, suddenly, a time for crying. All the joy that I had known on the Knap with Jeremy, and all the grief that I had thought myself freed of, merged in me and demanded release. My tears, too, postponed the moment of response to William. I was glad of this postponement, not knowing quite how to respond to him.

Then I knew. As we each busied ourselves with handkerchiefs, I took his free hand in mine and said, searching his puzzled eyes: "If what you experienced WAS a foretaste of death, don't forget that this was too brief to judge from. One has to adapt, to life on the other side, and you had no time. Given time – this curious commodity that we have yet to fathom – you'll find all the advantages of having discarded your body, and it seems to me that there are many. First and foremost, there are the reunions – with John and Geraldine and Jeremy, not to mention Philomena and your mother and father. Then there's the fact of having no more aches and pains, and no more restrictions. Imagine being anywhere, at will, and seeing everything! There are all the planets to explore . . . and the bed of the oceans. I can't wait until it's my turn for such exploration, with no clocks ticking and tying me to time!"

"Darling Catherine!" he sighed, love now in his eyes in place of puzzlement. "How favoured I feel, to have you in my life, and to share in your outlook. You're right. Instead of being afraid, I should be excited. With so much in store for me, I shall die happily. And we'll never say 'goodbye', will we?"

"No, William, we won't. There's no such word in our vocabulary."

The houseman, who had a home to go to with his sister in Swanage, helped us lock and seal the cellar after the very last item – the jar of pot pourri from the drawing-room – was stored there. I had almost forgotten Katharine's flood-warning, preferring William's assertion that the cellar could not be in any danger from water. Funny, how forgetful one can be, when forgetfulness is a necessity.

There was packing to finish, both of things, we were taking with us and of things for collection by the Red Cross that afternoon, and there was Billy's equipment – which was in itself sufficient to make our cousins think we were trying to take over their home – to prepare for transportation. This between making final essential telephone calls, dealing with unexpected (and expected) callers, and feeding Billy and ourselves – though he

220

was hungrier than we were. He was also fractious and altogether unlike himself, which hardly helped matters. But I could not blame him for his fractiousness. I liked the restless atmosphere no better than he did. We would all feel the benefit of being settled at Grange, after this time of unsettlement.

That evening, Katharine came to bid me 'adieu'. It would have been a blow, had she not come. I had rather depended on her coming.

"T'is a sorry business," said my girl in green, appearing somewhat suddenly right beside me as I prepared for bed. Both our beds – William's and mine – were being left behind. "No-one is sorrier than I am. I despise your King. George must be a tyrant, just as Henry has been. With Edward upon the throne, our days are mild and halcyon."

I could not stand by and see King George so maligned. "Our King," I told her, "doesn't indulge in tyranny of any kind. He cannot be compared with Henry. It isn't George's fault that we have to leave Tyneham. That's the fault of this war and of the guns we are using. These are too powerful to be contained within the old boundaries. For our safety's sake, we've no alternative but to move beyond their range. But when the need for testing weapons has gone, we shall move back again. The King's men have given their word."

"T'is fiendish, that this cannot be trusted."

"It CAN!" My cry was wrung from me, along with: "I trust it."

"You are too trusting, you poor thing. Arthur and I are glad that George is not OUR King. Because he is not, he cannot make US leave. My man is sad, as I am, to see you go on the morrow. For we have come to accept you as our own. Though we do not understand quite whence you came, nor how we three at once inhabited this same home, we are afflicted with a feeling of kinship and compassion. So neither Arthur nor I would want you to leave without our bidding you 'God speed!' Be of good cheer

. . . and be sure that when in your future you have need of us, we will be here. You will not venture far, in your heart. Fare you well, Catherine . . . till our next meeting."

I would have held her there, if I could have, for a few moments more. But there was no holding her. She departed as fast as she had appeared. I heard her, from afar, address her next words to Arthur. Just two of these reached my consciousness: 'ghoulie' and 'yonder'.

The ghoulie was going yonder, and I was the ghoulie. To Arthur, maybe, but not to Katharine. She and I had a better understanding. I would miss her more than I dared contemplate. How thankful I was, that I had painted her portrait – which had been hung already at Grange. At least I had that to remind me of her, should I ever need a reminder. And one day I would share her with the world. I was not yet ready for that, though. I wasn't ready to share her with anyone, even Arthur. I felt almost resentful of him, for his ability to be with Katharine in Tyneham.

I fell asleep surprisingly quickly, having half expected to spend a restless night, tossing and turning and trying to postpone morning. But, except for feeding Billy at two, I slept straight through. There was no postponing evacuation.

As William and I ate our last breakfast, Clement Attlee's uninspiring voice reached us over the wireless, broadcasting this bulletin, signed by Lord Moran, Mr Winston Churchill's personal physician: "The Prime Minister has been in bed for some days with a cold. A patch of pneumonia has now developed in the left lung. His general condition is as satisfactory as can be expected."

"I hope he recovers," William observed. "Britain will be in a pretty predicament if he doesn't. I can't see us winning this war without him."

"We'll win," I said, "and soon. I doubt that, with his resilience, it'll be long before he's back at the helm."

We confined our entire conversation to generalities, not

222

speaking of the moment that was now imminent. It could not be spoken of, but would somehow have to be lived through.

The grandfather clock had gone. This was among the many items stored in the cellar. How silent the House, without its chimes! I had never known such silence – aggravated, this morning, by our sense of being in limbo.

Through the silence, the telephone rang. Had there been some mistake? Were we, at this eleventh hour, to be permitted to stay?

William insisted on being the one to answer its shrill summons. Soon he rejoined me in the kitchen, saying: "That was the postmistress. She thought we should know that, because of the 'flu outbreak, the ambulance service is overstretched and Tyneham is being restricted to just half the ambulances promised. I can't see how we'll manage. There are those, among them Mrs Hodden and Charlie and Jack Miller, as well of course as the Tizzards, who are far too incapacitated to be moved other than by ambulance."

"Then they mustn't be moved until the proper transport is available – even if that means delaying the military take-over. Our sick and suffering can't be put at further risk, war or no war. If you wish, I'll ring Major-General Miller and tell him."

"You would, too, Catherine, wouldn't you?" William said, with the semblance of a smile. "But there's no need just yet. I've left instructions with Mrs Cooper which I hope will take care of things. So with any luck we shouldn't have to resort to stronger tactics. I trust our transport will arrive on time. There's little worse than waiting . . . this kind of waiting."

I agreed with him. The wait was about as bad as it could be. But it ended eventually.

The last of our smaller belongings having been loaded in to a furniture van which then drove them to Creech Grange, Major-General Miller came in person to oversee our departure and assume responsibility for the house-keys, promising that every care would be taken of our home.

We heard him and went through the motions of responding, after first satisfying ourselves that there were no casualties of the evacuation. All civilians had gone.

'Civilian' - an interesting word to describe an inhabitant of Tyneham. The last three of these – William, Billy and I – drove from there and did not look back during our drive.

# Twenty-one

We did not look back . . .

And we did not go back. Katharine was right. I WAS too trusting. We all were. There was never any question of our return.

From time to time there seemed to be, but there was none, ultimately. Should we have trusted less . . . loved less? Maybe.

It would have been better, though, had our trust not been misused . . . and had our love for our valley not been put through such a test. Better for whom? For us, and for our descendants.

How long ago it all seems now – the war's end and the slow realisation that successive governments had no intention of honouring the War Cabinet's pledge. It seems a distant dream, from which I have awakened.

Not so William. He died within a fortnight of our eviction. Cause of death? Pneumonia was the cause given, on his death certificate.

We joked together, during his brief sojourn at Creech Grange, that it was typical of him not to be outdone by the Prime Minister. William wasn't outdone. He died. I was with him. Churchill, of course, lived.

My son's great-grandfather never saw 1944, for his death occurred on 31 December. From the very moment of his uprooting, he began to wither.

Mrs Hodden and the Millers fared little better, although Lily's mother was as good as her word and went to Corfe without a murmur. Her 'flu turned to pleurisy in the cold, damp atmosphere of the Hodden home there (if 'home' it can be termed) and no cure was found for her. As for Charlie Miller, whose family had fished from Worbarrow seemingly forever, he at ninety-one years of age could not sustain the shock and hardship of being evacuated, and was dead already by Christmas. His brother, Jack, was another casualty. Separation from the sea, at the age of eighty, was too much for him. He soon followed Charlie. But there were to be no burials for any of them, nor those that went later, in Tyneham.

This is of no lasting consequence, their bones being unimportant. It is of consequence, though, that their souls are now free to roam.

Ah, freedom!

I am not free. My soul still inhabits my body. And I am still young, in my mind, although my youth has gone. I shall be seventy-three soon. Imagine! Yet I feel no more than nineteen. Maybe time was arrested, for me, upon my marriage to Jeremy.

A glance in my mirror tells me the truth of the matter. My hair is white, my skin lined. Time moves, on the outside. Only within is it immobilised.

I have been back to Tyneham, several times.

The first time was just after the war, with the WAAFs gone from there. But they left a legacy for me – a legacy that I have recovered from, yet never quite forgotten.

Such a sorry sight – the fan palm that, despite any number of gales through the years, had grown to a great height. For it had been beheaded. Why? The WAAFs had beheaded it, I learned, in the course of making a party decoration for their Mess.

They had, too, badly damaged the ancient roundels in the Chintz Room, and the library's stained glass window, during fire drill. This damage went unreported and irreplaceable fragments of stained glass were lost as a result. Not that these and other misdemeanours could compare with their flooding of the cellar.

We were wrong, to doubt Katharine. Not that we could have adopted different measures, had we been less doubting. There were too few avenues open to us, at that time,

Jeremy's cousin, Graeme, and I went together to the cellar with a view to checking that the fungus was not on the rampage. It was not.

But water was. Several feet deep, this greeted us as we finally finished unlocking and unsealing the Tice treasures. In a state of shock, we shone torches on the water's surface and saw, lit by the beams, rotting fragments floating like bizarre boats. Not a solitary case, box, clock, nor any kind of furnishing from former days could be saved. Each and every one of our belongings had either broken or disintegrated.

Upon investigation, we established that Air Force lorries had flattened the surface drains. There was no need to investigate how they had been driven, to achieve such a feat. They must have been manoeuvred mindlessly.

And Katharine had told me that they would be. She had said, at least, that the cellar would be flooded. So did this mean that, when she said it, it was in a sense flooded already? Yes. For the future existed in the present, just as the past did. I could at last grasp this, but I still could not be part of it – not a permanent part, like Katharine. There would, though, come the day for me that had come already for her and for Jeremy and for William. And that day would be cause not for grief, but for celebration.

Just as life is celebrated, so should death be, for it is a freer form of life and a further step on our path to perfection. I want no mourners at my graveside.

Not that I am in any hurry to die. I have loved life and it has been good to me. It gave me Jeremy. Death seemed to take him away, but this was illusory. Death does not take. It simply rearranges.

Adjustment is the key to being bereaved. To adjust properly is to see that when a loved one moves on we are not left alone. The love that we gave and were given has not gone. It still has existence. Our function is to tune in to its new condition. Then, when we are calm, we will feel the love that surrounds us still. It is quite palpable. We are impoverished solely when we won't allow ourselves to feel.

I have been wealthy where love is concerned. Jeremy's has always surrounded me – and there was William. There IS William. The name Billy does not suit him, now that he is a man. Just as I knew they would, Jeremy and his grandfather live on in my son.

William is tall, as they were, and wise, and kind. He speaks sometimes and his words might have come straight from them. I have stopped being surprised. But I have never stopped being thankful for his likeness, in looks and manner, to his father. I look at my son and see my husband.

William, though, has a wife of his own – and two sons. They are beautiful boys. I have never seen beauty as being unmasculine. What gender are trees and the sea, stars and the moon? This is not brought in to question when we commend their beauty. I have two grandsons who are, again, new versions of Jeremy and William. But they are, too, themselves – unique in their individuality. Which is how it should be.

So life goes on. Their lives, sadly, will not be lived in Tyneham. Bureaucracy has taken their heritage from them. The King, in effect, broke his word – just as Katharine said he would, already in 1943. We fought, but our fight was not won. It was lost, before we began. The people in high places referred to by Katharine have been shown, though, that they were wrong. We showed them and in doing so have known some satisfaction. This by no means atoned for the loss of our homes and our whole environment, but at least they saw themselves to be unjust and were dealt a moment's unease on account of their injustice. Does that moment avenge our loss? It would not, if we sought vengeance. We seek, instead, to be left in peace.

There is no bitterness in us. There could have been. There was pain, especially in the beginning. But to be bitter is to eat oneself from within, which brings disease. Why be bitter, when this achieves only bad things? Better to be serene and to store a fund of equanimity.

This, Tyneham has made easy. For I see our valley, in my mind's eye, not as it is, but as it used to be. My sightings sustain me. I wander safely in the Tyneham that others cannot see.

How silly! Others CAN see . . . have seen . . . will go on seeing. For my paintings have achieved popularity. The scenes all live again, and hang in countless homes. There are many originals. Over the years, I have produced these untiringly. There are also thousands of prints, which sell very reasonably.

So Tyneham lives. It has been said that our village died – and so it did, in a sense. Certainly it lacks human residents.

Death, though, as we now know, is not the end – and a new day has dawned for Tyneham. Protected by its plight from modernisation, it has been taken out of time and immortalised as a testimony to pre-war life.

We could never have gone back to that life, even had Tyneham been given back. Our innocence went with the war – and, some say, our integrity. Jeremy spoke, by the Twelve Acres bridle gate, of the wind of change blowing and that wind has blown. We have moved on from Tyneham's era. If we still lived there, we would have had to adapt to hordes of motor-cars and fun-seekers and litter. How well would we have adapted? How would Tyneham have fared in the race to stay 'up-to-date', with all that that entails? Our village was unsuited to modernity and would have lost much in the process – more, perhaps, that it has lost.

As things are, it is preserved. Not in the way we would have chosen, but the choice was not ours. It was made for us, irreversibly, so why argue the toss? We want no more arguments. We accept the loss. And acceptance has enabled us to search our hearts and find pleasure in Tyneham's preservation. This applies not to our homes, which have crumbled or been subjected to demolition, but to our ambience. Not that it is ours.

It is there for all to share and will not now alter. The sound of gunfire weighs on the air, and there are shells bringing danger, yet these factors do not deter the wild-life that populates Tyneham. This thrives in the wilderness which for almost fifty years now has known no cultivation. There is no better breeding ground for rare species and for birds of prey that elsewhere are threatened. And the plough has not been allowed to send to extinction our medieval field systems, nor the remains yet in existence of Saxon landholdings. Plough ridges cut in the thirteenth century, during the building of St Mary's, still survive to this day . . . and might not have done, had we returned and had Tyneham been over-run with those lacking discernment.

So Tyneham has been both advantaged and disadvantaged.

Who can say whether the gains outweigh the losses?

I am sure that, if I can find her, Katharine can.

# Twenty-two

But I need not speak of finding her, for she found me . . . and took me on this journey. We journeyed, together, back to the beginning.

Now, the end is nearing – or would be, if I believed in endings. Blindness might have been an end for me. For some artists it has been. And mine might mean that my artistry is restricted. Already, I am finding my failing sight a slight inconvenience. At first, I found it frightening, but the fear soon went. For it is not as if I were facing the unknown. Although not yet known within my own experience, loss of vision is quite a common affliction. At least I was born sighted. Had I been born blind, my story might have been very different. Never to have seen Jeremy . . . nor Katharine . . . nor Tyneham – this I cannot imagine. Fortunately, I need not try to imagine it – for I HAVE seen them, and William. Both Williams.

It occurs to me that I would probably have seen Katharine, even had I been blind from birth, for I am not at all sure that I saw her with my eyes. I sensed her, rather, within my mind. And I shall go on sensing, once I am blind. This is a joyous realisation. How surprising, that I took so long to realise.

Yet it is not so surprising. When told the truth of my condition, I was far from Tyneham. I had strayed far, temporarily, both in mind and in body. I could not afford to stray.

Recognising this, I came home, only to be dismayed by the changes, though I had known of them. Then Katharine eradicated my dismay, by bringing me back to the true Tyneham.

The ruins that I saw initially are man-made and therefore of no account. I made the mistake of taking them into consideration. Freely, I admit my mistake.

Having admitted it, I can no longer see them. Far from being surrounded by ruins, I am witness to their restoration. Where I am, with Katharine, there is no decay, no heartache, no question of gain, for there could be but one outcome to our tale – the right one.

I now know where I am. I am where I've long sought to be – outside time. Yet I have not died. That is, I don't think I have. I've simply stepped from the nineteen-nineties.

All along, I knew that it would be simple. I merely had to let this simplicity happen for me. There is the tendency, in humans, to complicate things. I shall try to cause no more complications.

Tyneham stands as it ever stood. Every life ever lived here still lives. Every memory that we made lingers.

*Somewhere in my heart there lives a valley . . .*

**PRESS RELEASE** issued by Mr William A.J. Tice of Steeple, Dorset, 31.5.93:

'The death has occurred today of Catherine Tice, the landscape artist whose work immortalised the Purbeck village of Tyneham. She died soon after writing an account of her life entitled OUT OF TIME. In fact, the hand-written manuscript still lay open at its closing page and her pen lay close by. My mother's death was due to natural causes. 'Heart failure' is the cause given by her doctor. It is my considered belief that her heart failed her following a recent visit to our ancestral home – a visit resulting in OUT OF TIME. No blame, though, attaches therefrom to the military occupation of Tyneham. For the fact of the matter is that I have seldom seen mother happier than after her sentimental journey to the House that she once shared with father and his grandfather. She spoke,

232

often, of the 'old days'. This is not to say that she regretted their passing. Mother regretted nothing. There is also the consideration that she was of the opinion that those days had not passed. Anyone interested in my meaning will read OUT OF TIME. So far as I and my family are concerned, that, not this, stands as Catherine Tice's epitaph. We have yet to see how her book is received. But the world hardly needs words from me on the work that art experts consider to be mother's greatest achievement – this being her portrait KATHARINE, which hangs in the National Portrait Gallery.

It will please many to learn that, by special dispensation from Her Majesty's Government, Catherine Tice's earthly remains are to be interred in St Mary's churchyard, Tyneham.

R.I.P.'

## A factual afterword by Philip Draper

It was in 1946 that the War Department first demonstrated their reluctance to give back the homes and the land they took from the people of Tyneham and the surrounding district in December 1943. The matter was taken up then by the press – notably, the NEW STATESMAN and STAR newspapers – and has been raised periodically since.

Despite this public support, it was broken in 1948 to the former inhabitants that their homes were to be the subject of a compulsory purchase order. The displaced persons and their supporters fought back. Sir Cecil Oakes, M.P. was nominated by the then Ministry of Town and Country Planning to hold a public enquiry, at which Mr J. Scott Henderson, Q.C., representing the former Tyneham residents as well as some fifty important national and local organisations, put a very strong case for the return of this area to peaceful uses.

In spite of these many representations, the decision was taken at Cabinet level to retain the lands for the use of the tank firing ranges. The then Minister of Town and Country Planning, the Rt. Hon. Lewis Silkin, M.P., broke the news, at a hastily convened Wareham meeting, to former inhabitants, stating:

"There was a definite pledge given to the people who were displaced. We recognise that pledge, but we have to consider the requirements of the War Department."

At a later public inquiry, on 11 January 1961, one of the witnesses who spoke for the Objectors was Col. J.W. Weld, OBE, TD, JP, Lord Lieutenant of the County of Dorset and at that time Chairman of Wareham and Purbeck R.D.C. Again, the case for the Objectors failed.

Some years on, it was felt that, in view of the growing appreciation of the need for conservation of our heritage, another effort should be made to restore the Tyneham Valley to its former state. So, in 1967, a 'Tyneham Action Group' was formed. This very active group spent the next two years marshalling and verifying all relevant facts and sounding public feelings. A contributing membership of over one thousand persons was enrolled.

After a high level conference in London on 'The Countryside in 1970', presided over by His Royal Highness, the Duke of Edinburgh, the Secretary of Defence undertook to ascertain how to reduce the Military demands on land, particularly in National Parks and on the Coast. Thus, early in 1971, the Minister set in being "The Defence Lands Committee" under the chairmanship of Lord Nugent of Guildford. This Committee made an exhaustive examination of many sites but regarded the Lulworth Ranges (including Tyneham) as the most important. They paid closest attention to the case of the Tyneham Action Group and its many sympathising organisations. Eventually, in 1973, this Committee published its Report, in which it recommended that the Royal Armoured Corps Gunnery School should be removed from Lulworth and Tyneham to Castlemartin in South Wales and that the Ministry of Defence sites at Lulworth should then

234

be released. It added, considerately, that "special steps should be taken to ensure that the land released can be protected and enjoyed".

So the battle was won!

Alas, the Secretary for Defence decided to recommend to the Government that the findings of his Committee should not be implemented as regards Lulworth and Tyneham. The Government accepted his view, the sole concession being that greater public access should be allowed when firing was not in progress.

In the event, the Ranges have been opened to the public on most weekends and on extended public holidays, and the Coastal Footpath and some circular walks have been sympathetically marked for public access at these 'open' times. The ruined buildings have been rendered 'safe', chiefly through demolition, though the church at Tyneham has been adequately restored as a non-consecrated building of remembrance.

## Extracts from *Tyneham: Dorset's Ghost Village*
by Rodney Legg (Dorset Publishing Co.,1993)

Tyneham House is now a ruin that can only deteriorate furthur as it is totally abandoned and crumbles within the overshoot area of the Lulworth Army Ranges.

The main section of the House, its east side, was demolished in 1968. At the back of the ruins of the principal part of Tyneham House are the derelict remains of a fourteenth century hall with great oak beams and elaborate timber trusses supporting the roof.

Tyneham House was one of the outstanding small country houses of Dorset. Its Elizabethan main section was constructed in grey Purbeck stone, with the high Victorian windows inserted along the ground floor. The rooms looked out across lawns edged with palms and other semi-tropical plants that accepted the mild, moist micro-climate of the valley. Beyond the lawns was an avenue of tall beech trees.

Woodwork from the House, principally carved wall panelling, was removed to the Dorset County Museum at Dorchester. In 1965 the Ancient Monuments Board received an exaggerated report of the House's collapse. Unfortunately, once attention had been drawn to Tyneham House, the process began that was to end in its demolition. The irony is that the sums involved in its restoration would today be regarded as trivial and that a lesser building, architecturally, that stands nearby was rescued in the mid-1970s as a museum. The statement from the Ministry of Public Buildings and Works shows that at no stage did anyone consider that a decade later the position might be completely changed:

"The report by the Ministry's architect and inspector for the area showed that the main block of the House seemed to be somewhat less severely damaged than had been feared, since the roof had not wholly collapsed, and the South-west Wing, containing the earliest work, although in a deplorable condition, partly collapsed internally, sodden, and covered with ferns and creepers, at least retained one bay of its timbered roof and its supports from ground level upwards, most of which appeared to be original. Damage was due to natural causes and had not been caused by shellfire.

"A detailed estimate of the cost of preserving the building from further deterioration, which included such things as clearance of vegetation and debris, formation of draining ditches to take away rain water, erection of a temporary roof and other coverings, closing up of door and window openings and strutting where required, amounted to the substantial sum of £8,000 – £2,500 for the South-west Wing; £300 for the East Porch; and £5,200 for the main House.

"With the exception of a few odd days when access was possible, it was only feasible to carry out such work during two brief periods of the year when the ranges are not in use – three weeks in August and two in December. The condition of the building was such, however, that it was considered that if action was not taken very soon to preserve the more perishable part of the work, all would be lost except the masonry shell.

"In these circumstances, it was felt that there were formidable difficulties in the way of preserving the building, and the Board eventually decided that salvage of the building as a whole would be an impossibility, and that the best that could be done was to allow certain features of the building which were capable of being dismantled and erected elsewhere to be removed from the site.

"With the greatest regret, the rest of the fabric has had to be abandoned. The Ministry of Housing and Local Government on whose list the House appears are aware of the position."

The loss of Tyneham House is the greatest single blow that the historical heritage of Purbeck has suffered during this century. Other Tyneham buildings of the seventeenth century and later were also destroyed during the 1960s and 70s. The large nineteenth century rectory was burned down in 1966. The schoolhouse still had long rows of empty pegs, but was ruinous until the military took down the walls to head height. Tyneham Farm was reduced to a ruined shell and then demolished; Jack Miller's cottage is virtually nothing now; Worbarrow's other old cottages and the former coastguard station are nearly down to their foundations; houses at South Egliston are battered. The seventeenth century house and barn at Lutton are decaying. Only the church has been actively preserved and it was partially re-roofed in 1969. The building seems to have been hit by a shell as an area in the churchyard was soft and covered with new turf. It is claimed that one of the graves had a direct hit and had its bones exposed. Since then it has received better care and is now restored as a museum of village life.

Older burial mounds, on the heath at Povington, were

virtually destroyed in 1971. Thorn Barrow and three other Bronze Age round barrows dating from about 1800 BC had only recently been marked with metal star signs "to render identification by the military easier". This was intended to protect them from accidental damage as they were scheduled as an ancient monument by the Department of the Environment. One barrow stood ten feet high but all four were "badly damaged" by military action. Thorn Barrow became a tank-scoop, and the four mounds in barrow group 702 were written off by the Department of the Environment in 1971 as being damaged beyond saving and recommended for excavation.

Miss Joyce Melhuish at the Department of the Environment wrote in 1974 that of the two Bronze Age round barrows at Ring's Hill, Arish Mell, "one is recorded as having been completely destroyed at some time between the date of scheduling (1962) and 1967".

EXAMPLES from Rodney Legg's book, of the feelings of former Tyneham inhabitants:
Diana I.H.Muehsam of New Jersey, USA, who spent her childhood with her grandfather, H.H. House, at South Tyneham Farm between 1933 and 1942, and who moved into Kimmeridge vicarage a year before the eviction:
'A childhood in such beautiful, idyllic surroundings would be hard to describe here after all the time which has gone by, knowing the uselessness of looking back. How painful it is to remember the small warm pools at Charnel where first I learned to swim, the "winkles" we cooked in tins on the beach, the endless picnics, fishing, looking for crabs at Broad Bench. Then there was Old Sticky (Mr Stickland) the fisherman, who built the "Minnimoo" and taught us a game which we called after him, "Sticky's Game". The magnificent profile of Gad Cliff is something I should love to see again one day. There is so much to tell, that I better stop right here.

238

It hurts too much.'

Mrs S.B. White:

'At Hollow Ditch there was a large russet apple tree, large wooden butter-pats with intricate patterns, and rows of lovely golden butter laid on a tray ready to go to Wareham market. Once a lady named Elsie Cake called on a straight-up, no nonsense bicycle with a fancy chain-guard. She hopped off in a most graceful manner, in spite of long skirts and button boots. I later tried to do the same but came a cropper. In the evenings, I would go across the heath to Marepool and watch the deer drinking at dusk. It was also from this spot that I watched Lulworth Castle burning [in 1929]. My grandparents are buried at Tyneham churchyard but Aunt Susan was buried at Steeple. She ended her days in a cottage at Kimmeridge, having been moved there at the time of the evacuation. But she always hoped to return to Hollow Ditch . . . '

John Gould, old soldier of the Devonshire Regiment and retired Wareham roadman:

'Tyneham's always in my thoughts. My home will always be there. If I could, I would go back tomorrow. It is a wicked shame that the pledge hasn't been kept.'

A last word from Rodney Legg:

'The events of 1943 may well turn out to have been, in retrospect, a beneficial accident as they have created a remarkable natural oasis midway along the busy South Coast. It is up to us to ensure that this beauty is protected.'

– The end –